THE BEACH HUT MURDERS

Rachel McLean writes thrillers that make your pulse race and your brain tick. A proud indie author who manages her own publishing company, she has sold millions of copies digitally and hundreds of thousands in print, regularly topping the bestseller lists. She is the author of the Dorset Crime novels and five spin-off crime series, with beloved characters appearing in multiple series. In 2021, she won the Kindle Storyteller Award with *The Corfe Castle Murders*. She divides her time between Birmingham and Dorset and lives with her wife, three children and two cats Cagney and Lacey.

ALSO BY RACHEL MCLEAN

Dorset Crime series

The Corfe Castle Murders
The Clifftop Murders
The Island Murders
The Monument Murders
The Millionaire Murders
The Fossil Beach Murders
The Blue Pool Murders
The Lighthouse Murders
The Ghost Village Murders
The Poole Harbour Murders
The Chesil Beach Murders
The Beach Hut Murders
The Gold Hill Murders
...and more to come

RACHEL McLEAN

THE DORSET CRIME SERIES BOOK 12

THE BEACH HUT MURDERS

ACKROYD PUBLISHING

Ackroyd Publishing

ackroydpublishing.com

Printed and bound in the UK by CPI Group (Uk) Ltd, Croydon CR0 4YY

THE STORY SO FAR

Over the first eleven Dorset Crime novels, DCI Lesley Clarke has gone from traumatised newcomer to the lynchpin of Dorset's Major Crime and Cold Case teams, holding together a unit scarred by corruption, organised crime and internal politics that never quite stay buried.

Kelvin Legacy and the Long Game

The Kelvin family remain the spine of the series. After Arthur Kelvin's death and the exposure of the officers who killed Tim Mackie, *The Chesil Beach Murders* digs deeper into their history. A break-in at Vera Kelvin's home links stolen items directly to a mutilated body dumped at St Chatherine's Chapel behind Chesil Beach, tying current murders to old Kelvin methods. Superintendent Carpenter finally admits that he and Eric Chiles ran an undercover vice operation in 1988, turning Frank Kelvin into an informant before Frank vanished in 1993; whether he ran, was killed by his own family or was silenced by the police remains unresolved.

Chesil Beach and the London Gang

The most recent case centres on Mark Ashforth, found with teeth and fingertips removed to block identification. His finances reveal he'd been working for an organised crime group. Johnny Chiles uses facial recognition to link three London offenders – Billy Miller, Luka Tanner and Mick Donnelly, known to police as the Three Musketeers – to the killing. A joint operation with the Met ends in their arrest and charges for both Ashforth's murder and that of witness-in-hiding Jackie Kendall, giving partial justice for the events that drove Jackie underground.

Internal Wars: PSD and Leadership

While Lesley is fighting gangsters, she's also under fire from within. DI Hannah Patterson files a bullying and harassment complaint, triggering a PSD investigation that briefly sidelines Hannah and leaves Lesley temporarily in sole charge of MCIT. The team quietly chooses sides, backing Lesley; Hannah ultimately returns to Devon, and Lesley is left with both a DI vacancy and a sharper sense of how vulnerable she is to political attacks. Nathan Strunk, the obvious internal candidate, is tested and found not yet ready for leadership.

The Evolving Team and Found Family

The ensemble continues to grow and realign. Johnny Chiles, once doubted because of his Met background and past Kelvin entanglements, proves indispensable on Chesil Beach and earns Lesley's trust. Tina Abbott, newly back from maternity leave, is the one who identifies Ashforth and reconnects professionally with Johnny. Meera Kumar and Jill Scott clash over ambition and work style but reach a new equilibrium as Jill pushes Meera to own her strengths while they pursue the Frank Kelvin cold case together. And Lesley has offered the DI vacancy to an old colleague, DI Zoe Finch. Will Zoe leave Cumbria and join the team?

Justice, Compromise and What's Still Missing

By the beginning of the twelfth Dorset Crime book, *The Beach Hut Murders,* killers have been charged and Lesley has survived yet another PSD brush – but the bigger picture is unresolved. Vera Kelvin is still free, Eric Chiles has only begun to talk and Frank Kelvin's disappearance hangs over Carpenter, Johnny and the whole force. The Dorset Crime story so far is one of hard-won victories overshadowed by the knowledge that the deepest secrets – and the most dangerous enemies – are still out there.

Illustration by Maria Burns

rachelmclean.com

CHAPTER ONE

Jude Bristow stood back from the pile of rubble obscuring the usually beautiful sea view and placed his palms on the small of his back.

He leaned back as far as his balance would allow, stretching out his grumbling back muscles. "Jesus Christ," he said. "I thought this was going to be easier."

Damian grunted. Jude's mate was a man of few words, most of them not fit for public consumption.

"Bastard thing," he muttered.

Jude nodded. "It is that. Did you have any idea so much of the concrete was going to be reinforced with metal?"

Damian shook his head. "It's a bastard."

Jude sighed. It was cold today, the wind whistling through the beach huts and the waves pounding onto the beach. Few of the beach hut owners had braved it out here. The Mudeford Ferry wasn't running and most of the boats he normally saw out in Christchurch Harbour were moored up.

But Jude and Damian worked for Bournemouth, Christchurch

and Poole Council, also known as BCP. And there was no rest for council employees, whatever the weather.

In fact, the worse the weather, the more work there was for him, Damian and the aptly named Digsy, who even now was climbing into a digger. If the people who used these beaches knew how much sand had to be shifted after a storm...

"Bastard building," Digsy grunted. "Should never have built the thing." He turned the digger's ignition and the machine shuddered into life.

"Digsy's not wrong," Damian said.

Jude looked up. "Digsy. Go easy, yeah?"

He squinted, perusing the progress they'd already made. They were under instructions to use non-invasive tools where possible, which meant pickaxes, shovels and pneumatic drills. This headland, with Mudeford Spit to the north and Hengistbury Head behind him, was a site of historic interest. Back at the visitor centre there was a display of the Bronze Age encampment that had been the last significant settlement here, long before some mad idiot had come along, plonked some wooden huts in a spot where the elements were determined to destroy them, and somehow managed to charge half a million quid each for them.

Half a million quid! That was what people were buying those huts for.

Sure, they were bigger than the average beach hut, and it was one hell of a location. They had kitchenettes and cute little mezzanine bedrooms in the eaves. But they didn't even have plumbing. If the wealthy owners wanted to go for a piss in the middle of the night, they had to trek to one of these basic concrete toilet blocks.

One of which was slowly – too slowly – being reduced to a pile of rubble before his eyes.

He wiped his brow; he was sweating, despite the chill. He looked at Digsy, who'd stopped the digger and was waiting. Tel, their supervisor, had gone to answer the call of nature himself in one of the three remaining toilet blocks. At least he had a key to the private cubicles, usually accessible only to the beach hut owners and residents. It was still a stinking concrete block, though.

But with Tel away, Jude was the *de facto* leader of their little gang. Hence, Digsy waiting before he started the digger in earnest.

"Go on then," Jude said. "I can't stand another minute of this bloody reinforced concrete."

The walls of the toilet block had metal running through them. The sort of ragged, twisted metal that felt more like scrap than anything manufactured for the purpose. And it was a bitch to cut the stuff out of thirty-year-old concrete.

Digsy started up the digger and moved forward. Jude heard a shout and saw Tel, running towards them along the path between the huts and the harbour, waving his hard hat. He was bellowing something unintelligible.

Jude ignored Tel – easier to seek forgiveness than permission, his partner Sal always said. He watched as Digsy brought down a sizeable section of the toilet block's northernmost wall.

That's more like it.

"What the bloody hell's going on?"

Tel was back. Jude looked up to see him bending over, red-faced and wheezing. He spat into the sand.

"You know our instructions," he continued. "Why are you using the digger?"

Digsy had his ear defenders on, so wouldn't be able to hear Tel anyway from his perch inside the digger. Damian was on the other side of the digger, checking that Digsy didn't overbalance on the uneven ground.

"Jude?" Tel said, standing in front of him. "I know they listen to you. Why didn't you stop this?"

Jude shrugged. How long could he feign ignorance? He'd thought this job would be a welcome change from their normal routine. But he couldn't bloody wait to get back to shovelling sand and hauling rocks along the beach for protection against the currents.

"Stop!"

Jude and Tel both turned. That wasn't Tel's voice, but Damian's.

"Stop!" Damian yelled again.

Jude looked towards the digger. Digsy was oblivious, ploughing the digging arm into the foundations of the building, teeth gritted in concentration.

Jude waved his arms. He knew better than to get in front of the digger, so jumped up and down, still waving.

"What the fuck?" Tel said.

Jude looked at him with a shrug. Tel joined him in the waving and shouting.

It took long enough, but eventually Digsy noticed them. He turned off the digger, and it juddered to a halt.

He frowned and removed his ear defenders. "What? What's up?"

Jude looked at the digger. It was level, no sign of it toppling. He looked at Tel, who seemed as puzzled as he was.

Whatever the problem was, it had to be on Damian's side. He checked the digger had come to a total stop and walked around the back of it.

"Damo? Damo, mate! You OK?"

"I'm fine." Damian was standing a few feet away from the digger, staring at the ground beneath it.

Tel was right behind Jude. "Why did you boys decide to start digging right when my back was turned? And what's all the panic?"

Boys. Jude rolled his eyes. Damian was five years older than Tel. Jude himself wasn't much younger. Digsy... no one knew how old Digsy was.

"What's up, mate?" Jude asked, approaching Damian.

Damian was pointing towards the spot he'd been staring at.

"That," he said. His voice was shaking.

Jude couldn't see anything. He shifted sideways for a better view and followed Damian's outstretched hand.

"Shit."

He turned to look at Tel, who'd paled.

"Shit," the supervisor echoed.

"Now do you see why I needed him to stop?" Damian asked.

Tel nodded. Jude took a step forward. Digsy lifted himself up, about to climb down from the digger's cab.

"No!" barked Tel. "Neither of you move."

Jude froze. He looked again at the ground beneath the digger.

Ah, hell.

This would slow things down. It would mean waiting for the archaeologists to do their thing before they could finish demolishing the toilet block and the external contractors could come in and build a fancy new one.

Maybe, if he was lucky, it might mean back to the other side of the headland. Back to shovelling sand and hauling rocks.

"Can I get down?" Digsy asked. "Or am I stuck up here forever?"

"Go down by the other side," Tel said.

Digsy turned away from them and clambered down, his movements as careful as Jude had seen from him. He rounded the digger and joined them in staring.

"Bugger me," he said.

The other three men nodded.

"Is that what I think it is?"

"Yeah," said Jude.

"Reckon so," said Tel. He sighed. "I'll have to phone it in."

Tel walked away from them, into a sheltered spot between two of the beach huts. Jude could hear him talking into his phone, but he couldn't make out the words.

Digsy stepped forward. Jude put out a hand to stop him.

"Bugger me," Digsy repeated. He turned to Damian. "Good job you stopped me."

Damian grinned. "Saved your life, mate."

"I wouldn't go that far."

Jude ignored the two of them. He squatted down to get a better view of what they'd uncovered.

He twisted his head to one side and then the other, trying to work out its shape. Was it even intact?

Either way, it was a body. Skull, at least two bones, although he couldn't tell for the life of him whether they were arms or legs.

He swallowed. *Hold it together*.

You poor bastard, he thought. Whoever it was, they'd been here a long time.

The archaeologists were in for a treat.

CHAPTER TWO

Detective Inspector Zoe Finch stood on Church Green in Wareham. To her right was the Priory Church of Lady St Mary, a far larger and grander church than she'd expected to find in a small town like this. Behind her was the quay with its bustling market currently in full flow, and right in front of her was the cottage she'd just viewed.

She stared at the cottage, her gaze moving across its front. Yes, it was pokey, low ceilings, narrow stairs, no hallway to speak of. But it had charm, and Zoe loved charm. The way the morning sun slanted across its front, the way the windows sagged just enough to suggest character, but not enough to be worrying.

In Birmingham, she'd lived in a Victorian terrace on a road full of students, certainly not the smartest of houses, but one that had felt familiar to her, like a favourite old jumper. In Cumbria, she'd begun in a house that she'd never felt comfortable in, and then she and Carl had moved somewhere more homely, somewhere built out of local stone with the distinctive surrounds around the windows. Somewhere with, ridiculously, for Cumbria, a hot tub in the tiny back garden.

This would be something new. It might be a challenge. There

could be damp or problems with the electrics or anything... but by God, it was gorgeous.

Tom, the estate agent, was standing next to her, following her gaze around the front of the house.

"Cute, isn't it?" he said, giving her a sidelong glance.

She nodded. Zoe was tall, five foot eight, but she'd tested the doorways and she could just about make it through all of them. She just couldn't invite any tall friends round.

She turned to him. "I like it."

Zoe didn't have a lot of experience when it came to buying houses, but she'd watched them do it on TV shows, and she had a feeling that expressing too much enthusiasm might somehow disadvantage her.

"I don't blame you," he replied. "It's idyllic. What do you think?"

She sniffed. "What do you mean, what do I think?"

"Do you think you'll be putting an offer in? It's been on the market for a couple of weeks, and we've had ten viewings already." He paused for effect. "Wareham isn't the sort of place where you get ten viewings very often. But this location, this location's something special."

She nodded. The cottage was right on the pavement, no front garden, nothing between her door and people passing by. Privacy wouldn't be great. But Zoe worked long hours. She was about to join the Major Crime Investigations Team in Dorset Police Force. She didn't imagine she'd be spending much time sitting in that front room, and besides, she preferred the room at the back. She could imagine stepping out of her front door, turning to see the church looming majestically over her, and then slipping into the alleyway opposite, making her way down to the quay to watch the boats go past.

Bliss.

She'd spent some time staying in a similar cottage around the corner in Church Street when she'd been down here working with DCI Lesley Clarke, the woman who'd been her boss in Birmingham and was about to become her boss again. She knew she liked Wareham.

"Yes," she said.

"Yes?" Tom replied.

"Yes, I'll be putting an offer in." She swallowed.

"Fantastic." He rubbed his hands together. "Any idea how much?"

Zoe knew her budget. Carl was in the process of moving out of the hot tub house and into a flat in Penrith. She wasn't sure how he felt about that, but that wasn't her problem. The important thing was that he'd bought her out. She could afford this. She could afford it with money to spare.

"The asking price," she said. "If you promise me you'll do no further viewings and take no further offers, I'll offer the asking price."

"I like a woman who knows her mind." He licked his lips.

She shrugged. "I don't have time to hang about. I'm starting a new job later today."

"You are?"

She turned to him. "Let's just hope we don't meet professionally, eh?"

He laughed. "Sounds ominous."

She nodded. Zoe preferred to avoid telling people what she did. It always prompted the kind of questions she either couldn't answer or didn't want to answer.

"The asking price," she repeated. "Do you think the seller will accept?"

He surveyed the house for a moment, then turned to her. "I'll need to speak to them, of course, but between you and me, I think you just got yourself a new home."

CHAPTER THREE

DCI Lesley Clarke looked up at the sleek glass building that housed Dorset Police HQ.

Much of the building work was finished now, and where the rubble had once been were the beginnings of landscaped grounds. She still hadn't been up to the suite of management offices on the top floor, not since her enforced visits to a woman from Professional Standards six months earlier, but she was confident, from what she heard, that they were pretty slick.

These offices were proving controversial. The local press was wondering why the police were spending this kind of money amidst budget cuts and staffing reductions. But Lesley knew that budgets didn't work that way, and besides, the old building had been horrendous: vast, draughty windows, with all the attractiveness of a motorway service station. This place might not be perfect, but she was already growing quite fond of it.

The automatic door slid open and she strode inside, enjoying the warmth of the building. Outside, it was minus five degrees. February in Dorset could get chilly with the icy winds blowing in off the sea.

Where she lived in Southbourne, the waves were choppy, and the foam on the beach was something to behold.

She headed for the stairs. Lesley had never been into fitness; she was the kind of woman who preferred a chocolate bar to an apple. Walking up the couple of flights of stairs to her office at least made her feel less guilty about it.

DI Jill Scott was coming down. She stopped when she saw Lesley. "Boss," she said. "I'm glad you're here."

Lesley stopped walking. "You're in early, Jill."

Jill nodded. "My team's got a case, or at least, it looks like it."

"OK," Lesley said.

The Cold Cases Team's investigations weren't always straightforward. Sometimes a body that looked like it might be worthy of police investigation turned out to be an archaeological find instead. Sometimes it was a mix of the two.

"Tell me about it," she said. "Shall we head upstairs? Please don't tell me this is another sensitive one."

Jill smiled. "Not as far as I can tell, thank God. You know the beach huts at Mudeford Spit?"

They were pacing up the stairs now, walking quickly. Lesley couldn't help but be impressed by herself, by the way she was walking and talking at the same time, not something she'd have been able to do a few years earlier, before she arrived in Dorset.

"I do," she said. "They're only a couple of miles from where I live."

"And d'you know they've been demolishing the toilet blocks?" Jill said. "Modernising them."

Lesley laughed. "About bloody time. Those things are awful. I can't believe people pay a fortune for a glorified cabin on the beach and then have to use a loo in a concrete block behind it."

Jill shrugged. "Never been there myself, but it looks like I might be about to. They found something there."

Lesley made her way out onto the second floor, where the offices of her two teams were located. "What kind of something?"

They stopped outside a row of four doors: the Cold Cases Team and the Major Crime Investigations Team, plus offices for their DIs. Jill pushed open the door to her own office, and Lesley followed her in.

Jill's laptop was on the desk. She turned it to face the two of them and brought up a photograph of what looked like human remains. They were badly decomposed and covered in mud.

"They found that in Mudeford?" Lesley asked.

"Underneath the toilet block," Jill said.

Lesley let out a long breath. "Bloody hell. How long ago were those blocks built?"

"I'm not sure, but by the looks of them, eighties or nineties."

Lesley shook her head. "So that's been under there all these years."

"We need to send a CSI team out," Jill replied, "and a forensic archaeologist, too. From what I can make out from these photographs, the remains are old. But not so old that it's not a potential criminal case."

"Thirty or forty years," said Lesley.

"Exactly," Jill said. "My theory is that this was left when the block was being constructed."

Lesley scrolled through the photographs. They zoomed progressively in on sections of the body, showing the skull, the ribs, and the limbs. Despite being badly decayed, the body seemed intact. No body parts had been removed, and it looked like it hadn't been disturbed in decades.

"If your theory is right," she said, "then it's one of your cases."

Jill nodded. "Are you happy for me to go over there with one of my team?"

Lesley looked at her. "Take Katie. She needs the experience."

DC Katie Young was keen and bright, if sometimes a little naïve. But sometimes that naivety could lead to her spotting things others didn't.

"No problem," Jill said. "She'll do a good job."

"Let's hope so," Lesley told her. "You go over to Mudeford and let me know what you see."

"You don't want to come along?" Jill asked. "Could be an interesting one."

Lesley smiled, shaking her head. "Believe me, Jill, I'd love to, but I'm not supposed to be involved in investigations, not directly. Superintendent Carpenter has me investigating the surface of my desk these days. It's your job to lead this investigation, and I'm confident you'll do a good job."

"Thanks," Jill said. "I'll get Stanley to brief the MCIT, just in case it's connected to one of their investigations."

"Zoe Finch starts today," Lesley said. "I imagine I'll be busy inducting her. I'll introduce you when there's an opportunity around your case. I think you'll like her."

Jill's nose twitched. "Just tell me she's nothing like Hannah."

DI Hannah Patterson had been the previous head of the MCIT. She'd accused Lesley of bullying and intimidation, a charge that hadn't stuck, and then left for her home county of Devon. If anybody had been bullying and intimidating, it had been Hannah, bullying her own team. No one missed her.

"Let's just say Zoe's a vast improvement on the last holder of that position," Lesley said, "and more. I worked with her for years in Birmingham. She's good, and she's only got better since she's been in Cumbria."

"It'll be a change for her," said Jill. "Discovering what the sun looks like."

Lesley laughed. "You're not wrong there. Zoe describes the Cumbria weather to me every time I speak to her. It sounds dreadful."

"Rather her than me."

"And me," Lesley said. "But you go and brief your team. Grab Katie and head over there. I assume Gail's already on her way."

Gail was the county's most experienced crime scene manager. For a case like this, she'd be needed.

"She phoned in half an hour ago," Jill said. "I'm not sure who'll get there first, but I know she'll be on the scene soon."

"Good," Lesley replied. "Keep me updated, Jill. And make sure your team have plenty to keep them busy while you're over at Mudeford."

Jill nodded. "No problem, boss."

CHAPTER FOUR

"How do you get to these beach huts, anyway?" Jill asked as she and Katie approached Hengistbury Head.

Katie had her nose buried in her phone. "Two options, guv," she replied.

"Which are?" Jill asked.

"Well, the first option is from Mudeford, on the boat. We're in totally the wrong place for that, and besides, it's not running at this time of year. The water's too choppy."

Jill turned off the Christchurch Road, passing large Edwardian houses set back from the road on either side. She wondered if one of these was where DCI Clarke lived.

"So," she said, "not really an option at all. Please tell me your second option's a bit more user-friendly." She huffed as an Ocado van stopped in front of her. With a builder's van parked opposite outside a house covered in scaffolding, it was impossible for her to pass.

"Don't they look in their rear-view mirrors?" she muttered, tapping her fingers on the steering wheel in frustration.

Katie looked up. "You OK, guv?"

Jill sighed. She'd had an argument with Meera that morning, the latest in a series of rows about the state of their home. It was looking more and more like they couldn't afford to stay in a house that needed so much TLC, especially with Meera working part time.

But she wasn't about to tell Katie all that. One hint of the problems with her home and Katie would be down the rabbit hole, digging up information on sympathetic restorations faster than you could say *Grand Designs*.

"I'm fine," she said. "Bad night's sleep."

"Suzi?" Katie asked.

Jill nodded, then gave a thin smile. "Par for the course with little ones. You'll find out some day."

Katie frowned.

Jill wished she could pull her words back in. "Sorry," she said. "Making assumptions. Tell me about this second option for accessing the beach huts."

They were within sight of the sea now, driving along a long straight road that, according to the signs, led to the car park and the visitor centre. The satnav still had them over a mile from the beach huts and was saying they'd have to walk much of the way.

If the only way in was on foot, how did the council get their machinery in?

"It is," said Katie. "User-friendly, I mean. You need to drive up to the turning point for the land train, by the visitor centre. There's an access road."

"Thank God for that."

Jill ignored the car park to their right and pressed on, slowing to avoid pedestrians. It was half-term; not as busy as the summer months, she imagined, but there were still plenty of kids happy to run into the road without stopping to look.

She pulled up outside a café with a sign outside announcing it as The Hiker. There was no sign of a land train, whatever that was. A barrier blocked them from going further.

Katie already had a hand on the door. "Shall I let them know we're here?"

"You do that." Maybe Jill could get a micro-nap while she waited.

She leaned back and closed her eyes. The wind from the sea was buffeting the car. Why would anyone come up here at this time of year, for pleasure?

She was brought out of her trance by Katie knocking on the driver's window and pointing towards the barrier, which was now open. The wind was whipping the hood of Katie's waterproof around her face.

Jill gestured for her to get in the car, but Katie shook her head, waved a set of keys, and pointed at the barrier. Jill nodded: *understood.*

She crept forwards, scanning her mirrors for wayward kids, and drove through the barrier. Katie closed it behind her and locked it. Jill waited for Katie to get in, her hand covering a yawn. But Katie was waving those keys again and pointing ahead of them.

Bloody hell, woman. Calm down, you'll wear yourself out. Was DC Young planning to walk all the way, in this weather?

Her funeral. Jill started moving, driving at a crawl. The pedestrians here weren't expecting a car to appear behind them, and she had to watch a few of them do a double-take then give her an accusing look before moving to the side of the road. Each time, she gave a gracious wave, feeling like royalty.

She carried on like this, ignoring shouts of "Can I get in?" from fractious kids. Then she realised she'd lost Katie.

She stopped. *Where are you, for God's sake?*

She needed to calm down. To stop blaming Katie for things that weren't her fault. More importantly, to stop blaming Meera for things that weren't her fault, either.

Katie emerged from a low building with a sedum roof, a man in a blue fleece beside her. He looked uncomfortable.

Jill smiled. Katie sometimes had that effect on people. Good job her tenacity and energy made her a damn good copper.

Jill went to wind down her window, then thought better of it and climbed out.

"Everything OK?" she asked Katie.

Katie indicated the man. "This is Doug Stewart. Manages the visitor centre. He's the person we'll need to speak to when we want to get in or out."

Jill held out a hand. "Mr Stewart. I'm Detective Inspector Jill Scott, from Dorset Police's Cold Cases Team."

"This lassie here told me all that," he replied in a broad Scottish accent. "Looks like you've got a cold case along there, alright." He shuddered. "Poor bastard. He's in a hell of a state."

"He?"

The man shrugged. "Man, woman, whatever. I'm nowhere near enough of an expert to know. But that body's been there a good while, I can tell you that."

"Not long enough for it to be Bronze Age," Jill said. She'd spotted the signs behind him.

"No chance," he said. "I reckon it's been there since they built those toilets, though."

Jill raised an eyebrow; *you, too.* "I don't suppose you know when that was?"

"How old d'you think I am, lass?"

She suppressed a sigh. Walkers and families were passing all around them, eyeing the car.

We're supposed to be here, she thought. Did they think that Katie, in her cheap grey trouser suit, and Jill, in her more expensive green one, were just walkers taking a shortcut?

"I'm not suggesting you were there at the time, Mr Stewart. But you work here. I thought you might know."

"Visitor Centre wasn't here back then. We've only been here since 2013." He wrinkled his nose. "But those toilet blocks are definitely twentieth century. Panj will be able to tell you."

"Panj?"

"Panjit. Warden up at the beach huts. She wasn't here then, either, before you ask, but she works for the council. She'll be able to sort you out."

"She's up there now?"

"You think she'd miss this? Yeah, she's up there, to be sure."

"Thanks." Jill exchanged glances with Katie, who was practically bouncing on her toes with impatience. The two of them turned back to the car.

"Good luck," he said.

"You think we'll need it?" Jill asked him. She looked at the car; was it about to get stuck on the access road?

He sniffed. "That body. It's in a bad way. I hope you two lasses have strong stomachs."

Katie opened her mouth, but Jill raised a restraining hand. "Thank you, Mr Stewart," she said. "I'm sure we'll be just fine."

CHAPTER FIVE

FEBRUARY 1994

Harold Carson yawned, stretched and reached out his left arm, just as he'd done every morning for the last twenty-five years.

He stopped as he found an empty pillow beside him. He drew his hand back, blinking.

At some point, he would get used to this.

Betty being gone was something everybody else had accepted. Their son, their daughter, they were getting on with their lives, but Harold...

How was he supposed to carry on without her? She'd told him to find somebody else, to meet another woman who could look after him, as if he couldn't look after himself. Betty seemed to have it in her head that Harold needed a woman, any woman, to keep him happy and secure.

But Harold didn't need any woman. He needed Betty.

There'd been times in the first year when he'd contemplated killing himself, maybe joining her in heaven or wherever she was. But killing himself would be a sin. There was no way he'd join her if he did that.

So he'd woken up every morning, reached for the empty pillow, hauled himself out of bed, and dragged himself through the day, going through the motions in his pointless job. Which was exactly what he did now.

His son, Stephen, was living with him. Had been for over two years. At first, Stephen had worried about Harold. Had watched him when he thought he wasn't looking, checking that the old man was still sane.

Of course he was bloody sane. People died. Nobody went insane because of it, but Stephen... well, Stephen had some funny ideas. Some funny habits too, but he was a grown man, so Harold knew better than to ask.

He walked past Stephen's door, calling out a grunted "Morning" on the way to the bathroom. It was like having a teenager, having to rouse his son from his pit, as if it was 1982 again and the boy had been up all night listening to records.

No response.

Harold shook his head, went into the bathroom, and used the toilet. He emerged, glancing at Stephen's door. No point in calling again.

He padded down the stairs. In the kitchen, he went through his normal routine, flipped the kettle on, pulled the pot down from the cupboard, warmed it with a splash of boiling water, the way Betty used to do, and then made a pot of tea.

Stephen normally emerged in time for his own cup. There was no way Harold was going as far as to take one up to him.

He sat down at the kitchen table and clutched his own mug between his hands. It was cold today, a chilly February breeze whipping across the grass between here and the sea. The house on Southbourne Coast Road looked out over a flat expanse of grass, with nothing between it and Hengistbury Head to one side and the dunes to the other. When he and Betty had moved in, it had felt idyllic. Without her, it just felt bleak.

He drank the last of his cup of tea and frowned. Where was Stephen?

Maybe he'd drunk too much last night. The lad was in the habit of going out without telling Harold where he'd be or when he'd return. He just had to accept it. Stephen was doing him a favour by being here, or at least, he thought he was. Harold wasn't so sure.

He poured himself another cup of tea and sipped it, wondering how long it would be before he'd have to go upstairs and rouse his son.

Stephen had a casual job at the quarry towards Hengistbury Head, and Harold didn't want him to lose it. Stephen wasn't the sort of lad who was going to hold down a nine-to-five job.

He yawned and stood up, scratching the stubble on his chin. He peered out of the window. It was a dull morning, and litter was blowing along the street. He'd have to go out there later and tidy his front garden. He didn't mind. It was worth it for the view, bleak as it might feel.

After a few moments, he headed back for the stairs, sighing. This wasn't what he'd signed up for when he'd let his son come back home, but today, it seemed it was what was happening. At the top of the stairs, he called Stephen's name.

"Wake up, lad," he said. "You need to get to work."

No response. Harold shook out his shoulders and stepped towards Stephen's bedroom door. It wasn't the bedroom Stephen had lived in as a boy, because Harold and Betty had moved here after the kids had grown up and moved away. But Stephen had made it his own, trashing it as if he was fifteen again.

Harold knocked on the door. "Stephen," he said, "you all right in there?"

No response. Harold threw his head back to look up at the ceiling. Should he go in? Would Stephen shout at him if he did?

He looked at the door for a few moments, willing it to open. It didn't.

Another knock, harder this time, hard enough to wake anybody from a drunken stupor, from a hungover fog.

"Stephen," he called through the door.

He rattled the handle a couple of times, waiting for a response. Still nothing.

Harold clenched his teeth. Maybe he should call Amber, his daughter. She was practical, and Stephen seemed to tolerate her more than he did Harold.

Don't be ridiculous, Harold thought. He raised his hand, knocked, and then pushed the door open. This was his house, after all, and he could enter whichever room he chose.

The bed was empty. The duvet was smooth, just as Harold had left it the day before.

Stephen hadn't been here. If the boy had been here, there was no way that duvet would have looked like that. Even if he hadn't slept in the bed, he'd have sprawled on it or moved the duvet to one side or *something*. It was like the lad didn't know the meaning of the word tidy.

"Stephen," Harold said, his voice small.

Now he knew he was talking to nobody. The room was tiny, only just big enough for a double bed, a wardrobe, and a chest of drawers. Harold turned round, facing back towards the stairs.

"Stephen," he called louder.

He looked towards the bathroom. The door was open, nobody inside.

He opened the third bedroom. Empty.

"Stupid lad," he muttered under his breath. "Why couldn't he call me?"

He went into his own bedroom and pulled on some clothes. Irritated that he didn't have time for a bath, he hurried down the stairs, his chest tight, and went into the living room.

Maybe, just maybe, the lad had fallen asleep down here last night.

But the living room was as he'd left it before going to bed himself. Cushions plumped, surfaces tidy, TV remote placed on top of the TV. Stephen hadn't been in here, either.

Harold walked to the front window, peering out onto the street. A couple walked past on the other side of the road wearing brightly coloured cagoules, presumably heading up to the Head for a walk. He considered calling out, asking them if they'd seen his son, but he'd been up for over an hour now. There was no way anybody walking past here would have seen Stephen leave.

He slumped down onto the sofa. "Where are you, lad?"

He walked into the hall and picked up the phone on the side table. He dialled Amber.

"Dad?" she said. "You OK?"

"I'm fine, love," he replied. "It's just Stephen."

"What's he done now?" He could sense the exasperation in her voice.

"I don't know, love. He's not here. He hasn't slept in his bed."

"You're sure he didn't go out early?"

"His bed's like it was when I tidied yesterday."

"Ah." Amber knew how messy her brother was. "Maybe he's..." she began, but she didn't have any suggestion as to where he might be.

Harold pulled the phone receiver closer to his mouth. "I think I... well, I'm wondering if he might have left home."

"Left home?" she said. "Where would he go?"

Harold wrinkled his nose. It wasn't like Stephen earned enough money to rent his own place. It wasn't like he had a girlfriend to go to. In fact, what *did* Stephen do in his free time?

"You're right, love," he said. "He probably just went out and got drunk somewhere, maybe crashed at a mate's house."

"What mate?" Amber asked. "I've never seen any mates."

"He must have friends," Harold said. "Everybody has friends."

She grunted. "I think you should call the police, Dad."

He felt his stomach dip. "The police? Why?"

There was a moment's silence before she replied.

"He never goes out overnight, Dad. He's always home at some point. And you say he hasn't slept in his bed."

Harold shook his head. "The place is too tidy."

She gave a mirthless laugh. "Exactly," she said. "Call the police, Dad, they can help you."

CHAPTER SIX

"Hello."

Lesley looked up from her screen to see a familiar face poking around the door to her office.

"Zoe!" She stood up, her mood brightening. "You were supposed to wait downstairs so I could welcome you properly."

Zoe slid inside the room and closed the door with a shrug. "I figured I'd save you the walk."

"Ha!" Lesley held her arms out. Zoe stepped forward and allowed Lesley to embrace her, then took a step back.

"Is hugging appropriate, now you're my boss again?"

Lesley flapped a hand dismissively. "There's no one here to see. And besides," she gave Zoe a *tell me the truth* look, "if you try and tell me that you and Mo Uddin never hugged, I'll tell you you're a liar."

Zoe feigned horror, clapping a hand to her chest. "Me? Lie? Never." Her smile dropped. "Well..." She frowned. "Let's not talk about that."

Lesley dropped into one of the two chairs that sat opposite her desk and gestured for Zoe to take the other one. "Nothing I need to know about, I hope?"

Zoe looked into her eyes for a moment. She blinked then pulled the smile back on. "Of course not. Just... things didn't end all that well between me and Carl."

"He didn't move down with you?"

Zoe looked down at the floor. "No. He moved me up from Birmingham to Cumbria three years ago." She sighed and raised her head. "I guess I figured that was it. That I'd make a life up there. Nicholas leaving home, and Carl..." She shook her head. "It wasn't right, not in the end."

"I'm sorry to hear that."

"Are you? You're the one who talked me into moving down here."

"I'm not *sure* I talked you into it."

Zoe laughed. "You were a one-woman persuasion team. Ever since that phone call where I thought you'd been kidnapped." Her face reddened. "God, I was a numpty, wasn't I?"

"I take it you're talking about the way you panicked when I called you and didn't speak for, oh... all of about a minute." Lesley winked. "Not about anything I need to worry about."

"I am. But I want a solemn oath from you that you'll never tell my team about that. Otherwise I'll tell them about your yoghurt habit."

Lesley stood up and rounded the desk. She opened the door to her mini-fridge. "You're too late on that one, I'm afraid."

Zoe's mouth was wide. "Wow. How did you get your health and safety officer to agree to that?"

Lesley reached round the back of the fridge for the cable. She pulled it forward to display the safety sticker. "I had it PAT-tested."

"You're clearly an influential woman around here. I'll make sure to keep on your good side."

"You'd better had," Lesley said, pushing the fridge back into position. She turned to see Zoe blush, just for a moment.

That wasn't the first time. What was she embarrassed about? Did Lesley need to worry?

She shook her head. *Don't be daft.* She leaned on the desk, fingers splayed.

"So," she said. "D'you want me to give you the lowdown on the people you'll be working with?"

Zoe shook her head. "If you don't mind, I'd rather form my own impressions. Are the MCIT all here?"

Lesley glanced at her watch. "As far as I know."

"Any new cases or changes I need to be aware of?"

"The Three Musketeers trial started today. DS Strunk's giving evidence later."

"Nathan Strunk," Zoe said. "Former PSD. But who or what are the Three Musketeers?"

"Billy Miller, Luka Tanner, Mick Donnelly. The three men we arrested for the murders of Mark Ashforth and Jackie Kendall. Johnny called them that after we arrested them, and it stuck."

Zoe nodded. "I feel bad about Jackie. If we hadn't let her leave the Hub..."

Lesley rounded the desk and put a hand on Zoe's shoulder.

"It wasn't your fault, Zoe. I was there, too, and it was my case. Four months passed, she went to Edinburgh, then Norway, then came home." She shook her head. "The only people responsible for Jackie's death are the bastard Musketeers who killed her."

Zoe looked up at her. "It's ominous, you calling them that. What about D'Artagnan?"

"You're suggesting there's someone else pulling the strings?" Lesley pursed her lips. "I've met those three. I've questioned them. I'm afraid there's no doubt that there's somebody else pulling the strings."

"Someone with a grudge against Vera Kelvin."

"Either they've got a grudge against her, or they're trying to muscle in on her territory. Organised Crime have their eye on the second of those two options. I'll introduce you to DI Rebecca Bremner. As for the first... we can only take action if they commit a crime in Dorset."

"Which you have no evidence of."

Lesley shook her head. "Not since Jackie's death. And our

Musketeers are claiming they acted alone. Their stories are depressingly consistent."

"They had enough time to confer."

"They did." Lesley sat down again. "We've been liaising with the Met, as far as the super will allow. Another introduction I'll make for you."

Zoe smiled. "I've already spoken to DI Ortega. I hope you don't mind."

"Mind? Your initiative is what I hired you for. I'm bloody ecstatic. And I'd also like you to give the financial evidence from the Mark Ashforth side of the investigation the once-over. Tina and Meera have already been through it, but I know it's your forte."

"Of course. There's a forensic accountant I've been working with, on a Cumbria case."

Lesley wrinkled her nose. "I'll have to check we can spend the money. We get our arses kicked by the press just for buying pens these days, after putting this new building up..." She gestured around her.

"It is very nice. And not in the middle of nowhere, unlike the Hub..."

"Oh, I wouldn't be so sure; you should see my commute." Lesley stood up. "Anyway, they'll be wondering if we've run off to the circus. Let me take you to visit your team. If you're lucky we might catch some of Jill's team, too. And the super."

"Of course." Zoe stood up, rubbing her hands together. "I'm looking forward to it."

CHAPTER SEVEN

At last Jill and Katie arrived at the end of the access road to the beach huts. Jill had managed to avoid hitting any pedestrians, but there had been a few close shaves she hoped Katie hadn't noticed.

She parked the car in the spot where the land train would have been waiting, if it were later in the year, and she got out. Katie was already walking up the path leading further along the harbour side. Waves lapped at the shoreline, and boat masts clanked; it was more sheltered here.

Katie turned to her. "It's up here, guv. I've got a What3Words reference."

"Tell me it acknowledges the fact that this is a toilet block."

Katie frowned. "*Opera. Intelligible. Stop*. Sorry."

Jill shrugged. "Ah well. One day, maybe."

Katie plunged her phone into her inside pocket and kept walking. A few moments later, they arrived at the site of what Jill could only assume was a former toilet block. The building itself was a pile of concrete rubble, the cistern of a toilet poking up through the blocks. To one side, was a digger and a group of four grubby, bored-looking men. To the other, was Gail Hansford and one of her CSIs, the one who wasn't ridiculously tall. Another woman stood behind him, wearing protective gear. An archaeologist, maybe?

And beyond them all, a gaggle of onlookers were trying to gain access via the alleyways running between the beach huts. Two uniformed officers were attempting to keep them at bay.

Jill scanned the crowd, wondering where to start. *Gail.* If in doubt, start with the crime scene manager.

She took a few steps towards Gail, who was leaning over the rubble, a tablet in her hand. "Gail."

Gail flinched, then turned to her. "Jill," she said, a little breathless. "You crept up on me."

"Sorry. Didn't mean to. How long have you been here?"

"About an hour." Gail gestured towards the woman Jill didn't recognise. "Did you send a forensic archaeologist? I'm impressed how quickly she got here."

Jill frowned and approached the woman. "DI Jill Scott, Cold Cases Team." She glanced towards Katie, who was talking to the Uniforms. Sensible; you never knew what they might have observed among the crowd. "Can I ask who sent you?"

The woman waved her hand and shook her head. "I'm Ursula Rowland. Forensic archaeologist. Well, PhD student, my supervisor is on her way and told me to get started without her as I'm closer. Rather not shake, sorry."

Jill shook her head. "Sorry, but I'll have to ask you to wait until your supervisor arrives, then they can vouch for you."

The woman smiled. "Yes."

"Yes?"

A nod. "They contacted Bournemouth University. Who sent me."

Jill glanced at Gail, who shook her head. She turned back to Ursula. "I'm sorry Ursula, but it's your supervisor they'd have sent. Do you mind stepping behind the cordon while I do?"

Ursula's face dropped. "Fine. I can be of help, though."

"I'm sure we'll get it all cleared up in no time," Jill said. "Thanks."

Ursula stepped away and stood against the cordon, watching. Jill called Mike; engaged. She left a message.

"Hi, Mike. There's a forensic archaeologist here, called Ursula Rowland. Can you check if she's registered? Thanks."

She approached Gail, aware of the crowd watching. She picked her way through rubble-strewn sand, which became damper the closer she got to the former toilet block. She was wearing a forensic suit over her clothes, but still she wished she'd chosen more casual clothes this morning.

She wrinkled her nose. "Something's leaking."

Gail sniffed. "The guy with the digger panicked when he realised what he'd uncovered. Swung its arm and sliced straight through a pipe."

"Supply or drainage?" Jill asked. She was learning a bit about plumbing thanks to the remedial work on her house's creaky system.

"Drainage. Can't you smell it?"

Jill could. She nodded and looked down at her feet. *These shoes are going in the bin tonight.*

"You might not think it now," Gail added. "But drainage is better than supply. We'd be swimming in it if it was supply."

"Nowhere to turn it off?"

Gail shook her head. "This is an old system. Guy from the council tells me the stopcock's half a mile away."

Half a mile away? That made Jill's house seem positively well equipped.

"Try to ignore the mud, if you can." Gail glanced down at Jill's shoes. "Let me show you the body."

Jill nodded. That was what she was here for, after all. "I'm assuming I don't need to worry about treading on any evidence."

"Not apart from the poor bugger himself," said Gail. "But no. He's been here for years." She glanced over at the cordon. "The archaeologist, if that's what she is, says decades." She pointed to the skull. "Look at his teeth."

Jill crouched down and squinted. It was windy today, but it was bright, too. "What am I looking at?"

"Remains of a brace. Corrective device."

Jill leaned in as far as she could without toppling. There it was, the remains, as Gail said, of a brace. Only a section of it was there, a scrap of what could only be muddy plastic and a glint of wire.

"That's been cleaned up by the leak," she said.

Gail grunted. "It's contaminating bloody everything." She cast a disgruntled glance towards the four men flanking the digger. One of them stood facing the other three, answering their questions with an air of exasperation. The supervisor, Jill assumed.

"So this isn't an archaeological find," she said, straightening.

"I'm not an expert," Gail said, "but I'm pretty sure they didn't have braces like that more than about fifty years ago."

"And they're mainly worn by children and teenagers."

"He's an adult," Gail said. "We'll need expert input on the bones, but they look mature to me."

Jill nodded. She checked her phone; nothing from Mike.

Damn. If Ursula was the archaeologist they needed, she could be of use. But she wasn't letting anyone on the site without authorisation.

She looked over at the cordon.

"Where's she gone?"

Gail looked up. "Sorry?"

Jill pointed. "The archaeologist. She's gone."

Gail shrugged. "No idea."

"Hmm." Jill scanned the faces behind the cordon. She sighed. "Maybe she decided to wait until we allowed her access."

"To go somewhere warm in the meantime," Gail said. "It's bloody freezing out here."

Jill smiled. "True." She cocked her head, looking down at the body. "So he's an adult male put here sometime in the last fifty years or so."

"That's my initial conclusion," Gail said. "Again, we'll need—"

"Expert input. I know."

Jill's phone buzzed; a message from Mike. *University say archaeologist will be with you in about two hours.*

Jill showed the message to Gail.

"So who was she?" Gail asked. "She told me she was a specialist in bone decomposition."

"Maybe she was. Is. Just curious. Thought she'd try her luck."

Gail grunted. "Another nosey parker, more like."

"We've got plenty of them."

"Yeah. We'll get a tent up as soon as we can get this ground stable." Gail gestured towards the remains of the toilet block. "The age of this block might help, too."

"He can't have been put here before it was built."

"Exactly. And it's likely he was left while it was being built."

Jill nodded. "Any idea when?"

Gail gave her a wink. "I asked the council workers, the foreman remembered. This block was built in the nineties. Our guy may have been put here during construction. The council will know more. Someone will, at least."

Katie had moved from the uniformed officers to the council workers. Jill smiled: *well done.* If there was background information to be winkled out of those men, Katie would winkle it.

"What was here before?" Jill asked, to no one in particular.

"Probably nothing," Gail said. "This place was very different in the eighties." She smiled. "Felt like the end of the earth."

"You came here?"

"Oh yes. Big treat, coming to Hengistbury for the day. It hasn't changed much, there was more here in Victorian times, from what I've heard. But it would have been deserted."

"A nice, secluded place to hide our poor victim," Jill said. Gail nodded.

Jill pulled in a breath and looked down at the remains. The sand had done its work, corroding his skin and rubbing down to the bone in places. But it had kept him dry, until now.

"We need to move him," she said. "Before the leaking water contaminates him anymore."

"A team's on its way," Gail said.

Jill gazed down at the body. *Poor bloke.* "So we're looking at a forty-year time frame, or thereabouts," she said.

"Definitely one of yours," Gail replied.

"Anything else that can help us narrow it down?"

"We can get an analysis done: fibres his clothes are made from. There've been lots of new fabrics developed over the last forty years, ."

"He could have owned those clothes for years before he died."

"He could," Gail admitted. "But it'll help us narrow it down."

"Guv!" Katie was over by the beach huts, beckoning.

Jill gave Gail a pat on the arm.

"Thanks," she said. "Let me know if you find anything else. And you'll get your expert, in a couple of hours."

"Looking forward to it," Gail replied.

CHAPTER EIGHT

DC Tina Abbott leaned back in her chair and stretched her arms above her head. Sitting at the screen like this for days – no, weeks – on end was getting to her.

Maybe things would liven up once the Three Musketeers' trial was over. It had started at the beginning of the week, and her boss, DS Nathan Strunk, was giving evidence later. Tina's job today was to go over his notes and check that everything added up, to make sure there were no holes for a skilful defence barrister to crawl their way into.

But right now, her back was stiff and her neck ached. She stood up.

"I'm going to the kitchen. Anyone fancy a brew?"

DC Johnny Chiles, also intent on his screen, raised an arm, thumb aloft. DC Meera Vedra looked up and gave Tina a nod. DS Strunk grunted.

Tina sighed. She wasn't the only one who was fed up.

"Was that a plan to put the kettle on I heard? Two coffees for us, please, Tina."

Tina turned to see DCI Lesley Clarke in the doorway, a tall

woman with wavy shoulder-length red hair standing behind her. This had to be the new DI.

"Er..." she said. She didn't want to miss the introductions, but at the same time, she didn't want to be rude.

"I'll give you a hand." Johnny rose from his chair, shifting his neck from side to side to banish stiffness. "Speed things up."

"You read my mind. Thanks, Johnny." The return of the team's lost sheep had been problematic and a little irritating, at first, but now it was like he'd never been away, and he seemed to have slotted neatly into the team. She wasn't sure Meera agreed with her, though.

"Tina." The DCI put a hand on her arm. "Before you go, let me quickly introduce DI Finch."

"DI Zoe Finch. You must be Tina." The redheaded woman held out a hand. She had to be a good four inches taller than the DCI.

Tina took the hand and shook it. "Pleased to meet you, Ma'am. I'm DC Tina Abbott."

The DI raised an eyebrow. "People use Ma'am around here?" She pushed out a breath. "Well, I guess—"

"Not for me, they don't," the boss said, raising an eyebrow at Tina. "I can't stand it."

"That's true," Johnny was standing next to Tina, grinning and holding out a hand. "I'm DC Johnny Chiles. Been part of the MCIT, or its predecessors, since forever."

The new DI cocked her head. "I thought you'd recently done a stint in the Met? Arrested our Musketeers, or so I've been told."

The tips of Johnny's ears turned pink. *At least it's not the rest of them*, Tina thought. Sometimes she reckoned they could use Johnny to replace the Portland Bill lighthouse.

"Yes," he said. "Er, yeah... that's right." He glanced at the DCI, looking anxious. "Moved across for a few years. Career development – you know the kind of thing."

She nodded. "I guess you could say I've been getting a bit of that myself in Cumbria, the last couple of years."

The DCI grunted. "You can say that again. Who's heard of Myron Carter?"

"Nasty bastard," Johnny said. "Drug smuggling. Money laundering. People trafficking."

"And a fair bit more besides," said DI Finch, her tone flat now.

"That's the one," DCI Clarke said. "Zoe took him down."

The DI shook her head. "Not on my own."

"No, of course not. No one works alone. But I was watching the way you worked throughout the whole thing, and I'm pretty damn sure that arsehole wouldn't even be close to being in custody without your thoroughness and tenacity."

The DI blushed, trying to suppress a smile. Tina noted that she wasn't meeting DCI Clarke's eye.

"Thank you," she said. "It's very kind of you, Lesley." She blinked and clapped her hands. "How about that coffee, eh?"

Tina stepped forward. "Be right back." She gestured for Johnny, who seemed to have forgotten his offer to follow her.

"Don't worry," DCI Clarke said. "You won't miss anything. Zoe and I will have an introductory chat with Nathan, then I'll leave her to gather you all together. You can debrief her on the Musketeers."

DI Finch nodded. So she'd been told about Johnny's nickname for them. *Let's just hope no one lets that slip in court.*

The DCI and the new DI walked over to DS Strunk's desk. Tina watched as they went, observing the easy body language between them.

So far, so good. But then, the last boss of the MCIT had been DI Hannah Patterson so the bar wasn't set high.

CHAPTER NINE

Katie stood in the middle of the four council workers, giving them her best attentive body language. Strictly speaking, she should probably separate them and speak to them individually, but she needed initial information. Formal witness statements could come later.

The vocal one, Jude Bristow, seemed to be the one who'd seen the body first. Or at least, the first one to realise that the object they'd unearthed from underneath the toilet block was a body.

But she was more interested in talking to Digsy, the one who'd been operating the digger. When she'd introduced herself, he'd given her a toothy grin and insisted that she call him Digsy. She'd resisted an eye roll at the obviousness of the nickname.

"Do you think you might have disturbed the body with the digger before you realised what it was?"

Digsy frowned. Another man, older and overweight with an air of uneasy authority, stepped forward.

"I hope you're not suggesting he's contaminated evidence," he said.

Katie gritted her teeth. *Heaven save us from people who watch cop shows.*

"Sorry, what's your name?" she asked.

"Tel." He cleared his throat. "Terry. Terry Smith." He gave her a thin smile; no gappy teeth this time, thank goodness. "I'm the crew supervisor. I just need to know you—"

"No, Mr Smith. I'm not suggesting that you or your team have done anything wrong. I just need to establish whether any of the damage I can see on the body happened when it was discovered. That way, I can rule out—"

"You can rule out it being done to him while he was alive," said Jude. He was looking pale.

She hesitated. Did she have the time or energy to explain?

Yes. It might encourage them to give her a fuller picture.

"The truth is, Mr Bristow—"

"Jude. No one calls me mister."

She nodded. "The truth is, Jude, that it's easier to establish damage and injuries done at the time of death than you might think. Given that this poor individual has been here for quite some time, I don't think that'll be a challenge. But it would be helpful to check, in case any damage was done between the victim being killed and your discovery of him. We don't know when he was put here."

"I should think that's pretty obvious," said a voice from behind her. Katie turned toward the crowd of onlookers, which PC Sharma was holding back.

She frowned. "Why?" she asked, scanning the crowd for the source of the interruption. The voice had been male. Elderly, judging by the hoarseness.

The crowd shifted, and a tiny man with a few strands of wispy grey hair and a face that was more wrinkles than skin stepped forward. He wore a heavy overcoat that looked like it weighed as much as he did.

"He's been here since 1994," he said, more clearly now.

Katie stepped towards him. "You sound very confident."

He shrugged. "That's when that toilet block went up. Judging by where they unearthed him, he can't have got under there since the thing was built."

He had a point. And the archaeologist had said the body would have been there quite some time.

"You're sure it was 1994?"

A nod. "As sure as I can see you in front of me." He blinked. "1994 was the year my boy went missing." His expression tightened. "I came down here thinking it might be him."

Katie felt her stomach hollow out. Poor man.

She took a step towards him. "Would you like to speak more privately?" She had no idea how easy it would be to identify the body. And it probably wasn't a job for someone who might be his father.

He shook his head. "I'm fine here." He jerked his head behind him to indicate a woman in her sixties. "This is my Amber. She'll look after me."

The woman, Amber, put a hand on her father's shoulder and looked into Katie's eyes. "Have you been able to make an identification yet?"

"Not yet, sorry. It isn't straightforward, after so much time." Katie looked between the pair. "Can you give me your names, please? And the name of your son and brother?"

The elderly man licked his lips, making a clicking sound that Katie tried to ignore.

"I'm Harold Carson, love. This here is my poor, long-suffering daughter, Amber Carson. And my boy's name was Stephen Carson."

"You say 'boy'. How old was he when he went missing?" As far as Katie knew, the body was an adult. Maybe the man was wrong.

Did she hope he was wrong? Did she want this family to finally know what had happened to Stephen and get closure? Or did she want to spare them the experience of learning that their son and brother had been rotting beneath a toilet block for decades?

Harold sniffed. "He was twenty-nine, love. His whole life in front of him."

Katie did some quick maths in her head. The man in front of her would be in his eighties, or possibly nineties, which would explain the 'whole life in front of him' comment.

"Thank you, Mr Carson. The honest truth is, we haven't yet identified the individual that was found this morning. But if you let me have your contact details, I or another officer can visit you at home to update you and find out more about—"

"We did all that when he went missing," Amber said. "I spoke to a policeman. PC Carpenter, his name was. Thin man, well spoken." She hesitated. "It's stayed with me."

PC Carpenter. Katie wondered if that might be the superintendent. But it was a common enough name. And imagining Superintendent Carpenter as a lowly PC was beyond her.

"I'll be sure to speak to the relevant teams," she told the woman. "A file would have been kept. But it was over thirty years ago, so..."

"She's right, girl," Harold said. "We'll need to go over it all again." He gave his daughter a steely look. "I'm hoping you've got the stomach for it."

"Of course I have, Dad." But Amber's tone wasn't so confident.

"Thanks," Katie said. "I need to speak to my boss about this." She gestured back towards the DI. "But if you can give me your address and telephone number..."

"Southbourne Coast Road," Harold said. "Been there since 1984 when they built the houses. Stephen moved in with me after my Betty died in 1988. Breast cancer." He looked down towards the ground.

Katie's stomach shrank even more tightly. A wife dead of breast cancer, a son missing for thirty-two years. How had he stayed living here all these years, without it destroying him?

Hope, she thought. The hope that he might discover what happened to his son. The hope even that his son might come home.

She just hoped she could help.

CHAPTER TEN

Jill muttered under her breath all the way back to the office. She'd left Katie at the crime scene with Gail and Brett, where the DC was taking statements from each of the council workers separately so they couldn't influence each other.

But they both knew that the council workers had nothing useful to tell them. They'd been demolishing a building and had found a body underneath it, that was all – a body that had been there a very long time.

But how long? Was this Stephen Carson, the son of the elderly man Katie had been talking to?

One thing was certain, if this was Stephen Carson, then she needed to speak to Superintendent Carpenter. And that meant speaking to the boss first.

She parked haphazardly in the Dorset Police HQ car park – wheels intruding onto the next space, not like her – and hurried inside and up to the Cold Cases team room. Stanley and Mike were inside.

"Hi," she said, struggling to regain her breath.

Stanley looked up. "Guv. You OK?"

"I'm fine. What are you both working on?" She perched on the edge of Katie's desk, trying to appear more relaxed than she was.

"I'm looking at maps of the area over the last thirty-odd years," Stanley said. "Identifying development work. The shape of the spit has shifted, too."

She nodded. "Mike?"

"I've been searching for planning applications. Trying to work out when the toilet block was built."

"It belongs to the council," Jill said. "Would their own projects even have to go through planning?"

"That'd explain why it's so ugly," Stanley grunted.

"It's certainly incongruous," Jill agreed.

"Do you know how much those beach huts sell for?" Stanley said. "Half a million, there's one advertised for half a million quid. And they don't even have a loo."

"Takes all sorts," Jill said. Katie had told her about the price of the beach huts on the way over there. She wished she had that kind of money. She could make their house properly habitable. Maybe even convince Meera she could love it there, too.

"I've got contact details for the council's building department," Mike said. "Maybe they can tell us."

"Good luck with that," Stanley said. "Was that area even under the same local authority when that toilet block was built?"

Mike shrugged.

"There's a good chance you'll find it was built in 1994," Jill said. "We've got a witness, an elderly man who lives nearby in Southbourne."

"Memory isn't always that reliable over such long periods of time," Mike said.

"And especially if he's an old fella," Stanley added.

Jill shook her head. "Sometimes the elderly have exceptionally strong memories of things that happened a long time ago. And besides, he has a good reason to remember. The block was built around the time his son went missing."

Mike raised an eyebrow. "Is he still missing?"

"He is. Name of Stephen Carson."

"Wow," Stanley said. "Well, that makes things easier."

Mike turned to him. "Not necessarily. We need to confirm the body's ID before we can jump to any conclusions."

Stanley made a *maybe, maybe not* seesawing motion with his hand. Jill pushed herself up from the desk.

"I need to speak to the DCI," she said. "Mike, you continue your work tracing when that toilet block was built, see if the father of the missing man has his dates right. We need to know who was involved in its construction, too."

"They'd have had access," Stanley said. "For putting him there."

"Exactly." Jill turned to him. "Although we don't know what procedures were in place for keeping the public out."

Stanley wrinkled his nose. "Thirty-two years ago. Could have been anyone."

"I'll call the council," Mike said. "See what they know."

"Thanks," replied Jill. "Stanley, I want you focusing on getting an ID. Speak to Gail, find out what forensics there are and what might be helpful. And once we've got a construction date, work on mispers from around that time."

"God knows what the files'll be like, guv."

"We're the Cold Cases Team, Stanley. This is what we have to deal with. And we've got a head start on the Stephen Carson mispers case. His dad told me which officer he spoke to at the time."

Mike looked up. "Who?"

"A PC Carpenter."

He raised his eyebrows. "The super?"

"The very same." Jill walked towards the door. "Which is why I need to speak to the boss."

Stanley laughed. "I can't imagine the super as a PC. I can't imagine him as a young man."

"Nor can I," Jill said. "But I'm sure he can, and I'm hoping he can remember this case."

CHAPTER ELEVEN

Katie stood back from the rubble of what had once been the toilet block, watching intently. PC Douglas had persuaded most of the onlookers to move on, and many of them had adjourned to the Beach House café further along the spit. Mr Carson had left with his daughter, unable to stay out in the cold any longer.

She was glad of that. There was no way she wanted Harold or Amber Carson to watch what was about to happen.

"Right," said Gail, standing on the other side of the rubble. "Digsy, I want you to ease your digger's arm back very carefully, so you don't disturb him any more than he already has been."

Terry, the supervisor, looked up from his position near the side of the digger. "I thought you said we hadn't done any damage," he said.

"And you didn't," Gail replied. "I'm referring to all the other stuff that's happened to the poor man."

Terry grunted, and Gail shook her head. She'd been talking to the council guys, getting information from them – but Katie could tell they were starting to annoy her.

She imagined the last thing these four wanted to do was spend their afternoon watching a body being exhumed from beneath a building that should have been demolished by now.

"That's it," Gail said as the digger's arm pulled back, the operator peering out of his cab with his tongue sticking out in concentration.

"Am I good now?" Digsy asked.

Gail gave him a thumbs-up. "You can reverse the digger away."

His shoulders visibly dropped in relief. He twisted to look over one of them and backed the digger away from the semi-demolished toilet block. Then he jumped down and stood with his colleagues.

"Perfect," Gail said. A specialist team was on its way; they would take over the lifting.

"Thanks," she said to the council workers.

The four men nodded. None of them looked at the crime scene manager; instead, they all stared at the body, which was now almost fully revealed. One of the men – Jude, if Katie remembered right – crossed himself.

"We don't need you anymore," she said. "You've given statements, right?"

Terry, the supervisor, looked at her. "We'd like to wait until he's removed, if you don't mind. Make sure he's safe."

Katie looked across at Gail; no one was better at ensuring the safety of a body than her and her team. The CSM nodded. "That's fine. But keep back, please."

He gestured at his colleagues and they all shifted back a few places.

Gail looked down at the body. She sighed. "Poor fella."

Katie pursed her lips. "I wonder who he is."

"Indeed." Gail shook her head. "Pathology won't come out here, not with their workload and such old remains. And it might be dry, but the wind and the sand will have done damage already. This isn't going to be easy."

"What are you going to do with him, once you've got him out?" Jude called over.

"Don't you worry about that." Gail glanced toward the roadway leading back to the visitor centre. Pathology might not have the resources to send a pathologist, but drivers were easier to come by.

"I'll walk up to the turning point, make sure they know where to go," Katie said.

"Uh-uh," Gail said.

Katie frowned.

"You're the only member of the investigating team here," Gail said. "Far as I'm concerned, you're temporary SIO."

Katie wriggled her toes in pleasure.

"I'll go," PC Douglas said.

"Good," said Gail. "Now let's get to work." She stepped forward towards the body and started taking photos.

PC Douglas was back in five minutes with the specialist team. Four men; no sign of Ursula Rowland. Katie wondered what had happened to her.

One of the men, who were indistinguishable in their forensic suits, approached Gail. She started giving instructions. He put a hand on her shoulder in an *I know what I'm doing* gesture.

Gail wouldn't like that.

Gail pushed the hand away and gestured towards the body. Katie bit down a smile and watched as the operation to remove the body began.

One by one, the lumps of concrete and metal pinning the victim down were removed. Gail gave Brett, one of her three techs, the job of cataloguing them in the hope there might be evidence left on them.

After forty-odd years? Katie doubted it.

At last, the man was completely exposed. His body was twisted, his hips pointing upwards, but his torso was shifted over to the right and his face obscured. His skin was shrunken and dried in places, sloughed off in others so that Katie could see the bones. It reminded her of a history project at school, an ancient man preserved in a bog.

Except this man had been preserved by dryness, not by damp.

The activity was attracting the attention of a fresh crowd of onlookers. Katie joined the Uniforms at the cordon, taking the section closest to Gail.

"Any sign of the cause of death?" she asked, trying to speak loud enough for Gail to hear but not so loud that the crowd could follow along.

"He's been here too long," Gail replied. "There's too much wear and tear. But no, I can't see anything obvious. But he's well preserved, considering."

Sure, it was early days. They'd need to get him into a lab and confirm the cause of death, if that was even possible after so long.

Katie shook her head. How had this man died? Had he come here beforehand, or been brought afterwards?

And more importantly, was he the missing Stephen Carson, or someone else entirely?

CHAPTER TWELVE

"Thank you, Detective Sergeant Strunk. No further questions."

Nathan nodded at the defence barrister and walked out of the witness box, trying to convey confidence in his movement. His questioning had been relatively straightforward and fact-based, focusing on the nuts and bolts of how they'd identified the Three Musketeers as suspects in the Ashforth and Kendall investigations, and the process they'd followed from that point on.

But Nathan knew that when a defence barrister asked a copper how he did his job, what they was really looking for were ways in which he'd done it wrong. In particular, procedural omissions or slip-ups that could lead to the trial being dismissed and the defendant walking free.

Things hadn't been easy while they'd been investigating the murder of the taxi driver found on Chesil Beach, and later, of the estate agent who'd witnessed some of his last moments. The DCI had stepped in as SIO after the last DI had gone off sick, and she clearly wasn't herself. But if DCI Lesley Clarke was anything, she was a stickler for doing things properly. Since making the arrests four months ago, he and his team had worked tirelessly on solidifying the evidence. Working with the CSIs to find corroborating evidence, working through any holes in the case. Things were as tight as his nan's cat's arsehole.

He'd be bloody glad when this was all over. All that evidence processing was getting dull.

Now that he'd given his evidence, he was allowed to go to the public gallery and watch. Tomorrow he'd be watching Johnny Chiles's testimony, giving the man some support. Christ knows, he needed it.

Today, he was supposed to go back to the office and help Johnny prepare. But he could spare a little time to watch the next witness.

He slid in through the double doors at the back of the court. A clerk was in the process of pulling across a curtain in front of the witness stand. Clearly, Yiannis Kallias had asked to remain unseen by the defendants, or – possibly more importantly – by any associates they might have brought along with them.

Nathan could understand why Jackie's partner was being cautious. But he also knew that Yiannis's picture was already out there. The man had run an online appeal when Jackie had first gone missing over a year ago. He'd been interviewed by the local press.

Maybe he'd changed his appearance. Jackie had dyed her hair while she'd been in hiding. But Yiannis? Nathan would never know.

There was some rustling in court at the appearance of the curtain. Ahead of Nathan, two men he didn't recognise, but who weren't wearing the lanyards indicating staff or press, bent towards each other and muttered.

They both had closely shaved heads. One was in his fifties, with a scar just visible above his collar. The other was ten years younger, with tattoos on the back of his hands, visible when he raised them to scratch his head.

Nathan didn't like stereotypes. He didn't like to assume someone was a criminal just because they looked like a criminal. But this pair had caught the attention of the three defendants, Billy, Mick and Luka. Every time the defendants glanced towards the gallery, there was a moment of shared looks and distinct hostility.

The question was, were these two men from London, like the three defendants, or did they work for the Kelvin family? Nathan made a mental note to look them up when he got back to HQ.

The judge's clerk confirmed Yiannis's name and that he was a witness called by the Crown Prosecution Service. She then sat down and let the Crown's barrister take over.

"Mr Kallias, I'm not going to keep you or ask you to speak at length."

The barrister looked towards the curtain, as did everyone else in the courtroom.

Silence. Yiannis would have been briefed: only give a response when asked a direct question.

The barrister turned back towards her colleagues on the front bench. She reached out a hand, and one of them handed her a sheet of paper. She nodded and turned back towards the curtain.

"Mr Kallias, I'm going to ask you a few simple questions, and I would like you to answer each of them with a straightforward yes or no."

No response, except for muttering in the public gallery. The judge wrinkled her nose, and the clerk called for quiet. The two men in front of Nathan pulled apart.

The barrister glanced down at her paper. "You are the former partner of Jackie Kendall, is that correct?"

"Yes." Yiannis's voice was low and indistinct, with his Greek accent impossible to detect. But the *yes* could clearly be heard.

"Thank you," the barrister continued. "On the twenty-fourth of June last year, did you book into the Premier Inn on West Cliff, Bournemouth, with Jackie?"

"Yes." Yiannis's tone and volume were unaltered. Nathan wondered what he must be going through behind there.

"Again, thank you. Now, is it correct that at twenty past five you left the hotel to buy provisions, returning at six fifteen, and on your return, you found Jackie dead on the hotel bed?"

Silence. The barrister waited. The room held its breath.

"Yes," came the response at last. The judge looked towards the area behind the curtain and gave the faintest of nods.

Nathan shoved his hands into his pockets, willing his fingers to stop fidgeting. He thought back to the first time he'd met Yiannis. The man's house had been chaotic, his only concern tracking down Jackie.

"Thank you, once again. After discovering Jackie's body in the hotel room, how did you respond?"

It was the first open question. But Nathan knew that if he asked too many closed ones, the barrister might be pulled up by the judge for leading the witness.

"I called the police," Yiannis said.

"Did you witness anyone leaving or entering your room, other than yourself or Jackie?"

"No. I didn't." Yiannis's accent was clear now, and his voice shook.

"Did Jackie tell you about an incident she'd witnessed, when she was preparing to show a house on Canford Cliffs in her role as an estate agent?"

"She did."

"Was it because of witnessing this incident that Jackie disappeared three weeks later and went into hiding in Cumbria, followed by Edinburgh and Trondheim, a village in Norway?"

"Yes."

The judge shook her head at the barrister. "I'm afraid we need this in the witness's own words." She turned towards the curtain. "Mr Kallias?"

Silence.

"Mr Kallias?"

"Sorry," Yiannis replied. "I believe that is why she left Bournemouth, yes. She was scared. She had been sent threatening messages."

"The content of these messages has been submitted as evidence," the barrister said.

"Very well," the judge said. "Carry on."

"Thank you, Your Honour. One final question from me to the witness." She turned towards the courtroom and glanced towards the defendants before turning back to the curtain.

"Mr Kallias," she said. "Did Jackie record a full statement of what she saw, and leave the video for your safekeeping?"

"Yes." Yiannis was quiet again.

"Thank you. Once again, this has been submitted into evidence."

"And the court will have the opportunity to watch it," the judge said.

Nathan clenched his jaw. Around him, the muttering had risen again, and the two men he'd been watching were exchanging urgent whispers.

This was going to be interesting.

CHAPTER THIRTEEN

Jill opened the door to DCI Clarke's office to find the DCI sitting behind her desk and an unfamiliar woman with shoulder-length red hair seated opposite. As Jill entered, the woman tucked her hair behind her ear, then frowned as it sprang back.

"Jill," Lesley stood up, gesturing at the woman. "I'm glad you're back. This is—"

"Zoe Finch," the new DI was already on her feet, a hand extended. "And you must be DI Jill Scott. I hear we're going to be working together."

Jill returned the woman's smile and shook her hand. DI Finch's grip was firm, but not overly so.

"Pleased to meet you," she said. She glanced at Lesley. "I need to update you on the body found at Hengistbury Head."

Lesley nodded. "Zoe, our other team, as you know, is newer. The Cold Cases Team. Jill's last case was—"

"Rowena Sharp," Zoe said, sitting down. Jill took the chair beside her. "Disappeared in 1973, found in a remote part of Poole Harbour last summer." She wrinkled her nose. "You must have some pretty powerful mud around here to preserve her for that long."

"Fortunately for us, yes. You're from Cumbria, right? Only your accent..."

Zoe laughed and raised her hands in a *you got me* gesture. "I'm a Brummie. Born and bred. Transferred to Cumbria a few years ago after..." She gave Lesley an uncertain look. "Well, after it became simpler to start afresh."

"The Canary case," Jill said. "And the eventual arrest of Trevor Hamm."

"And his subsequent death," Lesley added.

Jill nodded. "Portland Bill lighthouse. I hear the boss brought you in on that case, Zoe."

Slow down. What was this, twenty questions? She needed to give the poor woman some space to settle in.

But then, Zoe had started it. Genning up on the Rowena Sharp case. Jill had a feeling she was going to like her.

"She did," Zoe said. "Only from a distance, though. Lesley and Stanley came up to Birmingham for a day." She smiled. "I think the traffic terrified Stanley. He's on your team now, right?"

"He is. I've got him, Katie Young and Mike Legg."

"Tina Abbott's husband," Zoe said. "I have to say, you do have a habit of keeping it in the profession down here."

Jill felt her cheeks redden. "I'm married to a member of your team."

"Meera. She seems good. But obviously, I know we'll need to keep things professional when we're discussing her." Zoe's eyes widened. "Oh. I'm sorry. You didn't think my comment about keeping things in the profession was a dig at you, did you?"

"Err..." Jill frowned. She wasn't sure.

Zoe leaned forward, grazing Jill's arm with her fingertips. "I really didn't mean it to be." She straightened. "I was living with another detective, until recently. Carl. My ex." She pulled her hand back, placing it on her lap.

"I'm sorry," Jill said. So that was why the woman had moved hundreds of miles south.

"Don't be. It's fine." Zoe glanced at Lesley and then looked down again. "I brought it on myself."

During this exchange, Lesley had been leaning back in her chair, her gaze shifting from one DI to the other like she was at a tennis match.

"This is all very cosy," she said. "You two discussing your love lives and that. But you've got a case to update me on, Jill."

"Of course." Jill glanced at Zoe. "Something new has come to light. Something involving the super."

Lesley sighed. "Bloody hell, Jill. It's like you've got a fixation on the man. Don't tell me your cold case is one of Superintendent Carpenter's."

Jill glanced at Zoe, who looked none the wiser. "Err..."

Lesley raised her eyebrows. "It's fine, Jill. You can trust Zoe. You can't always trust her to follow orders, but you can damn well trust her to keep a secret."

Zoe made an involuntary sound, somewhere between a hiccup and a cough.

"You OK?" Jill asked.

"Fine." Zoe gave her a wry smile. "You carry on. Pretend I'm not here."

Oh, but you are here, Jill thought. *And I have no idea who you really are yet.*

She seemed nothing like Hannah Patterson, the woman she'd replaced, and that could only be a good thing. And Lesley had worked with her before.

Jill turned to Lesley. "I left Katie at the scene, with Gail Hansford and a woman who said she was a forensic archaeologist from Bournemouth University."

"I didn't know they were sending someone."

"Long story. I imagine they'll have fully exhumed the body by now. The council workers insisted on hanging around to watch."

"Sorry," Zoe said. "But who's Gail?"

"Crime scene manager," Jill replied.

"And a bloody good one," Lesley said. "Even better than Ady Hanson." Ady had been the lead CSM for Force CID in Birmingham. And he'd had a crush on Zoe.

"Really?" Zoe gave a little shudder. "And less aggressive than Stella Berry, I imagine." She caught Jill's puzzled expression. "CSM in Cumbria. Doesn't suffer fools gladly."

"Nothing wrong with that," Lesley said.

Jill nodded. "Anyway, we've got a potential lead. A member of the public, Harold Carson. He told Katie that the toilet block was erected in 1994. The same year his son went missing."

Zoe winced. "That's a long time not to know where your son is."

"Did he report his son's disappearance to the police?" Lesley asked.

"He did," Jill replied. "We don't have an ID for the body yet; it's going to be tricky, of course, so it could just be coincidence, but—"

"But this could be Mr Carson's son," Zoe said. She blew out a breath. "Poor man. Maybe he can get some closure at last."

"Is there a record of the original report?" Lesley asked.

Jill shrugged. "I don't know yet. I've got Mike and Stanley looking into it. That and the erection of the toilet block. After such a long time, it's always possible he's misremembered the date."

Lesley nodded. "Good. Sounds like things are starting to move more quickly than they normally do."

Jill nodded. "There's something else."

Zoe shifted forward in her seat. "You mentioned the super earlier. Superintendent Anthony Carpenter, right?"

"Yes," Jill replied. "He was the officer Mr Carson spoke to after he'd reported his son missing."

Lesley whistled. "Back when he was in Uniform."

"He was a PC, yes. I'm hoping he might remember the case."

Lesley placed her palms on the table. "He might do. OK."

Jill frowned. "OK?"

"Zoe needs to meet the super anyway. And you need to ask him about Mr Carson." Lesley stood up. "Let's all go for a little walk."

CHAPTER FOURTEEN

"So, if it's not a nosy question, what made you decide to move to Dorset?"

Lesley looked round at Jill and Zoe. *Perhaps not the best question for Jill to ask.* But Zoe seemed unperturbed.

"Do you want the official reason or the real one?"

Jill cocked her head. "Whichever you feel comfortable giving me."

Lesley smiled. She'd seen Jill do this with witnesses – put them at their ease by not probing too hard. But she was pretty sure Jill would get her answer eventually.

"The official reason," Zoe said, "is that my son moved to Exeter to do a master's. That and the weather. Cumbria's beautiful, but my God, it knows how to rain up there."

Jill nodded. Lesley looked at Zoe. She would know damn well what the other woman was doing.

"But the real reason," Zoe said, her voice lower, "was the break-up."

Jill winced. "Sorry to hear that. Is Carl your son's dad?"

Lesley grunted. Zoe laughed.

"Good God, no!" Zoe said. "Nick's dad hasn't been on the scene since... well, since he found out I was pregnant."

"The less said about him, the better," Lesley muttered.

"You knew him?" Jill asked. She glanced at Zoe. "Sorry. If this is..."

Zoe shook her head. "Half of West Midlands Police knew all about my personal life. It's fine."

"They also know the role you played in bringing down Trevor Hamm and his thoroughly unpleasant associates," Lesley said. "And that you uncovered David Randle."

"The superintendent who went into witness protection?" Jill asked.

Lesley nodded. Zoe said nothing, but her posture had stiffened.

"He's ready for you."

Lesley looked past her two DIs to see Carla, Carpenter's PA, looking up at them from behind her desk. How much of that had she heard?

"Right," she said. "Time to stop chatting about Zoe's past and see what we can find out about a certain other somebody's past."

She pushed the door open and stood back to let Zoe and Jill go first. It was odd seeing them together, Jill trying to piece together Zoe's background. Zoe had been in Lesley's life for even longer than her daughter Sharon had; Zoe's past was rolled up with her own.

"My goodness." Carpenter was standing behind his desk. "Three for the price of one. Lesley, you must warn me when you decide to come mob-handed."

"Jill needs to speak with you in connection with a case," Lesley told him. "And I thought it would be a good opportunity for you to meet Zoe Finch, our newest DI."

He put out his hand. "I've heard a lot about you, Zoe. I hope it all proves to be true."

Zoe smiled as she shook his hand. "I'll take it you've heard good things then, Sir."

He smiled. "Lesley wouldn't have persuaded me to take you on unless she thought you were a bloody good copper. I had two excellent CID DIs with their eyes on this post. Let's hope I made the right decision."

"That's a lot of pressure for her first day, Sir," Lesley said.

He turned to her. "We're all under pressure, Lesley." He smiled at Zoe. "If half of what your DCI has told me is true, then I have every confidence you'll be a fine addition to the team."

"Thank you, Sir." Zoe inhaled and put her hands in her pockets. She'd be drilling a thumbnail into a palm, Lesley knew. *It'll get easier.* Carpenter wasn't always like this.

"So," he said, turning to Jill. "What's this you need to speak to me about, DI Scott? The body found up at Hengistbury Head, I imagine."

Jill nodded. "Mudeford Spit, Sir."

He waved a hand. "Same difference. Problems with an ID, I imagine? I'm not sure why you'd need to speak to me about that."

"Don't worry, Sir," Jill replied. "I'm accustomed to the identification challenges that come with a cold case. But we do have a witness who has suggested he might know who the body is."

Carpenter raised an eyebrow. "That's convenient."

Jill met his gaze. "His name's Harold Carson, Sir. His son Stephen went missing in 1994. He lives very close by, in Southbourne. So—"

"I remember that one." The superintendent leaned forward, palms on the desk. Jill took a step back. *Hold your own,* Lesley thought. *His bark is worse than his bite.*

"Stephen Carson," he said. "Reported missing by his father when he didn't come home for a while."

Jill nodded. "You spoke to the father, is that right?"

"I did. Once when he made the initial report, and once to tell him we thought the chances of us finding his son were slim."

Lesley frowned. "Why did you think that?"

He eyed her. "This was 1994, Lesley. Missing persons reports, especially regarding young men... well, there wasn't the political pressure to treat them with as much diligence as we might the disappearance of a young woman."

"So the case was dropped," Jill said. "You thought he'd just decided to leave home of his own accord."

Carpenter nodded. "That was the most likely scenario."

"But he lived with his father," Jill said. "He moved in after his mother died. Why would he just leave without saying anything? Why wouldn't he make contact?"

"We had information about Stephen Carson. Information we didn't pass on to his father."

"What kind of information?" Zoe asked. All three women were standing close to the desk now, almost touching it.

The superintendent's gaze travelled across the faces of the three of them, then landed on Jill's.

"We had evidence placing him at a crime scene," he said. "The robbery of a petrol station. Boscombe, or was it Pokesdown? I can't remember."

"You thought he'd disappeared to avoid arrest," Lesley said.

"What kind of evidence?" Jill asked.

"I don't remember. Fingerprints, probably. It'll be on the case file."

Jill had her phone out and was making notes. "When did the robbery take place?"

"A month or two earlier, I think. Listen, it was years ago. You'll find the details in the case log."

Which may or may not be on the database, Lesley thought. But Jill and her team were used to this.

"Did the police ever track him down?" Jill asked. "Make the arrest?"

Carpenter twisted his lips together. "No. Look, we need to be very careful with his father. You don't know for sure that this body is Stephen, and if it is—"

"If it is, then a man who was reported missing has been allowed to stay missing for thirty-two years."

He turned to her. "Exactly. Now do you see why this case has to be handled with care?"

Lesley eyed him. He was rattled; she could see sweat under his collar. *Handled with care*, she thought. But was that care for Harold Carson's feelings, or care for Anthony Carpenter's reputation?

CHAPTER FIFTEEN

MARCH 1994

"I DON'T UNDERSTAND," Harold said. "You've only been looking for him for two weeks."

The police officer passed his hat from one hand to the other, not meeting Harold's eye. If he could have squirmed without looking like a total idiot, he probably would have done.

"I'm very sorry, Mr Carson," he said. "But I've spoken to my senior officers and my colleagues in CID, and—"

"So why aren't they here?" They were standing in the hallway of Harold's house. They hadn't even made it as far as sitting down. "If they're the ones who know about these kinds of things, why aren't they here, explaining themselves to me?"

The PC stretched his cheek. "I was the officer who came out to speak to you initially. I'm familiar with your case. It was thought that—"

Harold took a step forward. "If you're the one who's so bloody familiar, why aren't you the one making the decisions? Do you think we should continue looking for Stephen, eh?"

PC Carpenter glanced up at him, then down again. The hat passed from hand to hand a second time.

Stop it with that bloody hat.

"It's not for me to judge, Mr Carson. I'm just a PC. I don't have the kind of experience needed to—"

Harold took another step forward. The constable gave him a wary look, as if judging whether he was a threat. His free hand moved down to hover by his waist.

Don't you dare use your truncheon on me.

"Explain it to me, lad. You're the one who knows my case. You're the one who's been here, twice now, and you've heard me tell you why Stephen's disappearance is suspicious. So why aren't you fit to judge whether the police can look for him?"

The constable met his gaze. "I'm just not, Sir. That's how it works. I'm sorry, but—"

He turned at the sound of the key in the lock.

Amber. Dreadful timing, girl.

She looked between the two of them, her expression puzzled, turning wary when she spotted the expression on her father's face.

"PC Carpenter," she said. "Hello. Why don't you come in properly?"

"He's not coming any further," Harold said. "It's my house, remember. You live with that fella of yours."

She blushed. "I was only being polite, Dad. What's happened? Is it..." She gasped. "Oh my God. Have they found Stephen? Have they..."

She dropped the bag she was carrying and wiped under her eye with her fingers. Harold grabbed her hand.

"Don't be silly, love. It's not what you think."

She looked at him with a sniff. "So why are you so angry?"

He felt his shoulders slump. Was that who he'd become? He'd been a calm father, placid even. When the kids were little, the other dads had laughed at him. *They need a firm hand.* He'd ignored them.

But then, in recent months, things had become difficult with

Stephen. His son had been moody and uncommunicative. Like a teenager again, at the age of twenty-nine.

The arguments had hardened him. They'd made him lose trust. Was that the kind of man he'd become?

He tried to smile. "I'm not angry, love."

The policeman sniffed. Harold turned his head to give him a glare. *Don't push it.*

"So what is it?" Amber asked.

He put his hand over his face and closed his eyes. *Breathe.* He removed the hand. "They've decided to stop looking for Stephen, love."

Her brow furrowed. "What? Why?" She looked at the constable. "Why?"

He shrugged. "I'm sorry, Miss Carson. But we have limited resources. And my colleagues in CID think he's simply left home." He looked at Harold. "You did tell me the two of you had been arguing."

"What? No. I didn't tell you that because I thought he'd buggered off. I told you that because I thought he was behaving erratically. Because maybe he'd..." Harold gasped in a thin breath. "Because maybe he'd done something stupid. You know what those cliffs are like."

The constable nodded. "We have searched around Hengistbury Head, Sir. And the cliffs further along at Fisherman's Walk. Your son wasn't there."

"That doesn't mean he left of his own accord. Does it not occur to you that someone might have him, right now? That he might be locked up somewhere, waiting to be found?"

Or worse, Harold thought but most definitely didn't say.

"Dad..." Amber said. "He's only doing his job. You can't blame him."

"Thank you," PC Carpenter said. "I'm afraid that's all I have to tell you. I'll leave you alone."

Harold glared at him. "Alone. That's what I am now, with this goddamn empty house. And it's all your fault."

"Dad..." Amber was giving the constable an apologetic look.

"Don't take his side. Incompetent they are, the lot of them. Incompetent and uncaring." He looked at PC Carpenter. "And if my son turns up dead, I'll know who to blame."

CHAPTER SIXTEEN

Mike worked his way through four different people at the council before he found anyone who could tell him about the construction of the toilet block.

"They were considered very swish back then," Gordon Bishop, a junior architect who claimed to have been in his job for over thirty years, told him. "It was one of the first projects I worked on. They included a private cubicle, only accessible to beach hut owners. They had their own key."

"And it was definitely 1994?" Mike asked.

"Year after I graduated. Yes, I remember it. It was quieter down there then. Not quite so many beach huts, and no café. God knows how those loos are coping with demand now."

"I guess that's why they're replacing them," Mike said. "Do you know who the construction firm was? Or were they built by the council?"

"Not by the council. We stopped doing that sort of thing in the late eighties," Gordon sighed. "Standards took a downturn."

Mike shook his head. Nostalgia, for a time before Gordon Bishop had even been working there. "Can you find out who the construction firm was? It would be useful to know who had access to the site."

"Oh, that's easy."

"It is."

"Site security wouldn't have been tight. It's a beach at the arse-end of nowhere. They probably didn't even bother with a fence. Anyone would have been able to get access."

Damn. "OK. Thanks for your help. If you can find the name of the construction company, it would be helpful."

"Of course."

"Thanks." Mike hung up and leaned back in his chair, yawning.

"Any joy?" Stanley asked, not taking his eyes off his screen.

"Huh? Yeah. Well, yes and no. I've got confirmation that the loo block was built in 1994. But it seems there was no fencing, no security. Anyone would have been able to gain access."

"At least that makes it more likely that the body's Stephen Carson," Stanley said. "Same year and all that."

Mike pushed his chair over towards Stanley's desk. The guv was still with the DCI, and Katie had messaged to say she was driving back. "You getting anywhere with an ID?" he asked.

Stanley screwed up his face. "Not yet. The body's been taken to the morgue in Poole Hospital."

"Right."

"Anyway, it's not likely they'll be able to identify it easily. Thirty-two years. It's not like the guy's dad can give us a nice fresh DNA sample."

"Can't they get a sample from family members, see how closely matched they are?"

Stanley shrugged. "Possibly. Gail and Brett are still at the scene, trying to find any other forensics that have been preserved."

"Like what?"

"Gail says they're keeping an open mind." Stanley chuckled. "Which I guess is code for having no fucking idea."

Mike snorted. "And it's not like the family can identify the remains."

Stanley wrinkled his nose. "We've both seen the photos. I imagine the guv won't want the family anywhere near him."

Stanley brought up photos of the body on his screen. It didn't look anything like a recognisable human being. Mike shuddered.

"Let's hope the boffins can work some magic," he said.

Stanley grinned. "Let's."

CHAPTER SEVENTEEN

"Hi, everyone." Zoe closed the door to the team room behind her. "Sorry about that."

Johnny looked up. "No need to apologise, Ma'am."

She grimaced, approaching the empty desk – Nathan's. The other three members of the team were sitting at their desks. They all looked bored out of their minds.

"Ma'am sounds a bit formal," she said. "How about you just call me boss?"

Johnny wrinkled his nose. "I haven't been here all that long, but even I know that would be confusing."

"That's what everyone calls the DCI, Ma'am," Meera added.

"And the other team call DI Scott 'guv', is that right?"

"Yes," Meera said.

"I bet that's not what you call her at home." Johnny grinned.

A flicker of irritation crossed Meera's face. "No. But at work, we keep things professional."

"Very sensible." Zoe pushed herself off from Nathan's desk, which she'd been leaning against, and walked towards Tina. The DC was being quieter than she'd expected.

"What do you think, Tina?" she said. "What would you feel comfortable calling me?"

Tina shrugged, glancing at Meera. "I guess we've no option but to stick with Ma'am."

Zoe shook her head. "That makes me feel about sixty. Either that, or it makes me think you're scared of me. How about you just call me Zoe?"

Tina gritted her teeth. Johnny muttered something unintelligible. Meera started scratching the back of her neck.

OK, Zoe thought. *That's certainly triggered something.*

"You don't feel comfortable calling me by my first name," she said.

"The last DI, DI Patterson," Tina said. "She insisted we should call her Hannah."

Zoe knew what Lesley's opinion of Hannah Patterson was. It seemed her team shared it.

"In that case," she said, "how about I don't insist on anything. You carry on calling me Ma'am if that's what you're happy with. And when you feel it's appropriate, I'm happy for you to call me Zoe." She looked around the group. "But I'm definitely not insisting on it."

Tina nodded, her mouth a straight line. Meera stopped scratching.

"That sounds like a plan," Johnny said. Zoe noted he didn't add either 'Ma'am' or 'Zoe'.

She sighed, remembering the process of integrating into her Cumbria team when she'd moved up there. It had taken a single case. Maybe it would be the same here.

She clapped her hands together. "Let's not worry about that. Why don't you tell me what you're working on? The deaths of Mark Ashforth and Jackie Kendall, is that right?"

The door opened behind her. She turned, sensing the three DCs' relief at a distraction.

Nathan entered. He wore a suit that looked like it didn't get much airing: brown, double-breasted with a collar that was about ten years out of date.

"Nathan," she said. "Good to see you again." He looked pinched. "Everything OK?"

He nodded. His cheeks were pale and he kept grinding his knuckle into his left eye.

"The Three Musketeers trial," he said, then stiffened. "I mean Miller, Tanner and Donnelly. It was my turn to testify this afternoon."

"Your turn?" she asked. Funny way to phrase it.

"Johnny's on tomorrow." He looked at the DC. "You'll be fine, Johnny. They went fairly easy on me."

"You weren't the one who arrested them, Sarge," Johnny replied, looking unconvinced. "You don't have history."

"It's not about history, Johnny. It's about the facts. The procedure. Just tell them what happened, and you'll be fine."

Zoe looked between the two men. "Fill me in. How does Johnny have history with the Musketeers?"

A smile flickered on Johnny's lips at her use of 'musketeers'. Nathan looked past her, at his desk. She'd migrated back to it without realising and was leaning on it.

"Sorry, Nathan." She moved away from his desk and towards the table at the far end of the room. She lifted herself up to sit on it. It shook a little but held; Zoe was tall, but she was slim. "Tell me about the case."

Nathan sat down at his desk and nodded. "It began before we even knew it was a case, over a year ago. Jackie Kendall witnessed what were probably not far from Mark Ashforth's final moments."

"Are they going to play her video statement at the trial?" Meera asked.

Nathan turned to her. "They played it during Yiannis's testimony, which was straight after mine." His expression darkened. "It was a hard watch. Definitely had an impact on the jury."

"That's good," Zoe said. "Increases the chances of a conviction."

Nathan shrugged. "The eyewitness evidence isn't great. For Mark Ashforth's death, I mean. It was dark, and although one of the witnesses got video of the Musketeers leaving Mark's body at St Catherine's Church near Chesil Beach, the quality isn't great."

"They are recognisable, though," Johnny added.

"At a push," Nathan said. "And then there's the challenge of proving that it was the Musketeers who Jackie saw with him."

"Where did she see them?" Zoe asked.

"In the garage of a house Jackie was preparing for a viewing. She was an estate agent."

"A house that belonged to the Kelvin family," Meera added.

"I've heard of them," Zoe said.

Meera nodded. "When Jackie saw them, one of them was making a phone call. To someone he called 'Mrs Kelvin'."

Zoe raised an eyebrow. "Vera Kelvin?"

Vera Kelvin was the octogenarian matriarch of the family. When her son Arthur had died, the business – both legitimate and not so much – had passed to her.

"But here's the thing," Johnny said. "The Musketeers aren't part of the Kelvin operation. They're from a completely different gang, based in London." He paused. "Which is how I have history with them. I was in the Met for a few years."

Zoe knew that. She knew Johnny had transferred quickly, presumably seeking a career opportunity. She was puzzled that he'd come back.

"So the evidence for Mark Ashforth's murder is inconsistent," she said. "What about Jackie Kendall?"

"Oh, that's tight as a duck's arse," Johnny said.

"We've got CCTV," said Nathan. "The three men entering the hotel where she died."

"That's not the important bit, though," said Johnny. "They used a vehicle they'd nicked from Vera Kelvin's house and booked a room in her name so they could access the building."

Zoe frowned. "Why? Trying to frame her? It was bloody clumsy if that's what they were trying to do."

Meera shook her head. "The whole thing's a mess, Ma'am." She looked at Nathan. "How was Yiannis, during his testimony?"

"Yiannis?" Zoe asked.

"Yiannis Kallias," Nathan replied. "Jackie's partner. He found her." He looked at Meera. "They had him behind a curtain. Good job, too. There were two men in the gallery who seemed to be keeping an eye on the Musketeers."

Meera sucked in a breath. "It won't make any difference. Yiannis's face was all over the news, when he was looking for her."

"Maybe he's changed his appearance."

"God, I hope so." Meera rubbed an eye.

Nathan looked at Zoe. "There is one specific aspect of the case I'm hoping you can help shed some light on, Ma'am. Based on your reputation, that is. Canary, and the way you took Myron Carter down in Cumbria."

Zoe frowned. *Bloody Canary.* Six years ago in Birmingham, that had been, and still it followed her like a bad smell.

But then, without her work on the Canary investigation, she might never have been made a DI.

"What's that?" she asked, stretching out her fingers to avoid drilling her thumb into her palm.

"Forensic accounting," Nathan replied. "Mark Ashforth's finances were irregular, before his death. He was a taxi driver. Skint, constantly in debt. And then suddenly he wasn't. Skint, that is."

"You think he was on the payroll of the Musketeers?" Zoe asked. "Or the Kelvins?"

"That's what we're not sure of. We have his accounts, and records of a large deposit. But we haven't traced the sender yet."

She nodded, already thinking about the trail she was about to follow. For the first time since putting an offer on that cottage yesterday, she felt excitement.

"I can help with that," she said.

Nathan smiled. The others visibly relaxed.

Just how bad had Hannah Patterson been?

"But right now," Zoe added, "it's time for you all to go home."

"Really?" Nathan was frowning. "But don't you want to get started?"

"And I need to prepare for tomorrow," Johnny said.

Zoe shook her head. "I'll download the files and let them percolate in my head overnight. Meera, it's my understanding that you should have been gone two hours ago, so you can be with your daughter."

Meera's mouth dropped open. "Suzi's gone to a friend's house this afternoon."

"Even so, you're not paid to stay here longer than your contracted hours."

"Thank you, Ma'am."

Zoe smiled. "And Tina, I gather you've got little ones, too."

"Louis and Daisy, Ma'am." Tina's face glowed at the mention of them.

"And me, Ma'am," Johnny said. "I've got two kids at home."

Zoe smiled. *So many babies*. "Well in that case, either you're all eager to hang around because you're trying to avoid the bedtime routine, or you think I expect you to work like machines."

"We're police officers, Ma'am," Nathan said. "The hours are never easy."

"True. But that's when there's an active case on the go. Yes, there's a trial happening, and we have a case to solidify. But we aren't actively investigating a major crime right now. Am I right?"

Nods and grunts.

Zoe hopped down off the table. She'd have to bring another chair in here.

"Good," she said. "I'll see you all in the morning, when your brains are fresh. Johnny, your testimony is in the afternoon, right?"

"Yes, Ma'am."

"In that case, try not to think about it tonight. Get a good night's sleep, and some downtime." She laughed. "Blimey, I sound like I did when my son had A-levels. You and Nathan can prepare for your testimony in the morning. I'll help, if you think that would be useful. OK?"

Johnny looked at Nathan, who nodded.

"OK," he said.

"Good." Zoe headed for the door. No point in waiting for them all to close down their computers and gather their coats.

She turned in the doorway. "It was good to meet you all. Thanks for briefing me on the case. I'm looking forward to working with you."

She closed the door and strode to her own office three doors up, her heart pounding. That had been hard work. But it would get easier. At least, she had to hope so.

CHAPTER EIGHTEEN

"Katie!"

Katie had just entered Police HQ at Winfrith and was heading for the lift. She turned at the sound of her name.

DI Scott was at the bottom of the stairs, heading her way. "Katie. I'm glad I caught you."

"Guv. I was just on my way up to your office." She looked towards the lift, considering what Harold Carson had said to her. "It might be best if we talk there."

The guv nodded. "Works for me. How are things at the crime scene?"

The lift doors opened and the new DI, Zoe Finch, stepped out. She gave DI Scott a smile and Katie a nod.

"DI Scott," she said. "I appreciate you filling me in on what your team is working on."

"You never know when we might need to work together," the guv replied. "Besides," she laughed, "I was hardly going to tell you to leave the room, was I?"

DI Finch joined her in the laugh. "Well, I appreciate it." She looked at Katie. "DC Young, yes?"

Katie stepped forward. "DC Katie Young. Pleased to meet you, Ma'am."

The guv gave the slightest of snorts. Katie felt her face grow hot.

DI Finch put a hand on her arm. They were standing so close, anything other than physical contact would have been even more awkward.

"You, too, Katie. I hope it wasn't too much of a trek being at such a remote crime scene all day."

"Oh, I love crime scenes, Ma'am. The more remote, the better."

The DI raised an eyebrow. "Good for you." She pulled back her hand and looked at the guv. "I'll see you tomorrow. I'm off to see an old acquaintance, of sorts."

She walked past them and out of the building. Katie watched her, wondering who the old acquaintance was.

DI Scott had a hand on the lift door to hold it open. "So... the crime scene?" She waited for Katie to pass her, then stepped inside.

"They're making good progress," Katie said as the lift doors closed. "The body's been removed and Gail and her team are working through the rubble."

"You think they'll find anything?"

"He's been enclosed under there for a long time. If his killer left anything behind, it might have been preserved with him."

"It's pretty exposed there," the DI said. "I don't imagine that helps."

Katie wasn't so sure. "The sand could actually work in our favour."

"That's encouraging." The lift doors opened, and the guv stepped out, waiting for Katie to walk alongside her towards the offices.

Katie nodded. "It creates a dry environment, which has helped preserve the body. In most spots along there, the narrowness of the spit would mean water ingress, and that would have all but destroyed it. But the toilet block had concrete foundations, infilled with sand."

"Which kept him nice and dry. Does that mean we'll be able to identify him?"

They were at the door to the team room. Katie followed DI Scott inside.

"It's been thirty-two years, guv. It's still going to be tricky."

Stanley and Mike looked up as they entered. She gave them brief nods. It had been different since Mike had returned from parental leave; she'd lost some confidence, being the only female DC with two men. And the youngest and least experienced, too.

She knew she shouldn't feel like that. She'd been seeking out new experiences and responsibilities at every opportunity and was probably more experienced than Stanley now, in real terms. And as for Mike... there was every chance she'd be his boss one day.

"Alright, folks," the guv said. "Katie's got a lead on a potential ID. Tell them what you've learned about Stephen Carson, Katie."

She sat down at her desk. "An elderly man came to the crime scene. Name of Harold Carson. His son, Stephen, went missing in 1994."

"Same year the toilet block was built," said Mike. "I checked with the council."

"I don't suppose they told you the names of anyone involved in the construction?" the guv asked.

"Not yet. I'm working on it."

"OK. Stanley, how—"

"When in 1994 was it built?" Katie asked. "Which month?"

"Good question." The DI looked from her to Mike, an eyebrow raised.

"Work commenced in January," Mike said. "It was completed by March. I don't have a specific completion date, though."

"Finished in time for the holiday season," Stanley said. Mike nodded.

"That fits," Katie said. "Stephen Carson went missing in February."

"So we reckon that's our victim?" Stanley said. "Makes my job easier."

The guv shook her head. "It makes no difference, Stan. I want you to continue prioritising the ID as if you didn't know about Stephen Carson."

Stanley frowned. "But that makes no sense. Surely—"

"It was over thirty years ago," the DI said. "All the more reason to be as thorough and impartial as we possibly can. I don't suppose you've made any progress with forensics?"

He shook his head. "They've been too busy processing the scene. I'm hoping tomorrow we'll have some news."

"The police didn't think anything untoward had happened to Stephen at the time," Katie said. "They told his dad that he'd probably just left home of his own accord."

The guv nodded. "That tallies with what Carpenter told me."

"The super?" Mike asked. "I didn't know this was sufficiently high profile."

Katie looked at the DI, who gave her a nod before turning to Mike.

"Harold Carson made the missing persons report to a PC Carpenter."

Mike's brow furrowed. "The super, before he was the super?"

"Before he was quite a lot of things," the DI replied.

"Mr Carson is very angry with him," Katie said. "Said he wants to give him a piece of his mind."

"Angry at the super?" Mike asked.

Katie nodded. "He reckons Superintendent Carpenter – PC Carpenter at the time – wasn't entirely honest with him. He thinks the police went from taking his son's disappearance seriously to dismissing it too fast."

"Why?" Stanley asked.

Katie pulled out her phone. "I was thinking the same thing. I mean, I know he was in his twenties and male, not an automatic fit for a kidnapping victim. But it seemed odd. So while I was getting a lift back here, I did some digging in the system. Looked into what I could find about Stephen Carson."

"And?" The guv had turned fully towards her.

"And he was a habitual criminal, guv. Starting with shoplifting and theft of personal items when he was in his late teens. Moving through to burglary and culminating with an armed robbery on a petrol station a month before his disappearance."

Stanley whistled. "Not exactly the innocent victim, then?"

"So do you reckon he was killed in revenge for the robbery?" Mike asked.

Katie shrugged. "If our victim is him, then maybe. But if it isn't him, then maybe Stephen Carson simply left home to avoid arrest."

"Or to avoid the people he'd robbed," Stanley added. Katie nodded.

"That makes an ID all the more imperative," the DI said. "Stanley, I want you to put pressure on forensics and pathology. Tomorrow, I want you at the lab in Dorchester."

"Guv." Stanley gave a mock salute.

"Let's find out if this is Stephen Carson," the guv said. "And if it is him, we need to know who might have wanted him dead."

CHAPTER NINETEEN

Zoe was glad retired Detective Sergeant Dennis Frampton's house wasn't too far from HQ.

Zoe had seen the woman who opened the door back when she'd been following her husband, back when Lesley hadn't known if she could trust him.

Things had changed since then, for Lesley and, Zoe hoped, for her, too.

"Hello?" the woman said, half-closing the door behind her. "Can I help you?" She looked Zoe up and down. Zoe had abandoned her customary leather jacket while in Cumbria – nowhere near warm enough – and was wearing a duffle coat that she worried made her look like Paddington.

"We don't buy on the doorstep," Pam Frampton said, pushing the door a little further closed.

Zoe sighed. She hadn't wanted to make this formal. She took out her police ID – brand new, given to her on arrival this morning – and held it up.

"My name's Zoe Finch," she said. "I'm a friend of Lesley Clarke. A member of her team since this morning."

Pam frowned. "I've heard that name... oh." Another look up and down. "You've come to see Dennis, have you?"

"I want to make a fresh start," Zoe said. "I know Lesley values his input, despite his retirement."

Pam sniffed. "Give me a moment." She pushed the door so it wasn't quite closed and left Zoe alone on the doorstep. Zoe looked up and down the quiet street of semi-detached houses. She wondered how many of the neighbours were watching her.

Don't knock it. Curtain-twitchers made excellent witnesses.

She forced herself not to look into any windows and faced the door, hands plunged in her pockets. It wasn't as cold here as it would be on the western Cumbria coast right now, but still... Dorset in February wasn't quite the Dorset she'd been expecting.

The door opened again. Pam had been replaced by her husband. He wore a cardigan with a loose seam at the wrist over faded cords. Zoe tried to calculate how long it was since she'd last seen him. He'd certainly aged more than four years.

She straightened, almost standing to attention. "Dennis."

"DI Finch."

"You're a civilian now. You can call me Zoe."

His nose twitched. He looked at her, a hand on the door.

"I wanted to make contact," she said. "Clear the air. I know we... well, we didn't get off to a good start."

"You followed me. You thought I'd..." He glanced over his shoulder. "We both know what you thought I'd done."

"I was wrong," she said, holding his gaze. "And I apologise for that. But it's important to remind you that I didn't know anything about you. What I did wasn't my decision." She swallowed. "It was what Lesley asked me to do."

Was she being disloyal? No. She was only telling the truth.

He laughed. "I've heard about your integrity. You won't tell me a lie, even if it makes you look better."

Was that true? She'd certainly lied enough to Carl.

But then, she hadn't lied. Not really. She'd just neglected to tell him about things. Specifically, things concerning David Randle.

She shivered. "Maybe you're right. So does that mean we can get off to a fresh start?"

His body language softened. "I don't believe in holding grudges. How much has the DCI told you about Tim Mackie? About the circumstances surrounding his death?"

"Not much. Well, some. But not all of it."

He eyed her for a moment. "I'd like you to know what really happened."

"OK." She looked past him, into the house. "I'd love to come in. It's cold out here."

And I've heard about Pam's baking, she thought.

"Not here." He pushed the door almost closed, and Zoe was alone on the path again.

Bloody hell, she thought. *What is this, some kind of endurance test?*

A moment later, the door opened again. Dennis emerged wearing a grey waterproof coat, the kind of thing Zoe had seen on hikers in the Lakes.

"Where's your car?" he asked. "We can go to my golf club."

"Golf club?"

"Do you have a problem with that?"

"No. But it's dark."

He laughed. "I'm not suggesting we play a round. There's a bar. They know me. It'll be quiet, this time of year."

"OK." *Thank God for that.* Zoe was still at Lesley and Elsa's for a few days until she found a short-term rental. Somewhere that accepted cats. She didn't want to get back too late.

"Right," Dennis said. "Which is your car?"

"That one." Zoe made for the green Mini parked in front of the house two doors along.

"Nice. A British classic."

"They're German-owned now."

"Still a British classic. Particularly in that colour."

Zoe smiled as they reached the car. She put a hand on the roof and patted it. "Between you and me, it's seen better days. But it reminds me of my dad."

Dennis caught the wistful look on her face. "He was a Mini driver?"

She shook her head. "He worked at the Austin factory, in Longbridge." She smiled, climbing into the car. "He missed my birth because it was the day the first Mini Metro rolled off the production line."

Dennis was beside her now, in the passenger seat. "A workaholic. That sounds familiar."

"It describes you?" Zoe asked, starting the car. He was about to tell her about the death of his old friend and mentor. Compared to that, this barely counted as prying.

"Me and every other copper," he said. "Turn right at the end of the road. It's Wareham Golf Club, you can put it in your satnav."

Zoe used the opportunity of stopping at the junction to programme Google Maps. A twenty-minute drive. Not what she'd been expecting.

"So tell me, DI Finch," Dennis said as they drove.

"Zoe."

"Tell me, Zoe. Do you have children?"

She felt her face twitch. "A son, Nicholas. He's doing postgrad at Exeter Uni."

"Good for him. I assume you were on the job when he was growing up."

"I was. It was just me and him."

"Then you'll understand even more than most."

"Understand what?" she asked, glancing at him.

"The effect this job has. The pull it exerts on you. Guilt. Regrets."

She wasn't ready to open up about all that.

"It's not always easy," she conceded.

He grunted. "Indeed. Right. Take the left turn in a mile, and we'll be almost there. You can buy me a drink, and I'll tell you the truth about what happened to DCI Tim Mackie."

CHAPTER TWENTY

"HELLO?"

Johnny's voice echoed through the house. He waited on the doormat, expecting Brandon to run out of the living room and come smacking into his legs.

Nothing.

"Alice? You home?"

He dropped his keys on the shelf and walked through to the kitchen. It was empty.

As he walked to the back door – maybe they were in the garden – his phone buzzed.

He picked up. "Alice? Where is everyone?"

"I've been trying to call you for the last hour. I'm at the hospital."

He grabbed the door handle. "Hospital? Are the kids OK? Are you OK?"

"We're fine. I've got the kids with me, but it's not them. It's your dad."

Oh my God.

"Dad? What happened?"

"He collapsed at home. One of his neighbours saw him through the window and called 999. They had to break in."

Johnny's breathing was shallow. "Is he... has he... Is he going to be OK?"

"Honestly, sweetheart, I'm not sure. But he's stable now, apparently."

"I'm on my way." Johnny strode to the hall and grabbed his keys.

"Good. Because the kids are getting on people's nerves, I think."

"They're just kids." Johnny was out of the house already and heading for his car.

"He's in an acute assessment ward. It's not exactly family friendly."

Johnny threw himself into his dad's antique car and started it. "Are you with him?"

"No. We're in a waiting room. South Wing, Dorchester Hospital."

"I'll be as quick as I can."

"Drive carefully, Johnny. I don't want to be visiting you here, too."

He flung his phone onto the passenger seat and sped away from the house. At the first junction, he slammed on the brakes. Alice was right. Racing there wouldn't help.

Twenty minutes later, he was at the hospital. He parked the car in a corner of the car park that wasn't really a space and ran to the main doors.

He muttered to himself, scanning the bank of signs. So many wards.

There it was. He followed the directions and found Alice sitting in an alcove off the hallway. Kitty was on her lap, squirming, and Brandon sat on the floor playing with the legs of her chair.

"Daddy!" The boy wriggled his way out from under the chair and grabbed Johnny's legs.

"Hey, kiddo." Johnny patted the top of his son's head, but his gaze was intent on his wife. "How is he? Where is he?"

"Hello, are you Mr Chiles's son?"

Johnny turned to see a woman in what he supposed was a nurse's uniform standing behind them. Her expression was calibrated, hitting the perfect balance between friendliness and concern that he knew so well.

"I am," he said. "Why?"

She smiled. "He's asking for you."

Johnny felt the tension drain from him. He looked at Alice. She grabbed his hand, her eyes wet.

"Go on," she whispered. "I'll stay here."

Johnny wiped his eyes and swallowed the lump in his throat. He hadn't realised it until now, but he'd been expecting the worst.

The nurse led him past the nurse's station and through to the ward. At the far end, curtains were drawn around a bed.

She gestured towards it. "He's not been awake all that long, and he's quite frail. Hopefully seeing you will do him good."

Johnny nodded, aware that his ears were turning red. "Thanks."

He headed over to the corner and slid through a gap in the curtains. His dad was propped up in bed, eyes closed. He looked smaller than usual, and his skin was the colour of unmixed cement.

"Dad?" Johnny murmured. He took the chair next to the bed and twisted to face Eric.

Eric's eyes fluttered open. "Son." He turned. "Ow."

"It's OK. Don't move." Johnny stood up and positioned himself in his dad's line of sight. "How are you?"

Eric gave him the thinnest of smiles, then closed his eyes again, his brow furrowed. "I don't know."

"What do you mean, you don't know? Are you in pain?" Johnny asked.

"Yes. No. Not as much as I was." Eric gestured towards a drip leading into his arm. "Morphine."

Morphine? That meant a lot of pain.

"What happened?" Johnny repeated.

Eric opened his eyes. "I collapsed, son. Veronica from next door..." He sighed.

"Alice told me your neighbour saw you through the window. The paramedics had to break in."

Eric's eyelids fluttered. "Are they allowed to do that?"

"Yes, and I'm bloody glad they did. Have they told you why you collapsed?"

Eric turned his face away. "It's back, son."

"Dad?" Johnny frowned. "What? What's back?"

"Do you need me to tell you?"

Shit. "The cancer."

Eric nodded, then winced.

Johnny put a hand over his dad's. The skin was crepe-thin and cold to the touch. "I'm so sorry, Dad."

A grunt. "So am I."

"How bad is it?"

"They don't know yet, son. They need to do more tests."

"I'm sorry, Dad. We'll help you. We can bring you for the tests. You can stay with us while you get better."

Eric drew in a whistling breath. "I don't think it works like that."

"Of course it does. We're local now, and—"

Eric waved a hand: *shush.* He coughed. Johnny leaned over and put an arm behind his back, helping him to get upright.

"Thanks, son. But I'm not going to get better."

Johnny stared at him. "You don't know that. You just said they need to do more tests."

"I already had some. Before today."

"Why did I—"

"I didn't want to worry you, did I? It's only given me pain the last few weeks. I didn't think..."

He slumped against the pillows, his breathing shallow.

"You don't have to talk, Dad. I can sit here with you. Keep you company. I'm sure they'll—"

Eric put a hand on his arm. "No, son."

"I know it's getting past visiting, but given the circumstances..."

"That's not what I meant. You go home. Get those little 'uns to bed. I need some time alone. I need to talk to Hilda."

Oh God. "Dad. I'm afraid Mum's dead. She's been dead for—"

Eric laughed, then coughed. "I bloody know that, Johnny. I talked to her every day we were married, and I still do."

"Oh." The idea of talking to his dead mum had never occurred to Johnny.

"Go home, lad. Ring David. Tell him what's happening. But he's not to come here, understand? I'm not dying yet."

Johnny doubted his brother would drop everything and rush over here from Bristol. Ever since getting clean from drugs – the taking and the dealing – he'd been selfish. Ungrateful, given what Johnny had done for him.

"You sure?" he said.

"Sure. You come back tomorrow, after work. Bring the baby with you; I can't cope with a toddler. You've got a life to live, son."

Johnny picked up his dad's frail hand. He stared at it for a moment, then kissed it.

"What'd you do that for?" Eric pulled the hand away. It flopped onto the bed.

"I don't know. To tell you I love you, I suppose."

Eric snorted. "Don't be daft. Now go. I'll see you tomorrow."

CHAPTER TWENTY-ONE

"You OK?" Lesley asked Elsa. Her wife had just picked up a pile of crockery from the kitchen island and placed it on the draining board. She'd slammed it down so hard, Lesley had expected it to break.

"I'm fine," Elsa replied.

"You don't look fine. Those plates don't think you're fine."

Elsa yanked open the dishwasher door and started loading it. They'd just finished dinner. Zoe was upstairs in the spare room, on a video call with her son. Her cat Yoda was underneath the kitchen table, where it seemed to feel safe.

"I'm fine," Elsa repeated.

Lesley grabbed her hand. Elsa shook it away and all but threw the glass she was holding into the dishwasher. When the dishwasher was loaded and the door safely closed, Lesley stood behind her wife, who was wiping down the worktops, something Lesley had already done. She snaked her hands around Elsa's waist.

"What is it, Els? Has something happened at work?"

Elsa threw the dishcloth into the sink and turned to Lesley. After a moment, she shook her head.

"Work's fine." Her eye flickered. "I got a new client today."

Lesley smiled. "That's great news, congratulations!"

Elsa snorted. "Not such great news for her. A mum of three accused of insurance fraud."

"Did she do it?"

Elsa's face fell. "Is that all you care about? Innocence or guilt? My client has no one to look after her kids if she gets a custodial sentence."

So she did it? "Surely that won't happen for insurance fraud."

Elsa shook her head. "It's not her first time."

"Ah." Lesley hadn't released Elsa's waist. "Well, she has an excellent lawyer. I'm sure you'll avoid that outcome for her. But if it isn't work that's bothering you, what is it?"

Elsa held her gaze for a moment. She glanced towards the cat, then back at Lesley. She shook her head. "Ignore me. I'm being unfair."

"Unfair about what? Is it something I've done? You have to tell me, Els, or I can't—"

"It's not you." Elsa waved an arm around the kitchen, then towards the door. "It's this."

Lesley frowned. "This? The kitchen?"

"No." Elsa scowled. "The kitchen's fine. Although... no. Now's not the time to talk about renovations."

More renovations? They'd only just had the scaffolding taken down for the roof. What had started as a leak into a bedroom had ended with structural issues and an entire new roof.

"We can't afford any more renovations, love," Lesley said.

"I know," Elsa said. "Don't worry. I'm not planning any. And it's not the kitchen that's bothering me."

"What, then?"

"The mess."

"Mess?" Lesley looked around the kitchen. It looked pretty tidy to her. "What mess?"

Elsa lowered her voice. "*Her* mess. Haven't you noticed?"

Lesley frowned. "No."

Lesley wasn't as fastidious as Elsa. It had caused some tension when they'd first moved in together. Lesley had learned to be tidier, and Elsa had learned to tolerate a limited amount of clutter. But they were never going to find themselves in Stacey Solomon territory.

"I really haven't noticed," Lesley said.

"That's because I've been tidying up after her. She left her breakfast things on the coffee table this morning. And her laptop. I took that up to the spare room. And then there's the cat. The smell of the litter tray." Elsa grimaced. "It's a tip. Worse than anything Sharon ever did."

"Or Nicholas."

Lesley and Elsa turned to see Zoe standing in the doorway.

"Oh, hell," Elsa said. "Did you hear all that?"

Zoe shrugged. "Don't be embarrassed. You're letting me stay in your home, and it's obvious I need to show you a bit more respect." She smiled. "Nick used to complain about my mess all the time, back in Birmingham. His room was the tidiest in the house. He never was your average teenager."

"I'm sorry," Elsa said.

Zoe stepped forward. "No. I'm sorry. I've made more work for you, and that's not fair." She put a hand on the now-pristine kitchen island. "And besides, I just agreed to rent a flat in Poole. Until the purchase of my house in Wareham is complete."

"We're not trying to kick you out," Lesley said. "Are we, Els?"

"Of course not. Just asking you to be a bit more tidy."

Lesley gave her wife's foot a gentle kick. Elsa glared at her.

Zoe reached under the table and picked up her cat. It headbutted her face. "I'll be out at the weekend," she said. "I hope you don't mind me staying a few more nights? I could always get a hotel."

"No," Lesley said. She stepped away from Elsa. "Don't be ridiculous. You can't take a cat to a hotel. And you're always welcome here."

"You are," Elsa said. "I didn't mean to make you feel unwelcome."

Zoe stroked between the cat's ears. "It's fine. I know what I'm like. And besides, living with your boss... it's a recipe for disaster, right?" She smiled.

"I like to think we're friends as well as colleagues," Lesley said.

But Zoe was right. Perhaps her moving out was for the best.

CHAPTER TWENTY-TWO

JILL SLUMPED BACK on the sofa and yawned. Meera was upstairs putting Suzi to bed. Jill had brought home the files relating to Stephen Carson before his disappearance. She pulled them out of her bag and laid the papers out on the coffee table.

"What's that?" Meera entered and sat down next to Jill. She put a hand on her knee.

"The Mudeford case," Jill replied. "Our working hypothesis is that the victim is a man called Stephen Carson, who went missing around the time the toilet block was built."

"Early nineties, right?" Meera shifted her weight forward and scanned the files. "You think they'd have been digitising stuff by then."

"The World Wide Web was only invented in ninety-one. And my dad used to grumble that he didn't get email until 1996."

"Wow. I can't imagine a world without email." Meera looked wistful. "Although when I try, I kind of like the idea. No spam. No 'reply all'."

Jill smiled. "A tech-free utopia."

"Don't overdo it." Meera stood up. "Can I get you a cuppa?"

"Decaf tea, please."

"Gnat's piss coming right up." Meera winked.

Jill smiled as her wife left the room. It was good to talk about a case with her. To share a joke. Lately, it seemed like all they did was argue about the house.

Had she been wrong to talk Meera into buying this antique cottage?

Don't go there. She needed to focus on the case.

She picked up the sheets, attempting to work her way backwards in time from Stephen's disappearance. The most recent files dated from after that, when the police had decided to stop looking for him. There were notes by a DS Samuel Cotton, a name she'd not come across before. It looked like he'd been delving into Stephen's background, researching his criminal record. Stephen had been wanted for armed robbery. No wonder Cotton had assumed he'd disappeared of his own accord.

"Here you go." Meera sat down and handed a mug to Jill. "Any breakthroughs?"

"This Stephen Carson guy sounds like he was a nasty piece of work. Growing record over a number of years, and when he disappeared, he was a key suspect in an armed robbery."

Meera wrinkled up her face. "Doesn't mean we shouldn't try to find his killer, though. I mean, we tracked down Arthur Kelvin's killer."

"True."

"So if he was a key suspect, why didn't they carry on looking for him? Even if they didn't think he was a misper, they'd have wanted to question him."

Jill nodded. "You're right. It doesn't make sense. Have you heard of a DS Samuel Cotton?"

"Nope. Who's he?"

"He's the one who decided to drop the missing person case."

Meera sipped her coffee, also decaf. They both had to give themselves the best chance of sleep they could, with Suzi waking so early.

"Sounds like you need to speak to him," she said.

"Maybe Dennis'll know who he is."

"Dennis?" Meera looked surprised. "You mean DS Frampton?"

Jill turned to her. "Believe it or not, he's been helping me out."

"What on earth with?"

"He remembers some of these cold cases. He might remember this one."

Meera grunted. "I never thought I'd see you working with DS Frampton."

"He's not a DS anymore, remember. Just a civilian."

"The sarge will never be just a civilian." Meera pointed at the papers laid out on the coffee table. "So have you got the file from the robbery in this lot?"

"Hmm. I think so." Jill sifted through the files. They were working out of chronological order, but there was a logic in looking into that case next.

She picked up a file. "I think this is it."

"You want me to help go through them?"

Jill's jaw tightened. "I know this sounds picky, sweetheart, but I think I need to look through them myself. I shouldn't really have brought them home."

Meera shrugged and leaned back. "I won't tell anyone."

"Thanks." Jill rubbed Meera's knee. She hoped she hadn't pissed her off, but she was learning that her cold cases had a tendency to become sensitive.

She read through the file. There was the initial record of police being called out to Pokesdown, then the statement from the petrol station attendant. He'd been a twenty-two-year-old, working part-time on the late shift. He wouldn't have expected to have a gun pointed at him. Even if the police did believe the gun to be fake.

She read through forensics reports, a summary of CCTV coverage from the forecourt, which wasn't helpful, and more witness statements from neighbours.

"They found his prints," she said.

"Huh?" Meera was scrolling through her phone.

"Stephen Carson. His prints were on the hatch the petrol station used at night for payment. They were on... oh."

"What?" Meera asked.

"There was a getaway vehicle. A Fiesta. Not exactly powerful."

"Maybe it had been souped-up."

Jill nodded. "It was abandoned three streets away. Not only did it have his prints on the door handles and steering wheel, but it belonged to his dad."

Meera looked up from her phone. "His dad, the one who reported him missing? The one Katie's been talking to?"

"Yeah."

"So not souped-up, then."

Jill shook her head. She continued to scan the file.

"So if Carson used his dad's car in an armed robbery," Meera said, "and his prints were at the scene, why didn't they try harder to find him?"

"Not sure." Jill continued reading. "Oh." She looked up, then back at the file. "Shit."

Meera inched in close to her. "What?"

"They found more prints. The investigating officer. Looks like there was contamination, his prints getting mixed up with Carson's at the crime scene."

"Who was the investigating officer?"

"I don't know."

"What do you mean, you don't know?" Meera craned her neck to get a better look.

"I don't know." Jill turned the file face-down. "The name has been redacted. Black marker all over the place."

"But you said 'he'."

"There's a couple of spots where they didn't cross the pronoun out."

Meera scratched her cheek. "So there was a procedural fuck-up, they had to drop the case, and they didn't go looking for Carson."

"Something like that."

"It doesn't help you."

"No."

Meera gave her a puzzled look. "You OK? You look pale."

"Do I?" Jill put a hand to her cheek. "I think I'm coming down with something."

"Poor you. I'll get you another tea. Chocolate hobnobs, too, that'll cure anything."

Jill smiled. "Thanks. I love you."

"I love you, too." Meera left the room.

Jill turned the file over again. She'd lied to Meera. Did that make her a bad wife?

No. It made her a good copper.

She stared at the paper in her hands. Someone had obscured the name of the investigating officer. Most of the pronouns, too.

But they hadn't obscured a handwritten note in the margin.

Two words: *case transferred.*

No mention of where it had been transferred to, or why. But the note was signed, and Jill recognised the name.

Right there, in the margin, in faded blue biro.

Case transferred. E. Chiles.

CHAPTER TWENTY-THREE

Mike rubbed his eyes as he stepped out of the shower. Daisy had woken at five am, and he'd been vaguely aware of Tina going to her. Now he could hear Tina's voice downstairs, along with Louis's.

He looked into the mirror and sighed. How had three years of fatherhood aged him a decade? He leaned in and scratched a spot on his chin. He frowned and pulled at his hair. Grey, already? No. It was a blob of shampoo he hadn't properly washed out. Mike's hair had been close-cropped until recently, but he was experimenting with letting it grow out a little. He hadn't let his curls show since he was a teenager. Was he growing old?

He wandered through to the bedroom, yawning. He needed to get a move on, give Tina a hand. It was so hard, dragging himself through the routine of getting out of bed, showering and getting dressed. Half the time, he didn't have a clean shirt.

This was one of those days. As he picked up yesterday's shirt from the top of the laundry pile and sniffed it, his phone buzzed on the bedside table. He dropped the shirt onto the bed – passable, just – and picked up the phone. It was Johnny.

"Hi, Johnny." Mike checked the time on his phone. "Am I late for something?"

"No. You're not, but I might be."

"Huh?" Mike put the phone on speaker and placed it on the bedside table. He picked up the shirt.

"I need you to cover for me, mate," Johnny said.

"Cover for you?" Mike shrugged on the shirt and started buttoning it up.

"It's my dad. He's in hospital again."

"Again?"

Johnny sighed. "He spent a lot of time in County a couple of years ago. Prostate cancer."

"Oh. Sorry to hear that." Mike and Johnny had been in touch the whole time Johnny had been in London. Had Johnny not told him, or had his sleep-deprived brain forgotten?

The bedroom door opened, and Tina entered, Daisy squirming in her arms. Mike felt himself brighten.

"Thanks, mate," Johnny said. "Look, there's a chance it's come back, and they're gonna have to keep him in for a few days. Run tests and all that."

"Sounds stressful." Mike walked over to Tina and grabbed Daisy's hand. He gave Tina a kiss on the cheek. "Johnny," he muttered in her ear.

"I gathered that," she replied. She raised her voice. "Hi, Johnny."

"Oh. Hi, Tina. He's got me on speaker?"

"Yeah. You've got me and Daisy."

"Ah. Give her a kiss from me."

"I will." Tina kissed the baby's cheek, placed her on the bed, and started rummaging through her bedside drawer. "Ignore me," she whispered to Mike.

He nodded. "You need to visit him, I assume?" he said in the direction of the phone.

"Yeah. Can you let the boss know and cover any urgent stuff that comes up for me?"

"You and Mike are on different teams," Tina pointed out. "But I can cover for you."

"You can? Oh, thanks, T."

"Oi," said Mike. "That's what I call her."

"Sorry. Thanks, Tina."

Tina was sitting on the bed, holding Daisy in place with one hand and attempting to fasten a necklace with the other.

"Let me." Mike knelt on the bed beside her and fastened the necklace. Daisy turned to him and started trying to climb up to his shoulder.

"Hang on, though," Tina said. "Aren't you in court today?"

"Am I? Oh, shit." Johnny made a noise of frustration. "I can't get out of that."

"No," agreed Mike. He rubbed Tina's shoulders, and she leaned back against him.

"OK," Johnny said. "Tina, can you cover for me in the office? I'll go to the hospital, and then straight to court."

She turned towards the phone. Her pupils were dilated. "I thought you and Strunk were planning on doing some prep."

"Shit! Oh, fuck. Why is this so complicated?"

"Sorry, mate," Mike said.

"It's OK," Johnny replied. "I'll have to call the DS. Maybe do the prep by phone. I'll sort it. Thanks, you two."

"Good luck," Mike said.

"And give our best to your dad," Tina added.

"Thanks." Johnny hung up.

Tina took a deep breath and stood up. "Poor Johnny."

Mike nodded. He rounded the bed and pulled her into him, just as his towel fell from his hips.

Tina's pupils dilated. She gazed back at him for a moment, then raised her eyebrows. She nodded towards the baby. "Err..."

Mike widened his eyes. He grabbed the towel and wrapped it around himself. "Sorry, Daisy."

"Good job she's only little," Tina said. She gave Mike a tap on the nose with her fingertip.

He looked at her. "I wish we didn't have to go to work."

"So do I. But we do." Tina gathered Daisy up from the bed. "Come on, Daisy. Routine beckons."

CHAPTER TWENTY-FOUR

Jill stood fidgeting outside the super's door, wishing she'd taken the time to go via the ladies' and check her appearance first.

She was wearing her green suit, one of her favourites. It complemented her strawberry-blonde hair and somehow made her eyes look bluer. Even Meera, distracted as she was by the breakfast routine, had commented on it this morning.

"Your favourite suit," she'd said, looking up from cutting banana slices for Suzi. "You must have an important meeting."

Jill had frowned. "Is it that obvious?"

"I'm sorry. That came out wrong." Meera had stepped towards her and kissed her cheek. "You look lovely."

Jill had thanked her, then kissed Suzi goodbye. As she reached her car, parked around the corner from their driveway-free cottage, she'd realised she hadn't kissed Meera.

She tugged on the cuffs of her jacket and brushed off her lapels, irritated with herself. She couldn't remember if Suzi had grabbed her jacket with a sticky hand.

"You're DI Scott, is that right?" said the woman sitting outside Carpenter's office. Carla, his PA. "Good name."

"Sorry?"

"I'm a football fan. She's great. Shame she retired."

"Oh. Yes."

Jill had got this a lot a few years ago, when the Lionesses had won the Euros for the first time. She'd never been all that interested in football, but Meera, who was in the habit of putting important matches in their diary so she could be sure Jill wouldn't double-book them, had filled her in. It still hadn't encouraged Jill to watch.

"I'm sure he'll call you in soon," Carla said.

Jill nodded, trying not to look impatient. "Has he got someone with him?"

Carla shook her head and beckoned Jill closer. "He's doing his morning meditation."

Jill snorted. "You're pulling my leg." She was still new enough to this building for people to do that kind of thing.

"Uh-uh. Says it centres him, gets him ready for the day. Don't tell DCI Clarke, though. I'm pretty sure he doesn't want her knowing."

"I won't." Jill wasn't planning on telling a soul, especially when she expected the response to be laughter and accusations of gullibility.

"Oh. He's ready." Carla was reading from her phone screen.

Jill swallowed and straightened up, gazing at the door.

It opened to reveal the super standing there, one hand on the frame. Jill couldn't tell if he'd been meditating, but he certainly seemed relaxed.

"Jill," he said. "Sorry to keep you waiting, just been triaging the day. Come on in."

Triaging the day? Surely that was his PA's job. Maybe Carla hadn't been pulling her leg.

She followed the super's outstretched hand towards the low chairs in the corner, by the window.

"Coffee for me, please," Carpenter said to Carla. "And for DI Scott..."

"Coffee's fine." She turned towards the door. "Milk, one sugar."

She was trying to lose weight, but she wasn't about to get out her sweeteners.

"Got that, Carla?" Carpenter said and closed the door without waiting for a reply. Jill hovered by the chairs.

"Sit down, please," he said. "I don't bite."

I've heard you do, she thought, pulling on a smile. "Thank you." She took the seat closest to the window.

"Right," he said, taking a seat at the far end of the small sofa beside the seat she'd chosen. At least he understood personal space; that was good. "We have two things we need to discuss, although they seem to be related. Intertwined, even."

"We do."

"What do you think they are?" he said.

A test. Jill remembered the warnings the DCI had given her. *Play along. It gets easier.*

"The first, of course, is the Mudeford Spit investigation," she said.

"I gather there's a lead on an ID," he said.

"I don't want to jump to conclusions until we've consulted with forensics and pathology," she replied.

He crossed one leg over the other and tilted his head. "But?"

"But a man living nearby went missing at the same time the toilet block under which the body was found was being built," she said. "His father and sister have spoken to DC Young."

"I know all that," he told her. "But that's not why you're here. The second item we need to discuss..."

There was a low knock at the door. Jill leaned back in her chair.

"Come in," Carpenter said, not taking his eyes off Jill.

The door opened and Carla entered. She held a tray; two mugs of coffee, a plate of digestive biscuits.

"The perfect breakfast," Carpenter said as Carla placed the tray on the table between him and Jill. "Thank you."

Carla straightened and nodded. "You'll have to leave at nine for the summer planning meeting," she said.

He checked his watch. "Of course. Jill, do you have any idea what a headache it is, planning for the summer season?"

"No, Sir. But I can imagine." It had been a while since Jill was in uniform, but she remembered all the overtime. It had helped pay for her first flat.

"Damned nightmare, it is. And we seem to start planning earlier every year. Thank you, Carla. I'll make sure this is wrapped up in good time."

Carla smiled and left the room. Carpenter turned to Jill, a digestive in his hand. "The second thing we needed to discuss," he said.

"My meetings with our mutual friend," she replied. "I've been getting background on the Kelvins, finding out if there's anything that can shed some light on the Three Musketeers trial."

"It won't," he said. "My guess is that the turf war with this London gang began long after he retired."

Jill shook her head. "There appears to be history. Gerard Kelvin and a man called Norman Osgood."

"Norman Osgood. Don't believe I'm familiar with that name."

"He was a foot soldier for the gang that preceded the one the Musketeers were part of. My theory is that Gerard used him as an undercover contact, to keep an eye on what was going on in London."

"And what does all this have to do with our friend?" the super asked. Neither of them wanted to say the name *Eric Chiles* out loud. Eric Chiles, the undercover Vice DI who'd masqueraded as a desk sergeant in Poole for decades, all while investigating police corruption and organised crime.

"Our other friend was feeding him information, or so I believe," she replied.

Our other friend. Frank Kelvin, who'd supposedly emigrated in the nineties, but who they now believed to have been killed by his own family.

"I don't suppose you're any closer to ascertaining his whereabouts," the super said. "Or his status, as it were."

"I'm coming at it obliquely, Sir," Jill said. "It takes time."

"So it does. And you're next seeing our mutual friend when?"

"This afternoon. A safe location."

"Good. Be careful, won't you?"

"Of course." Jill didn't like all the cloak-and-dagger around seeing Eric Chiles. But she knew that if the Kelvins found out he was talking to her, his life could be in danger.

She swallowed and placed her mug on the coaster in front of her. "That's not actually why I came to see you, Sir."

An eyebrow went up. "It isn't?"

Jill shook her head. "The Mudeford Spit case."

"This is about me telling Harold Carson we weren't treating his son's disappearance as suspicious."

"It's related to that, yes. But I found something else."

"Go on." He leaned forward, glancing at the door and then at his watch.

"I've been looking at the case files for the robbery Stephen Carson was involved in," she said. "A month before his disappearance, in Pokesdown."

"I remember that being a factor in us deciding not to pursue the misper angle," Carpenter replied. "The theory was that he'd left home to avoid arrest."

Jill nodded. "It looks like there were some... complications... with the forensics."

"What kind of complications?"

"A serving officer's prints were collected at the crime scene."

"A serving officer? Who?"

"I don't know." Jill swallowed. "The name was redacted in the file. All I know is it was a man."

The super frowned. "Redacted? In a CID report?"

"I don't think it was CID who did it," she told him.

"No? Who was it?"

"A DS Samuel Cotton," she said.

Carpenter's nose wrinkled. "I remember him."

"Was he... was he under investigation?" she asked.

"I'm not sure. I was only a PC, remember. He was in his fifties and retired not long after that. But he was the kind of DS who... well, let's just say that his methods were unorthodox."

"You think he was corrupt."

"I'm not sure what I think. But the man died in 2008, after a long retirement. I attended his funeral. He's not around to defend himself." The super drew in a breath. "So you're suggesting he redacted the name of the officer whose prints were at the petrol station?"

Jill straightened. "Actually, I'm not."

"No?"

"I mean, after what you've just told me... It's possible it could be him. But there's something else. In the file."

Carpenter's phone, on the table in front of him, buzzed. He picked it up.

"Damn," he said. "It's time for me to leave for that god-awful planning meeting. What else is in the file, Jill?"

"There's a handwritten note, in the margin," Jill replied. "Written by our friend, I believe."

Carpenter was standing now, shoving his phone into his pocket. "Saying what?"

Jill stood to face him. "Case transferred," she said, "with our friend's name."

The super pursed his lips. He gazed past her for a moment, deep in thought. Then he blinked and looked at her.

"You need to be careful, Jill," he said.

"I know that."

"No. This new case of yours. If it's related to... our second friend, whose status is unknown. If it's related to what happened to him, then this is more than a straightforward historical murder case."

There was a knock at the door, more insistent than the last one.

"One minute!" he called. He put a hand on Jill's shoulder, then withdrew it as he caught her flinch.

"You have a meeting this afternoon?" he said.

"I do."

"Inform Lesley. Make sure she knows where you'll be. Don't tell anyone else, not yet. And please..."

"Yes?" Jill's mouth felt dry.

"Whatever you do, don't inform your team of the link between the two cases. The less they know, the safer they'll be."

CHAPTER TWENTY-FIVE

Katie stamped her feet on the ground, clutching her arms around her body. It was colder today; the beach huts were quiet, and the crowd hadn't returned. At some point since she'd last been here, someone – the council workers, she presumed – had erected temporary fencing around the site.

Good. It wasn't just nosy parkers they needed to keep out; there was the wildlife to contend with, too. She'd spotted a fox as she'd crawled along the access road in her car.

Gail and Brett were in front of her, picking their way through what remained of the toilet block.

"Do you want me to help?" Katie asked. Maybe if she kept moving, she wouldn't feel like she was about to get frostbite.

Gail straightened up. She placed her palms on the small of her back and stretched.

"Bloody hell," she said. "I need to start doing yoga again."

"You do it regularly?" Katie asked.

"Used to. It can be hard to find the time, what with work and Timmy. But you don't need to hear about my challenges. I just wish I was a bit more bendy, is all." She smiled to herself.

"Why don't you have a break? I can take over for a bit."

Gail eyed her. "I assume you've had the training."

"I have. Search patterns, soil composition – well, sand composition – effect of climate on evidence. I did the course on burned-out buildings last month, it was—"

"OK. You can stop there." Gail held up a hand. "You've got the knowledge. Just take it slow, and if Brett tells you to stop what you're doing, stop what you're doing."

Gail strode over to her van, yanked open the back doors, and pulled out a rucksack. She delved into it for a can of Pepsi and a Twix, then closed up the van, walked around it, and perched on the bonnet. She took a deep breath, pulled down the hood of her forensic suit, and peeled open the Twix wrapper. Katie wondered if she'd been getting ideas from the DCI.

"Right," Katie said.

Gail gave her a thumbs-up, just as her shoulder-length hair was whipped into her face by a gust of wind. "Knock yourself out."

Katie, who'd put on her forensic suit as soon as she'd left her car, approached the all-but-demolished toilet block. The water had either been turned off or run out, and thankfully most of it had seeped away. But Katie wasn't taking any chances; she'd brought her sturdiest Doc Martens.

"Where do you need me?" she asked Brett.

He looked up and smiled. "Hey, Katie. Gail was working underneath that end of the foundations, or what passes for them. She's using a grid-based approach. If you start from that point there" – he pointed at a line of pipework bisecting the building's remains – "then you'll probably reach the point where she left off before she's finished her break."

"No problem." Katie picked her way towards the spot Brett had indicated, taking care where she placed her heavy boots.

She started working her way across the foundations, perpendicular to the wall next to her. She used a tape measure she'd put in her pocket at home to divide the area up without touching anything, then set to work.

"You like this kind of thing, don't you?" Brett said, not looking up from his own search.

"I like it all," she replied. "Getting involved in crime scene work, post-mortems, background research. It's all fascinating."

"How long have you been a detective?"

"Three years." She continued scanning the ground, not letting the conversation distract her.

"Ah."

Katie waited for Brett to say more. After a few moments of silence, she straightened up.

"What do you mean, 'Ah'?" she asked.

He shrugged. "You're new. Still keen. It's a wonderful thing, a copper who loves every aspect of the job." He chuckled. "Never lasts."

Katie eyed him. He was still bent over, his back to her. *It'll last for me*, she wanted to say. But she knew how he'd respond.

She went back to her search. "How long you been a CSI?" she asked.

"I see what you're doing. You think I'm an old lag. Hardened and cynical."

"You don't look like an old lag." Katie was twenty-four. Brett seemed to be, what, twenty-eight? Thirty?

He laughed. "It's just that I've seen plenty of coppers lose that initial glow. Maybe you'll be different. I can see a gleaming future in front of you, Katie Young."

Was he winding her up?

"You didn't answer my question," she said.

"You're right there. I've been a CSI for eight years. Before that, I worked in admin, back at Winfrith."

"That must have been different," she said.

"It certainly was," Brett replied. "I hated every bloody minute of it. Which is why I studied, got the qualifications I needed."

"Are you two having fun, sharing your life stories?"

Katie twisted to see Gail standing by the fence, hands on hips.

"We're comparing how long we've been in our jobs," Brett said.

"And no doubt you've been telling Katie how jaded and cynical she'll be after a few years," Gail replied.

"Stop," Katie said.

Gail took a few steps towards her. "Sorry, Katie love. Brett doesn't mean anything."

"Not that. I don't care about that."

Katie stood perfectly still, not turning to address Gail. She didn't dare move a muscle.

If she moved, she'd lose it.

"What's up?" Brett was upright again; she could see his movement in the corner of her eye.

"Have you found something?" Gail asked.

Katie heard footsteps; Gail approaching. She held up a hand. The footsteps stopped.

"It's tiny," she said. "Half-buried. If I move, I'll lose sight of it."

"OK." Gail's tone had changed; serious, all business. "I'm going to circle around the building and approach you from the front. I'll hand you a camera, and I want you to photograph whatever it is."

"OK." Katie's back was starting to ache from not moving. She could still see it, just about. A glint of metal.

"I'm fetching the camera." Gail strode back to the van and returned, her footsteps slowing as she approached Katie. "I'm coming round now."

"OK." Katie didn't dare nod.

It was almost nothing, just the tiniest section of what looked like a silver chain. Katie took a slow breath.

Don't lose sight of it.

It could be nothing. It could have been dropped by a council worker, or by just about anyone over the last thirty-two years.

But if it wasn't...

Gail was in front of Katie now, holding out a bulky SLR camera.

Katie licked her lips, then held out a hand, not taking her eyes off the tiny scrap of metal.

She turned the camera around in her hands, then brought it up towards her face, not daring to cover her eye yet. She fired off a few photos, hoping she had the lens pointing the right way.

"You have to look at the screen," Gail said. "To be sure you're getting it."

"What is it?" Brett called over. "What have you found?"

"I can see it," Gail said.

Thank God for that, Katie thought. She looked at the camera screen and zoomed in. It was clear. She took more photos.

"What is it?" Brett repeated.

"Looks like a chain," Gail said. "Silver, or something silvery."

Katie nodded. "A necklace, maybe. Or a bracelet."

"I'm placing the ruler down," Gail said. "Take some more photos for scale, then hand me the camera."

Katie did as she was told. She heard more footsteps. When she looked up, Brett was standing next to Gail.

"Nice one, rookie," he said.

"Oi," said Gail.

"I'm not a rookie," Katie said.

He grinned. "Sorry, mate. You know I don't mean anything by it."

"OK," Gail said. "Time to extract it." She passed the camera to Brett and squatted down. "Katie, you don't have to stand like a statue anymore."

"Weeping Angel," Brett said. "That's what Sunil would say."

"Sunil's a geek," Gail said. "Good job, too, given how good he is at digital forensics."

Brett sniffed. Katie stepped back. *Come on*, she thought. *I want to know what it is.*

Gail reached out with a lolly stick. She hooked it under the object, pulled it free of the sand, then placed it back down.

"OK," said Brett. "Nice one, Katie."

She suppressed a smile, her heart racing. It was indeed a silver chain. A necklace, by the look of it, with an engraved plate.

"Can you read it?" she asked, glancing at Gail.

"Not with the naked eye. Too much damage. Hang on."

Gail took a photo, then zoomed in on it on the camera's screen.

"Well, well," she said.

"What does it say?" Katie asked.

Gail held out the camera. Katie leaned forward to look. She gasped.

Engraved on the plate was one word. A name.

'Stephen'.

CHAPTER TWENTY-SIX

"DC LEGG SPEAKING." The number wasn't local, not the council with more information on the toilet block construction, then.

"Morning. Are you part of the team looking into Stephen Carson's disappearance?"

That wasn't quite what they were looking into, but...

"I'm in the Cold Cases Team," Mike said. "And yes, we are trying to find out what happened to Stephen."

"Good. My name's Sonya Onbanje, I work at the passport office. Someone from your team must have put out an information request. His name is on our system."

So Stephen Carson had had a passport, then. Only seventy per cent of people did.

"Thanks for getting in touch," Mike said. "What record have you got of him?"

"According to the email I've got in front of me, he went missing in 1994, is that correct?"

"His father reported him missing in 1994, yes."

The door opened behind Mike; Stanley, with two coffees. He placed one on Mike's desk.

"Anything interesting?" Stanley pointed at the phone.

Mike shrugged, then covered the phone with his hand. "Passport office."

"OK. Wasn't expecting that." Stanley sat down and slurped from his mug. Mike gulped his down. Five cups of coffee a day were all that was keeping him awake right now.

The passport official was speaking. Mike realised he'd zoned out.

"Sorry," he said. "Can you repeat that..." he searched his memory, "...Sonya. I was interrupted." He waggled his eyebrows at Stanley, who turned towards his own screen.

"Are you OK?" she asked. "You sound groggy."

"A toddler and a baby," he said. "Sleep deprivation."

"Ah. It gets easier, I promise. Anyway, I was saying that we have a record of a passport renewal in that name. Stephen Carson."

"Passport renewal? From when?"

"2006."

"Nine years after he disappeared."

"Indeed," Sonya replied. "And before you ask if this means someone was appropriating his identity, we run very thorough checks and refer to biometric data."

"You're sure? He was only twenty-nine. His appearance could have changed."

"We use the underlying bone structure of a person's face, DC Legg. That doesn't change."

Mike frowned. "OK," he said, "can you send us a copy of the passport renewal application?"

It would have included Carson's address in 2006, not to mention a photo.

"I've just sent it," she replied.

"Thanks. Can you hold on while I look at it?" Mike opened up his email and beckoned Stanley over.

"What's up?" Stanley asked. Mike pointed at his screen.

He opened the email and clicked on the attachment. The application, plus a scan of the new passport, with photo.

"He'd have had to get it countersigned," Stanley said. "By someone who knew him well."

"Have you got it?" Sonya asked.

"Sorry," Mike replied. "Yes, I have. I'll use the contact details in your email if I need to follow up."

"Sure. I hope it helps."

"I'm sure it will. Thanks." Mike hung up.

Stanley was behind him now, leaning over his shoulder. Mike scrolled through to the section of the application detailing the counter signatory.

"Shit." He fell back in his chair.

Stanley leaned closer. "What? Oh. Yeah, shit. Shit indeed."

Mike shook his head, staring at the document.

People eligible to countersign passport applications had to work in a small pool of occupations: MPs, judges, school headteachers, lawyers, doctors.

Stephen Carson had had his application countersigned by a lawyer.

"That's the DCI's wife, right?" Stanley asked. "There isn't another one by that name?"

"Yeah." Mike took a breath in and out. "Well, look on the bright side."

"There's a bright side to finding out the DCI's wife is involved in this?"

Mike nodded. "Yup. We know where she is, and we can ask her if she eyeballed him when she was doing that application."

"She would have been at Nevin, Cross and Short back then. You reckon she'll tell the truth?"

Mike swivelled his chair to face Stanley.

"Let's hope so," he said. "Let's bloody hope so."

CHAPTER TWENTY-SEVEN

Katie was heading towards Gail's van when her phone rang. Gail and Brett were still at the toilet block, bagging and cataloguing the necklace.

It was the guv. *Perfect.* Katie grinned. She was looking forward to telling DI Scott about their breakthrough.

"Guv," she said, talking quickly as she walked, "we've found something. The body is Stephen Carson. We found his—"

"Stop," the guv said. "You can't have. It must be... tell me what you've found."

Katie frowned. *You can't have?*

"In the foundations of the toilet, we found a pendant," she said. "A silver one. There's an engraved plate and it says 'Stephen'."

"It says 'Stephen'?"

Katie nodded. "Engraved. It's right under the foundations, guv. It won't have been dropped there recently. I—"

"Hang on," the guv said. "I'm sorry, Katie, but it must have belonged to another Stephen."

"Another one. Why?" Katie was at the van. She balled her fist and punched the vehicle's roof.

"Oi!"

Katie turned to see Gail standing up, hands on hips.

"Sorry!" she called.

"She's important to me, that van," Gail replied. "Be gentle with her."

"Sorry," Katie repeated. A moment ago she'd been walking on air. But now...

"This necklace," the guv said. "You're sure it was in the foundations?"

"Certain. I found it myself." Katie pushed her shoulders back. She'd made a breakthrough. Hadn't she? "I was about to call and tell you, suggest that I take it to the family, see if—"

"Oh, you're going to need to visit the family, alright. But for very different reasons."

Katie leaned against the van. The wind had picked up, waves breaking on the harbour behind her. She shivered.

"I'm sorry, guv. I don't follow."

"No. I don't blame you." There was a moment's muffled speech. DI Scott was talking to someone, her hand over the phone's microphone. "I'm with Mike and Stanley. Mike has new information. Give me a second while I put you on speaker."

Katie hunched her shoulders against the cold. She tried the van's door; open, thank God. She hurried round to the passenger side and got in.

That was better.

"Mike?" she said. "Can you hear me?" Her voice would be clearer without the wind whistling between those beach huts. She hoped the beach was less bleak in the summer.

"I'm here," Mike replied.

"Me, too," said Stanley.

"Hey, Stan," Katie replied.

"Good, we're all here," the guv said. "Mike, tell Katie what the passport office told you."

"Yeah," Mike said. "Katie, I had a call from the passport office. They were responding to an inter-agency—"

"I've guessed all that," Katie interrupted. "What is it they told you?"

"OK, hold your horses," Mike replied. Katie heard a snigger; Stanley, surely. "There's been a ping on Stephen Carson's passport," Mike continued.

"A ping?" Katie said.

"An alert, a... you know what I mean. Anyway, his passport was renewed. In 2006."

"Sorry, say that again. 2006?"

"That's what she told me, and we've seen the application. It means Stephen Carson was alive and well and planning to use his passport, nine years after your guy was killed. Not only that, he used the new passport. Six times."

"He's not my guy. And do you know it was Stephen Carson who applied for the renewal? Maybe whoever killed him was using his identity."

"Passport applications have to be counter-signed," Stanley said. "By someone who knows the applicant."

Katie shrugged. "So the counter-signature could have been faked. Or the counter-signatory could have been in on it."

"We don't think so," Mike replied.

Katie shook her head. "Has the guv told you what we've found here?"

"A necklace," Mike said. "Hardly conclusive, is it?"

"Come on, guys," the DI said. "This isn't a pissing contest. Katie's necklace could be significant, particularly if there are fragments of Carson's DNA on it. I take it Gail will be sending it for analysis, Katie?"

"She certainly will."

"Good."

"Have we got his DNA?" Stanley asked. "It was a long time ago."

"Good question," the guv replied. "There's nothing in the original file, but..." She fell silent. "I'll look into that, and maybe the family will be able to help."

"After thirty years?" Katie said. What she'd found was turning to nothing. Typical.

"Admittedly the chances of getting a DNA sample are slim," the guv said. "But we can ask his sister for hers, for comparison. And Carson had a record. His fingerprints are on file."

"The necklace was in a bad way, guv," Katie said. "I think the chances of finding prints on it are slim."

"Let's not assume the worst before we even know, eh? I want you to take the necklace to the lab with Gail or her team, see what you can get."

"No problem, guv." Katie felt her back straightening. Maybe her find would prove to be significant after all.

But that passport...

"Did they tell you who the counter-signatory was?" she asked. "On the passport application? We might find it useful to speak to them."

"Oh, I think we will, alright," Mike said.

"Let's not dramatise this," the guv said. "We need to tread carefully. I'll have to speak to the DCI, and the super, too."

"Cus the super was the one on the mispers case," Stanley said.

"Exactly," the DI said. Her voice sounded tight.

"OK," Katie said. "Is this counter-signatory someone we know? Is it someone significant?"

Silence.

"Are you still there?" Katie asked.

"Sorry," DI Scott replied. "It is someone we know of, yes. I haven't met her, but I believe Mike has worked on a case that involved her."

"More than that," Mike said. "I was a guest at her wedding."

Katie frowned. "Is this person a copper?"

She rubbed her forehead. Was Stephen Carson's disappearance

not followed up because he was working with the police? And if so, was that connection legitimate?

"No, Katie," the DI said. "It's not a copper. But it is a copper's wife. Elsa Short, formerly of Nevin, Cross and Short. Married to DCI Clarke."

"Oh, hell," said Katie.

"Oh hell, indeed," added Stanley.

"I will need you to speak to the family," the guv said. "They need to know their son may well have been alive in 2006. And they might be able to confirm that your pendant didn't belong to Stephen."

Your pendant. "But what if it is his?" Katie said.

"It can't be," said Mike. "He clearly left home to avoid arrest for that petrol station robbery, maybe he left the country so he could make himself scarce."

She shook her head. "Why would he wait until 2006? It makes no sense."

"That's one thing we do know," said the guv. "Mike, you and I need to speak to Elsa Short. Katie, find out what you can about that pendant. In the meantime, I need to have a chat with the DCI."

"What about me?" asked Stanley. Katie rolled her eyes.

"Background," said the guv. "We've been looking into Stephen Carson's activities up to 1994. I want to know what he was doing after that. Especially in 2006."

"Fair enough."

"Good," she said. "Keep me informed, folks. Hopefully we'll make some sense of this mess."

CHAPTER TWENTY-EIGHT

Lesley was fishing the dregs of a spicy chicken Pot Noodle from the bottom of the pot when there was a knock on her office door.

She frowned into the bottom of the pot. No use dragging it out; she'd eaten it all. She tossed the pot into the bin behind her desk, wiped the fork with a tissue, and placed it on top of the filing cabinet beside the bin.

Mustn't forget to wash that.

"Come in!" she called, licking her lips. Spicy chicken wasn't her favourite flavour, but it wasn't far off.

Jill stuck her head around the door. "Sorry to disturb you, boss. Have you got a minute?"

"You're not disturbing me. Of course." She waved Jill in.

"Thanks." Jill closed the door. She took the seat opposite Lesley, sniffed the air, then seemed to think better of asking about the lingering odour of processed chicken.

If chicken was what they really put in those things.

"Hang on a minute." Lesley stood up and opened the window, then returned to her chair.

Jill stiffened and looked past Lesley at the window. She said nothing. But Lesley could read her face; the temperature had dropped. Significantly.

They'd tough it out.

"Right," Lesley said. "What do you need from me?" She cocked her head and gave Jill a smile, wondering what Zoe was getting up to. Settling into her new team, hopefully.

"I'm not sure I want anything from you, boss," Jill replied. "But I would like to update you on some developments in the Mudeford Spit case."

"Sounds promising."

Jill waggled her head from side to side, then shivered. "Yes and no. We have conflicting evidence."

Lesley raised her eyebrows. "That does sound interesting."

Jill gave a small smile, then shivered again. She pointed towards the window. "I'm sorry, boss. Do you mind...?"

"Closing the window? Bloody glad you asked." Lesley rose, pulled the window shut, then sat down. "That's better. You should have said something."

"I just did."

"I mean earlier. Before you sat there shivering." Lesley waved a hand. "Forget it. What's this conflicting evidence, then?"

"OK." Jill nodded. "So we've found a necklace at the crime scene. Buried in the foundations, very unlikely to have been left there any time after our victim was."

"You think it belonged to the victim?"

"Well, we did. It's got an engraving. The name 'Stephen'."

Lesley leaned back in her chair. "Stephen Carson?"

Jill shrugged. "That would make sense. But that's where the other piece of evidence comes in." She twisted her hands in her lap.

Lesley frowned. *What's eating her?* "Tell me about this conflicting evidence."

Jill looked up to meet her gaze. "Stephen Carson applied for a passport renewal in 2006."

"The passport office has been in touch?"

"They have. It's legit." Jill still looked uncomfortable.

Lesley sniffed. "I don't mean to criticise the passport office, but – well, I do – are we sure it was him? Not someone committing identity fraud?"

Jill looked back down at her hands. Lesley shook her head.

"What's going on, Jill? This isn't like you. Tell me the thing, whatever it is. There's something that's bugging you. Is it a police officer? Someone we know?"

Jill looked up. "We know the passport application was genuine because... well, firstly because we trust the passport office. And secondly because the application was countersigned. By someone we know."

"Someone local? It would have had to be, what?" Lesley said, trying to remember the list of people who could countersign passport applications. "MPs? Teachers? Or solicitors. Oh bloody hell, not Aurelia Cross again. How did Stephen Carson know her? And how come he was still hanging about in Bournemouth in 2006, and in all that time no one brought him in for the petrol station robbery?"

Jill shrugged. "The 2006 thing, I don't know. But it wasn't Aurelia Cross. It was your wife."

"Elsa?" Lesley dropped her hand to the desk. She thought back. How long had Elsa been working in Bournemouth?

Not since 2006, she was pretty sure of that.

"Did you see the address on the passport application?" she asked.

"It was a fake address. Ringwood, but it doesn't exist."

"That's Carson's address, right? The fake."

Jill nodded.

Lesley balled her fist. "What was that you were saying about trusting the passport office? Bloody idiots. What about Elsa's address? What's on the paperwork for that?"

"A London address, boss. Crouch End."

Lesley nodded. "Makes sense."

But how had Elsa come across Stephen Carson while she was living in London?

She felt her skin tighten.

"OK, Jill. Leave this with me, please. I'll talk to Elsa."

"I'm not sure that's wise."

Lesley closed her eyes. "She's a witness. And we can't compromise the chance of a conviction if we do track Carson down." She clenched her teeth. "You're right. Go and see her now, before there's any suspicion of me sticking my oar in. I can give you her office address."

"Christchurch. I already have it."

If Lesley hadn't been as taut as a tightrope wire, she'd have laughed. "Of course you do. Go and speak to her. Let me know what she says. Not because she's my wife, but because I want to know what the bloody hell happened to Stephen Carson."

Jill stood up. "Of course."

"Thanks, Jill." Lesley looked up at the DI. She forced a smile. "Thank you for telling me. And never think you can't tell me this kind of thing. However awkward it is, I need to know. I won't bite your head off."

Jill's mouth was a thin line. "Thanks, boss."

Lesley was about to tell her to 'call me Lesley'. Zoe did, after all. But maybe that could wait. At least until she knew what was going on with Elsa.

Jill gave her a nod and left the room. Lesley leaned back, gazing up at the ceiling.

Oh fuck, Elsa, what have you done now?

CHAPTER TWENTY-NINE

KATIE WASN'T sure how she felt about knocking on Harold Carson's door again.

What was she supposed to tell him? That she'd found a necklace that might be his son's but probably wasn't? That his son just might be alive and travelling the world on a passport issued in 2006?

The poor man had been through enough, without all this uncertainty. But she'd seen journalists up at the spit. Including that Sadie Dawes from the BBC, who the boss seemed to hate.

Whatever there was to tell him, he needed to hear it from the police. Not from the six o'clock news.

She looked at the text from DI Scott again: *Give him the facts. Avoid speculation. See if he might have anything with Stephen's DNA on.*

She had a tightrope to walk.

A shadow appeared through the obscure glazing of the front door. Katie squared her shoulders and pulled on a smile, that police smile she'd been working on; friendly and supportive, not too encouraging.

The door opened and Stephen's sister stood in front of her.

"Oh," Katie said. "Miss Carson."

"Mrs Hutchins," Amber replied. "I hope you've got concrete news. My dad's out of his mind with worry. He won't admit it, but I can tell from his body language."

Katie nodded. "I do have news, yes. Can I come in?"

"Of course. He's having a nap, though. Why don't you tell me what there is to tell and then I can pass it on to him? I'm sure I'll do a better job of it than you." Amber turned towards the kitchen, leaving Katie alone on the doorstep.

Ouch. So the woman wasn't pulling her punches. Never mind, Katie had experienced worse.

She shook what remained of the earlier rain off, stepped into the house and closed the front door. Amber was out of sight.

Katie walked through to the back of the house, keeping her footsteps light. She glanced up the stairs as she passed them. The only sound was Radio 2, from the kitchen.

Amber had her back to the door and was pouring hot water into mugs. She half-turned.

"Tea?"

"That's kind of you. Yes, please."

"Well, I was already making one. Does me no harm to make two. How d'you take it?"

"Just a splash of milk, please. No sugar." This wasn't the time to ask for soya milk; Katie would just have to tolerate a rumbling stomach later. Sometimes, a lactose-intolerant copper just had to pretend she wasn't.

Amber handed her a mug and leaned against the kitchen counter, fingers wrapped around her own. The room was chilly.

"I hope you're not going to drag this out for him," she said. "He's too old for all this."

"I can assure you, we're aware of—"

"I don't need your reassurances. Just tell me why you're here. I'll figure out what he needs to know."

"I'd prefer it if—"

"Just tell me, DC Young. He's frail. Let me manage this, please?"

Katie sighed. Amber was right. Harold's daughter would know best how to protect him from any unnecessary stress.

"Of course," she said. She reached out and put her mug on a worktop, tea undrunk. There was nowhere to sit in here, and only Amber had something to lean against.

Amber cocked her head and sipped her tea.

"There have been two developments," Katie said. "And I have something to ask you."

"The developments first. Have you identified the body? Is it my idiot of a brother, God rest his soul?"

"We're still working on that." *Which is where the question comes in.* "It's complicated, with so much time having passed."

A grunt. "OK then. So what's happened?"

Katie weighed up the two pieces of information. Hope, first.

"We received a call from the passport office," she said. "They have a record of your brother applying for a passport in 2006."

Amber's mouth fell open. Her hand jerked and she yelped. "Bloody tea." She slammed her mug down on the worktop. "2006?"

"2006. He applied for and received a new passport. We're confident the application was genuine. That it was Stephen."

"Bloody hell. So the little bastard has been alive and well all this time, and never thought to get in touch with Dad?" She thumped the door of the cupboard behind her. "The bastard."

"I can imagine it's a shock."

"A shock? You reckon? So where is he now? Sunning himself somewhere I bet on the proceeds of his..." Her face turned red and she swallowed.

Katie's eyes narrowed. Proceeds of what? But she knew Amber wouldn't tell her. Not like this.

"It's good news, surely? Your brother might still be alive."

"Yeah, and ignoring his poor old dad." Amber shook her head. "Christ's sake. I'm gonna kill him." She put up a hand. "Turn of phrase. Of course."

"Of course."

"So what's the second thing? You told me you had two things to tell me."

Katie swallowed. "It's probably unrelated. But we found a necklace, at the scene. It has the name 'Stephen' engraved on it."

A deep wrinkle formed between Amber's eyebrows. Katie rubbed her arms; the room seemed to be getting colder. Dusk was drawing in, behind her outside the window.

"Well it can't have been his, can it? Not if you say he was gadding about on a new passport in 2006." Amber sucked her teeth. "The fucking bastard."

Katie wondered how Amber would have reacted if her father had been in the room. Not like this, she imagined.

"I'd like to show you a photograph of the necklace," she said. "In case it's familiar."

Amber shrugged. "I'm sure it won't be. Your body isn't Stephen, after all."

Katie said nothing; she held out her phone. "Even so, I'd be grateful if you'd tell me if it rings any bells."

Amber frowned at it and shook her head. She pushed the phone away. "Not familiar. It must be someone else's. Bit of a coincidence, eh?"

"I'm sorry?"

"Your victim having the same name as my missing brother. Good job you told me about the passport before showing me that, or I'd have thought..." Her shoulders jerked. "Well, you can guess what I'd have thought."

"Yes." Katie pocketed her phone.

Amber folded her arms. Katie heard the sound of the toilet flushing upstairs. Amber's gaze flicked upwards, and she stiffened.

"Anyway," she said. "I'll tell my dad what you've told me. It's important not to give him a shock, I'm sure you understand." She pushed herself off the cupboard doors and walked towards Katie, ushering her towards the door.

When they were in the hall, Katie turned to her. "I need to ask you for something, as well."

"Oh, that. Your question. For something?" Amber was all but pushing her towards the front door, her attention on the stairs.

Katie stopped with her back to the front door. "I know it's a long shot after all this time, but might you or your father have anything with Stephen's DNA? A hairbrush, a razor blade. Something like that."

Amber gave her an *are-you-stupid* look. "After thirty-two years? You're kidding, right?"

"It's a long shot, I know. But family members often keep souvenirs, when someone goes missing. Objects to remember them by. If you could ask your father—"

"What's that? What d'you want her to ask me? How long have you been here for?"

Harold Carson was halfway down the stairs, glaring at her like she was the person responsible for his son's disappearance.

"Mr Carson," she said. "I'm sorry to disturb you. I was just asking Amber if you or she might have anything with Stephen's DNA. A hairbrush, or a—"

"Or a razor blade. I heard you the first time, I'm not deaf."

His daughter turned to him. "The detective is just leaving, Dad. I told her we didn't have anything. Not after all this time."

"But we do." He took two steps down the stairs. "We do."

"You do?" both women asked in unison. Katie wanted to punch the air.

He took another step down. He was smiling. He looked at Amber. "Your mother was a soft-hearted soul, love. She kept things."

"A hairbrush?" Amber asked, her tone incredulous.

He shook his head. "Nothing like that, girl. She kept yours, too, in a tin. Come on."

He pushed past them into the kitchen. Amber followed and Katie brought up the rear. What did he have?

He was rummaging in drawers. He turned towards them, brandishing a squat, circular tin. A sweet tin.

"What's that?" Amber asked.

Harold prised open the lid and held the tin out.

Bloody hell, Katie thought. Not just DNA, but...

"Teeth," he said. "Baby teeth, to be precise. Betty kept them all. Daft woman. Wonderful woman." His eyes glistened.

Katie pulled on a forensic glove from her pocket and held out her hand. "May I?"

He eyed her. "You bring them back swiftish, yes? No losing them in your evidence store."

"I will personally ensure that they are returned to you within a week," she said.

He took a whistling breath and handed over the tin. Katie placed it in an evidence bag, barely able to breathe.

Stephen Carson wasn't their body, if that passport application was to be believed. But now... well, now they'd know for sure.

CHAPTER THIRTY

JILL FELT the tension ease in her back and shoulder muscles as she drove away from the office.

The DCI had reacted rationally to the revelation about her wife and the passport application. She'd gone further than that, insisting that Jill speak to Elsa Short, instead of her.

Jill had worked for bosses who'd have done the opposite: told her to keep quiet, insisted on 'putting the matter to bed' themselves. So she was relieved.

But still. She had this, and the fact that Eric Chiles's name was on that case file. And she'd forgotten to tell the boss that.

"Tell her later," she muttered to herself. "After you've spoken to Elsa Short. And after your next meeting."

She opened the window as she turned off the Lulworth Road, following signs for Tyneham and Wareham. There was a viewpoint here, a beauty spot with a vast parking area. And in February, no one came here.

Except for her and retired DI Eric Chiles, who'd been cleared to drive by his doctor before Christmas and had suggested this spot as sufficiently remote.

Jill wasn't so sure. Vera Kelvin lived no more than five miles away, just beyond Lulworth. And Eric's car was an antique, hard to miss if you knew what you were looking for. But he'd taken to using his daughter-in-law's car, while she was at work. He knew where she kept the spare keys, and he checked her appointment schedule.

Eric might have been retired, but he was still an undercover detective.

Jill parked at the Lulworth end of the car park, where her car was hidden from the road by a scrubby hedge. Eric would park at the other end and wait for her to walk across to him. He never left his – his daughter-in-law's – car.

She reached her arms into the air, placing her palms against the car's roof. She flexed her fingers and yawned.

She needed to get over to Christchurch. She needed to tell the boss about Eric's connection to the Mudeford case. But first, she would ask him why he'd transferred the case. And just what she needed to know about Stephen Carson.

She turned to check the car park; still empty. She checked the clock on the dashboard. He was late. Ten minutes late.

Eric Chiles was never late.

Jill felt her heart flutter, just for an instant. She put a steadying hand on her chest. *It's only ten minutes.* Maybe he'd had a problem 'borrowing' the car. Maybe he'd got stuck in traffic. Maybe...

Don't go there.

She took a long, slow breath through her nostrils. *Calm down. It'll be fine.*

She needed to distract herself. Meera had sent her a video, of Suzi with her friend from school, the two of them dancing to a Taylor Swift song. Jill had rolled her eyes: Taylor Swift, already? But now she had the time to watch properly.

She smiled as the video played. The two girls were out of time with the song, and their voices were flat. But they were four-year-olds. Expecting more of them would be churlish.

She fired a reply back to Meera's message with the video.

Cute. How's your day going?

No response. There was no signal up here.

Jill sighed. She allowed herself another look at the clock. Twenty minutes late.

This wasn't like him.

"Eric, where are you?" she muttered.

Maybe he'd forgotten. But a man who tracked a family member's schedule and knew where she kept her keys so he could 'borrow' her car... that wasn't a man who'd forget a meeting like this.

She'd give him ten more minutes. If he'd been on time, they'd have finished by now. He never hung around for long, no matter how many questions she had.

And she needed to get back to work. The work her team knew about, at least.

She closed her eyes. A power nap, that would occupy her. And God knows, she needed it.

She opened her eyes. One minute had passed.

"Bloody hell."

He wasn't coming. She could wait until nightfall – it was already dusk – but he wouldn't show.

She left the car park, waiting for a car to pass before turning right.

Jill could only hope that Eric's non-appearance was down to a problem with the car, or that he'd simply forgotten. Anything else... that didn't bear thinking about.

CHAPTER THIRTY-ONE

Zoe didn't like being in a separate office from her team. Maybe she'd appropriate one of the desks in the team room, or maybe that would make her team think she was crowding them. She needed time to get the measure of them.

She leaned back in her chair and turned to look at the view. Green fields and hedges beyond; that, at least, was familiar. Not much in the way of hills, but a brighter sky to make up for it.

She turned at a knock on the door. It would be Tina.

"Come in."

The door opened. Tina put her head around, smiling. She had dark brown, curly hair that came just below her chin, and blue eyes. Today she wore a cheap-looking grey suit that did little for her. There was a stain on the lapel that reminded Zoe of her own time as a DC, when Nicholas had been young.

"Tina," she said. "Good to see you. Come on in, take a seat."

Tina sat opposite Zoe, her back straight.

"You can relax."

"I am..." Tina frowned. "Sorry, Ma'am. I'm trying. It's all a bit stressful, what with the trial."

"I can imagine. And I won't keep you any longer than I have to."

Tina shrugged. "You're the boss."

"I hope you'll find I don't work like that. There'll be things that you're better at than me and on which I'll value your opinion."

Tina had started frowning.

Zoe continued. "I don't know what those things are yet, but I can imagine local knowledge will be part of it, together with your background knowledge of this and other MCIT cases. You're the longest-serving member of MCIT, and I'll need the benefit of your experience."

The frown deepened. "I only started in 2021, Ma'am. Johnny's been around for a lot longer than that."

Zoe shook her head. "Johnny was in the Met for almost four years, he's only been back six months."

"Oh." Tina's smile faded. "OK. Well, if I'm the most experienced you've got, you're going to struggle."

Zoe laughed. "I've heard very good things about you from Lesley, Tina. I'm puzzled that you haven't applied for promotion yet."

Tina's cheeks flushed. "I haven't been out of uniform that long, Ma'am. And—"

"Five years you've been in MCIT. And you were a PC for four years before that. Don't underestimate yourself. I can guarantee you that your male colleagues won't do the same when it comes to their careers."

"Oh, but Mike's not ambitious." The blush spread across Tina's nose. "That's DC Legg, my husband."

Zoe smiled. "I know." *Something in the water*, she'd said to Lesley. "But it's not Mike I'm thinking of."

"Johnny? He's got enough on his plate with coming back from the Met. Not to mention his dad. He's sick, that's why Johnny came back." Tina hesitated. "That's why Johnny had to take family leave today."

"I know. I hope his dad's feeling better very soon."

"I don't know, Ma'am. They reckon his prostate cancer could be back." Tina licked her lips. "Sorry, Ma'am. It's not my place to talk to you about Johnny's family."

"Don't worry, Tina. You're only doing it because you're worried about him. About both of them."

"I am. Johnny'll be devastated if his dad dies."

"It's that serious?"

"I don't know. I really don't. I'm just imagining the worst, I guess." Tina straightened in her chair. If she'd been wearing a uniform, she'd have tugged her jacket down. "Sorry."

"You apologise too much. I did much the same when I was younger. But you really don't need to."

"So..." Tina smiled. "Understood, Ma'am. Is there anything specific you needed from me? I haven't been closely involved in the Ashforth and Kendall cases."

"I find that hard to believe."

Tina shrugged. "The DS was the one who tracked down Mark Ashforth and spoke to his widow. Meera took a statement from Yiannis Kallias about Jackie Kendall's murder, and she's had some involvement in getting him protection. And it was Johnny who made the arrest. The Three Musketeers."

"You're missing the fact that although Nathan initially spoke to Mark's widow," Zoe checked her laptop screen, "I can't find her name..."

"Anne-Marie Mercier, Ma'am."

"Anne-Marie. Thanks. Like I say, Nathan spoke to her initially. But it was you who went back to inform her that her husband had been identified, yes?"

"I was the only one available."

Zoe shook her head. "That's not the only reason the DCI would have wanted you there. You're good with people, from what I've heard. And as well as informing Ms Mercier, you brought in the evidence about his finances. That evidence is crucial to establishing a link between Mark Ashforth and his killers."

"Well, I think the video evidence Johnny gathered—"

"Tina, please. You keep downplaying your role. You need to stop giving credit to everyone else and start giving a bit of credit to yourself."

"I'm not going to take credit for other people's work, Ma'am. I'm not that kind of officer."

Zoe eyed her. *That kind of officer*. Was it a veiled reference to DI Hannah Patterson, her predecessor?

Forget Hannah. She knew her team wanted to.

She was going about this all wrong. Tina couldn't simply be told she was a good copper; she needed to figure it out for herself. And Zoe needed to give her gentle nudges, instead of steamrolling her. Much like her old friend DS Mo Uddin had done for her, back in Birmingham. And Lesley, now she came to think of it. Lesley had been so subtle that Zoe had barely registered her support.

She stretched her arms out in front of her. She needed to move, to get out from behind this desk.

"I'm sorry, Tina," she said. "It's not for me to tell you how to think."

"That's OK. I just... I thought you wanted to get background from each of us, on the trial. That's what the DS said you talked to him about."

Zoe nodded. Nathan Strunk was ex-PSD. He'd worked under DI Robert Collingwood, a convicted killer. She still didn't know if she could trust him, and she hadn't managed to read Lesley's opinion of him.

"You're right," she said. "Financial forensics are kind of my thing."

"Canary. I heard."

Zoe gritted her teeth. "Like a bad smell, that case. Follows me everywhere."

After six years, would it ever go away?

"I thought you'd be proud," Tina said. "You took down some very nasty men."

Zoe sighed. "But it's not the ones you put away that you remember, is it? Not in a case like that. There were other men, who walked free."

"I heard you got them, too, in the end."

"You're right. We did." But it had been messy. Bloody messy. And the fallout, in the form of former Detective Superintendent David Randle, had followed her to Cumbria.

Zoe rubbed her temples; a headache was forming. "You're right, of course. We got them, in the end. Or they got each other. But that's not my point. My point is that I'd like you to talk me through the financial evidence you have in the Ashforth case, so I can get a head start."

Tina visibly lightened. "Of course, boss. Where d' you want me to start?"

Zoe stood up. "I want you to start with helping me get out of these four walls. Where does a person get a decent coffee around here?"

"A coffee, Ma'am?" Tina was rising from her chair. "Or a decent coffee?"

"That depends on the distance of a decent coffee." Zoe knew what rural areas could be like. "Let's say I'll settle for a half-decent one."

Tina smiled. "Then I know someone in the evidence team who keeps a halfway-decent coffee machine down there."

"Really? They've managed to get that past the building mafia?"

"You've seen DCI Clarke's mini fridge, right?"

"I have. I'm intrigued." Could Zoe maybe bring in her own coffee maker, get access to fully decent coffee whenever she needed it?

It would certainly help with this damn headache.

"Speak nicely to Terry in building services," Tina said. "Maybe buy him chocolates." Tina's eyes widened. "You're from Birmingham. He bloody loves Milk Tray, and you can hardly get them anywhere."

Zoe raised an eyebrow. "I'm sure I can source a box of Milk Tray or two, if it will assist with my quest for good coffee."

"Perfect." Tina laughed. "Where d'you want to go first then, building services or the evidence store?"

"The evidence store. That's the only place I'm gonna get a good coffee right now." Zoe walked to the door, clapping Tina on the shoulder as she passed her.

She held the door open and let Tina pass through. "While we walk, I'll fire questions at you about Mark Ashforth's finances, if that's alright with you."

"Fine," Tina replied. They strode to the left, where Tina pressed the button for the basement.

"And stay with me," Zoe added. "I'll need you to vouch for me, help me get that coffee." She stepped into the lift. "And that's something I fully expect you to take credit for."

CHAPTER THIRTY-TWO

Lesley was heading down the stairs towards the car park when her phone rang. She was sick of sitting behind her desk; maybe some fresh air would clear her head.

Or maybe this call would.

"Gail," she said. "You're a sight for sore ears."

The crime scene manager laughed. "I'd be very surprised if you can see me."

"You know what I mean. Please, tell me something that'll give me something to do. Something that's not shuffling paperwork."

"Oh, I think I can oblige."

Lesley smiled. She waited for the automatic doors to open and stepped outside.

Shit. She'd forgotten how much the climate control in the new building sealed them off from what the weather was doing. The sky was cloudless, but the temperature wasn't much above freezing.

"Fuck me," she muttered.

"I thought you'd be glad to hear from me."

"Sorry, Gail. It's really not you. I stepped outside for some fresh air and... you don't need to hear me grumbling."

"The air was a little fresher than you expected, I imagine. That's why I wear thermals under my protective suit."

"Sorry. First world problems, I know," Lesley said. "Tell me what I can do for you."

"I've got news, relating to the body found at Mudeford Spit. Have they done the PM yet?"

"It's this afternoon," Lesley replied. "Tell me your news."

"OK. So we've got the necklace DC Young found."

"The one with 'Stephen' on it. It can't be Stephen Carson though, he's not the victim."

"So I heard," Gail replied. "I'm afraid I'm just going to confuse things for you."

"You are?"

"This necklace. We cleaned it up and it's got prints on it."

"OK..."

"Two sets, to be precise," Gail told her.

Lesley shuffled into an alcove where the wall dipped inwards. *Bloody hell, I should have brought a coat.*

"OK," she said.

"I called you," Gail continued, "because one set... well, they're from someone we've come across before."

"OK. Who?"

"Kyle Kelvin," Gail said. "Vera Kelvin's—"

"Grandson. Currently residing at His Majesty's pleasure in Leicestershire somewhere. Are you sure?"

"We triple-checked it," Gail said. "I was as surprised as you."

"But Kyle... does he have a middle name? Why would he have a pendant saying Stephen?" Lesley frowned. "He's not the victim, bastard is still alive."

"Indeed. But I don't think the pendant was his."

"Because of the name," Lesley said. She shuffled to turn her back away from the wind.

"No," Gail replied. "Because of the other set of prints."

Lesley frowned. "Go on."

"They're on file because of an arrest made for possession in 1991."

"Whose?" Lesley said. She wanted to get inside.

"Stephen Carson's," Gail told her.

"What?"

"I know you reckon he's still alive," Gail said. "And I know it makes things messy. But there's no doubt about it. The second set of prints on that necklace belong to Stephen Carson."

CHAPTER THIRTY-THREE

"THANKS FOR JOINING me for this, Stanley," Jill said as she got out of the car. She'd been feeling spooked by Eric's no-show, so had diverted via HQ to pick up assistance for the next interview.

"No problem, guv." He stretched, surveying the view from the quay car park in Christchurch. It was certainly more interesting than the building site that the car park at Winfrith continued to be, months after the new building's completion. "Does me good to get out from behind a computer." He yawned.

Jill smiled. "We keeping you awake?"

"Sorry." He wrinkled his nose. "Nah. I mean, no. It's just the journey, y'know. I thought the A338 would never end."

"Tell me about it." Both of them lived closer to the office, unlike the DCI. How did her commute not drive her insane?

Maybe she liked it, at the far edge of the county. Less chance of bumping into colleagues.

"Right," Jill said. "Where are we going? You had the address when we were in the car."

He pulled out his phone, squinted at it, and cocked his head.

After a moment, he pointed ahead of them, towards the centre of the town. "That way."

"You're sure?"

Stanley flashed her a smile. "Positive, guv. I was just waiting to get a decent signal."

"Ah." Not struggling to read the map, at least; that was something. "Come on then. Let's hope she's in."

"You didn't call ahead? Sorry, guv, I didn't mean that to sound..."

They walked out of the car park and along a narrow road flanked by cottages that looked centuries old. Just Jill's kind of place.

"I get where you're coming from, but I didn't want to give her the opportunity to prepare."

He nodded. "Makes sense." He looked behind them, towards the west, where they had come from. "But..."

"But we drove a hell of a long way, to risk her not being here." Jill scratched her nose. "I know. And I apologise in advance if I've wasted your time. But—"

"It's OK, guv. I get it. I know the rumours about... about her. I get it. You don't know if she's in league with Stephen Carson."

"We don't know if anyone's in league with him. We don't even know if he's—"

Stanley stopped walking. "We're here." He spun his phone towards a low building with a pale green front door and the upstairs window – there was only one – shoved right up on the eaves.

What a place to work. It beat the modern monstrosity at Winfrith, hands down.

Jill stepped towards the door. A small plaque to its side announced the occupant: 'E. Short and Associates. Criminal Law'.

This place didn't look big enough to fit any associates. Maybe it went back a way.

Jill glanced at Stanley, then knocked on the door. She stood back and rubbed under her eyes, knowing she probably had smudged mascara. *Damn sleep deprivation.*

The door opened, and a young woman with a short wavy bob and brown skin looked at them. She smiled.

"Mr Grimstone, how... Sorry, you're not... You're not who I was expecting." She looked between the two detectives. "Who are you? Can I help you?" She eyed Stanley's pale grey, tight-fitting suit and narrowed her eyes.

Jill held up her ID. "Hello. I'm DI Jill Scott from Dorset Police. This is DC Stanley Brown."

Stanley cleared his throat and showed his ID.

"We'd like to speak to Elsa Short, please," Jill continued. "Sorry for the unannounced visit."

The woman, who couldn't have been over thirty – not the DCI's wife, Jill assumed – waggled her eyebrows.

"Are you really," she said, more a statement than a question.

Jill allowed herself a smile. This must be the associate. Or one of them, if more could fit in there.

"Is she here?" Jill asked. "It's in connection with a murder inquiry."

"The body you found over at Mudeford Spit?" The young woman stood in the doorway, showing no sign of letting them in.

"Is she here?" Jill repeated.

The woman sighed, just as another woman appeared behind her. Older, maybe in her mid-forties, with thick dark hair that swept over her shoulders and dark, suspicious-looking eyes.

Jill could see what the DCI saw in her.

"Can I help you?" the older woman asked. She put a hand on her colleague's shoulder, then withdrew it. "Sam, who are these people? Police, judging by this chap's suit, but I haven't met them before."

"DI Jill Scott," Jill said. "And DC Stanley Brown. I assume you are Elsa Short?"

Elsa smiled. "One and the same. Are you Dorset, or Hampshire?"

"Dorset. Cold Cases Team."

"Really? Two of Lesley's lot. How odd that we haven't met. Do come in, I'm sorry we've kept you standing on the doorstep."

Elsa pulled back, and her colleague, Sam, followed suit. Jill and Stanley walked inside, feet loud on the wooden floor.

Once they were safely inside, Elsa went back to the door. She leaned out, peered up and down the street, then closed it. She turned to them and leaned against the blue wood.

"Expecting someone?" Jill asked.

Elsa frowned. She looked at her colleague, who straightened.

"Mr Grimstone is due any moment. He'll be expecting to speak with you," Sam told her.

Elsa pursed her lips. "I get the feeling this is urgent. Can you take that one for me?"

The younger woman looked momentarily surprised, then pleased. "Of course."

"The case file is on my desk. Why don't you go up and grab it before he arrives?"

The younger woman nodded, then headed through another pale blue door, at the back of the small room they stood in. This room had a low ceiling and a desk to one side, with no one sitting at it.

"Can we speak somewhere more private?" Jill asked.

Elsa nodded. "Of course. We'll head up to my office, once Sameena has the file she needs."

There was the sound of squeaking floorboards overhead. Jill and Stanley both looked up.

"This part of the building dates back to the seventeenth century," Elsa said. "And my office is in the eaves. I hope you won't have to stoop too much, DC Brown."

Stanley looked surprised to be addressed. "Er... no. I'm sure I'll be fine."

More squeaking came from beyond the wall – Elsa's associate coming down the stairs, no doubt. A moment later, she reappeared through the blue door holding a file.

"Got it. Office is all yours."

"Thanks. You take the conference room, get Mr Grimstone a cup of tea to settle his nerves."

Jill surveyed the room they were in again. Yes, there was an old armchair in addition to that desk. But this wasn't what she'd have called a conference room.

Elsa was looking at her, her gaze intent. There was a knock at the front door, and she gave her colleague a nod. The other woman went to answer it.

"Come on, DI Scott," Elsa said. "I'll show you up. This place isn't as dilapidated as it looks." She headed for the second blue door.

"Dilapidated isn't the word I'd use," Jill said as she followed the lawyer, Stanley following immediately behind.

They entered a narrow hallway. To their left was a set of steep stairs. To the rear and right, more blue doors.

"No?" Elsa said. "Not dilapidated. Pokey, then? Antediluvian?"

Jill smiled. "Quaint. Characterful. Welcoming."

Elsa laughed. "Really?" She nodded. "Ah, yes. I remember now. You live in an ancient cottage, don't you? Lesley told me."

Jill felt her chest tighten. *What else has the boss told you about me?*

"Not ancient," she replied. "But old, yes. Why don't we go up to your office, and we can discuss what DC Brown and I came to talk to you about."

Elsa eyed her. *She knows what I'm doing,* Jill thought. Reclaiming control of the situation.

"Of course," she said.

Bloody lawyers. Jill was the copper here, the one who should be asking the questions.

Elsa turned and headed up the stairs, causing them to creak loudly. Jill paused at the bottom; could they take the weight of more than one person?

Elsa hadn't said otherwise, and it was her office. Her problem if the stairs collapsed.

Please don't collapse, Jill thought as she put a foot on the bottom step. Not for the first time since taking this case, she regretted wearing heels.

Finally they reached the top. The room was partially in the eaves, with only half the floor space usable. At the centre was a large oak desk.

"How did you get that up here?" Stanley asked.

Elsa brushed her fingertips across the wood. "With great difficulty, and a shed load of ingenuity."

That's not an answer, Jill thought. Was this how Elsa Short habitually responded to questions?

Elsa rounded the desk and sat in a high-backed ergonomic chair. *Poor bloody removal men*, Jill thought. Elsa gestured for Jill and Stanley to take the two seats opposite her.

She placed her hands on the table. "So," she said. "What is it I can help you with? You've come a long way."

Stanley opened his mouth to speak. Jill didn't let him.

"You mentioned it yourself already," she said. "The body found at Mudeford Spit." She twitched her nose: dust. "How much do you know about it?"

Elsa leaned back. "You mean, how much has my wife told me? Nothing. We agreed a long time ago not to talk about the specifics of our work. Too dangerous, given what we both do."

"Dangerous? That's an interesting way to describe it."

A shrug. "You know what I mean. Professionally jeopardising, for both of us."

Jill nodded. "So what do you know about the case?"

"I know you have a name. A man who went missing around the time those toilets were built. Do you have an ID yet? Is it him?"

"How on earth d'you know that?" Stanley asked. "We haven't—"

Jill put a hand up to stop him. Elsa turned to him. Jill wasn't sure if she'd actually looked at Stanley properly up to this point.

"A body is found a few miles from my office," she said, "and even closer to my home. You think I wouldn't want to know more? To prepare myself, should I find myself acting for your suspect or suspects?"

"You've had an approach?" Jill asked.

"Sorry?" Elsa frowned. "Ah. You think the killer has already come knocking on my door. No. That's not how it works."

"So what do you know?" Jill repeated.

Elsa smiled. "I can see why Lesley rates you." She took a breath. "Here's what I know. You found a body. It's old, the theory I assume is that it was put there when the toilet block was being built, which was, when... eighties? Nineties? Well before I arrived in Dorset, anyway."

"1994," Stanley said.

Elsa gave him a nod. "Thank you. So, like I say, the body is old. A cold case." She gestured towards Jill and Stanley, the Cold Cases Team. "I've heard a rumour that there's a potential name. A man who went missing at around the same time."

"And does that rumour include the name of the missing man?" Jill asked.

Elsa's brow furrowed. "It does not. But I'm assuming, given you're here, that he might be someone you think I know. He can't have been a client. I was... well, I was a long way off practising law in 1994."

Stanley grunted. Jill glanced at him, then looked back at Elsa. "How about 2006?" she said.

"2006?" Elsa blinked. "So the body is more recent?"

"Can you tell me where you were living in 2006? I assume you were practising law by then?"

"Just. I was twenty-eight years old in 2006. And I was living in London."

"But you were a qualified solicitor."

"Like I say, just. I certainly wouldn't have acted for anyone involved in your investigation. I was a junior associate in a big London firm, barely more than a paper pusher."

Jill reached into her bag, leaning against her ankle. She pulled out the copy of Stephen Carson's passport application. Taking her time, she leafed to the countersignature page, then placed it on the table.

"As a solicitor," she said, "you were eligible to countersign a passport application. This is one you signed in 2006."

Elsa picked up the file and flicked to the first page. "Stephen Carson? Who's he?"

"We thought you'd know that," Stanley said.

Elsa turned to him with a shrug. "The name is familiar. Is he involved in your case?"

"Stephen Carson," Jill said, "is the man who went missing when those toilets were being built."

"But he can't be your victim." Elsa put the file down. "Or he wouldn't have been applying for a passport nine years later."

"No," Jill said.

Elsa sighed. "So he's your suspect, then. I hope you don't think I've got something to do with all this."

"He isn't our suspect," Jill said. "But we did think he'd turn out to be the victim, until this was sent to us."

"Let me take another look." Elsa grabbed the file. Her cheeks had flushed. She went to the page with Carson's photo and held it closer to her face. She read through the file, then checked the photo again.

She put the file down with a smile. "Oh, I do hope you haven't taken too much time out of your day for this."

Jill said nothing.

Elsa leaned back, looking between Jill and Stanley. She seemed amused.

"He was my neighbour," she said. "Lived in the same apartment building as me. I barely knew the man. I knew his girlfriend – well, ex-girlfriend, by that point."

"You barely knew him," Jill said.

Elsa nodded. "Sorry. But I have no idea where he'd lived before, or anything about him being missing. His girlfriend – Sophie, her name was." She smiled, her eyes darkening. "They'd split up. He was leaving the building. Leaving the country, he said. She asked me to help him with his passport application, so I did."

"You're supposed to know someone for two years before signing that document."

Elsa raised an eyebrow. "Why are you so interested in him, anyway? He's clearly not your victim."

Good question, Jill thought. Where to start? The robbery, the prints on the car, the redacted file. And now the connection to Elsa Short. She'd been wondering if that would connect in turn to the Kelvins.

It seemed not.

Jill sighed. "So he was your neighbour, and you did him a favour."

"Just that. Here's the address of the block, and our respective flat numbers. Sophie's name would have been on that flat, she moved in two years earlier."

Jill pocketed the Post-it note in front of her and stood up. "Thank you for your time."

"My pleasure. It's been interesting meeting more of Lesley's team." Elsa stood up. "Let me show you out."

Jill shook her head. As she shifted her weight, the floorboards creaked. "I'm sure we can find our way."

"I'm a criminal lawyer, DI Scott." Elsa was smiling, but her eyes were flat. "I can see that one coming a mile off. I'll show you out."

"Fine." Jill exchanged glances with Stanley. Maybe Elsa was right. Maybe they were wasting their time chasing Stephen Carson. He'd left the area to avoid arrest after the petrol station robbery, and by coincidence, his girlfriend had been Elsa's neighbour. Maybe that was all there was to it.

She gritted her teeth as they clattered down the stairs. *Back to square one.*

CHAPTER THIRTY-FOUR

Lesley was sitting at her desk, wondering if she'd get a call from Elsa, when her phone rang.

She snatched it up. She was trying not to admit it to herself, but she was anxious about Jill interviewing her wife.

"Jill," she said. "I was wondering when I'd hear from you."

"Sorry, boss. I didn't realise you were waiting on me."

Lesley squeezed her eyes shut. *Calm down.*

"That's not what I... Sorry, Jill. These things take the time they take. Tell me how you're getting on."

"Right. Look, I know my team has been busy as well. Do you mind if I bring them in, get everyone on the line?"

"Of course." Lesley would have preferred for Jill to collate what her team had and bring it to her. But that would take time.

And besides, if Jill felt comfortable debriefing Lesley on the Elsa interview with the whole team present, it meant there was nothing to worry about.

Hopefully.

"Thanks." The line went quiet, and then there were voices; Jill doing a roll call.

"Right," Jill said. "I'm in the car with Stanley, Mike's on his way to the post-mortem, and Katie... where are you again, Katie?"

"I'm in Dorchester, guv. At the forensics lab."

"You're following up the prints on the necklace, is that correct?" Lesley asked. She realised she hadn't told Jill what Gail had told her.

"Er... No, boss. Sorry. Gail told me that was all in hand. I'm with Sunil, we've been looking at Stephen Carson's passport application, checking it wasn't forged. And trying to trace his whereabouts after he applied for it."

"Any joy with that?" Jill asked.

"We're making progress," Katie replied. Lesley felt her skin prickle.

"I don't understand," Mike said. "If Stephen Carson isn't our victim, then why are we interested in him still?"

"Well..." Jill said. "Stanley and I have just come from a witness interview. Elsa Short."

"Of Nevin, Cross and Short," Mike cut in.

Not anymore, Lesley wanted to say. *Not anymore.*

Bloody conference calls. She should have waited for Jill to get back to the office. But she didn't want her teams thinking she was being obstructive.

"She's long since left that firm," Jill pointed out, "and it turns out her countersignature on Carson's passport application has nothing to do with her legal work. Well, other than the fact it qualified her to be the counter-signatory."

"It was 2006," Lesley said. Elsa would have been twenty-eight. A long way from being tangled up in Nevin, Cross and Short. Or in that firm's work for the Kelvin family.

"It was," Jill said. "Elsa was in London, not long qualified. It seems that Carson was her neighbour. Well, her neighbour's boyfriend."

"I've checked the property records," Stanley said. "The girlfriend still lives there, believe it or not."

"Twenty years on?" Katie asked. "Really?"

"I know," Stanley said. "In London, too."

"It means we can talk to her," Jill said. "See if she's had contact with him."

"That's brilliant," Katie said.

Lesley shook her head. "Let's not get ahead of ourselves. Katie, did Gail tell you about the prints found on the necklace?"

"She did, boss. Said there were two sets. One of them belonging to Stephen Carson."

"Did she tell you who the other set belongs to?" Lesley asked.

"She told me she needed to make a call about that," Katie said. "I assume that meant it was inconclusive."

A call to me, Lesley thought.

There was a knock on the door. Lesley looked up to see Zoe looking in.

She waved her inside, gesturing for her to close the door. Zoe sat down, looking puzzled.

"Zoe Finch has just entered my office," Lesley said. "I'm letting her listen in as part of her induction to the wider team. I assume no one has a problem with that."

"Hey, DI Finch," Stanley said. "I met you in Birmingham. Stanley Brown."

"Hi, Stanley." Zoe smiled. "Good to hear from you again."

"Jill is also on the line," Lesley said. "Along with Mike Legg and Katie Young."

Zoe grunted hellos to everyone. Lesley raised her eyebrows at the DI: *what do you need?* Zoe gestured at Lesley's phone lying on the desk, and then at her ear. *Let's listen.*

"OK," Lesley said. "Where were we?"

"The prints," Katie said. "I can follow up with Gail if you like, see if—"

"It's OK," Lesley said. "The call she had to make, it was to me." She glanced at Zoe, wondering how much she'd have researched before starting here. All of it, probably.

"So were the prints conclusive?" Jill asked.

"They were," Lesley said. "Gail called me because they belong to someone we've come across before. Kyle Kelvin."

There was a whistle from somewhere down the line: Mike?

"Wow," Jill said.

"How much do you know about Kyle, Jill?" Lesley asked.

"Enough," came the reply. "I did my homework, and Stanley briefed me when we were working on the... when we were considering some witness evidence last year."

Lesley knew what Jill was referring to. She and Stanley had interviewed an inmate at HMP Exeter, a man called Lucas Parsons. He'd claimed to know about the disappearance and alleged murder of Frank Kelvin. Kyle Kelvin's father.

Jill's team knew about Frank. They didn't know that Frank had been an informant, working with former DI Eric Chiles. Johnny's dad.

"Kyle Kelvin is currently in prison," Katie said.

"Thanks to the efforts of members of this team, yes," said Lesley.

"I'm looking up his file now," Katie continued. "He was born in 1989. Which would have made him just—"

"Seventeen," Mike said. "He'd have been seventeen in 2006."

"It's not 2006 we need to think about," Jill said. "That's when Stephen applied for his passport. The last date we know he was alive."

"You're right, guv," Katie said. "The date we need to look at is 1994."

"That makes no sense," Mike said. "Kyle would have been five."

"Certainly too young to have been involved in the murder of whoever it is under those toilets," Lesley said.

"Actually, he's at Bournemouth mortuary now," Mike corrected. "I'm hoping to have a cause of death very soon. Maybe an ID sometime soon, too."

"It's six pm," Jill said.

"Pathologists don't keep regular hours," Mike said. "It's fine, I've let Tina know."

Lesley nodded. Who looked after little Louis and Daisy, now Mike was back at work? None of her business.

"OK," Jill said. "So we've got the fingerprints of a missing man and a five-year-old, we've got the knowledge that Stephen was alive in 2006, and we've got a victim whose identity we still don't know."

Zoe, across the desk from Lesley, had her hand raised. "Er..."

"Go on," Lesley said. "I'm sorry, I've been keeping you waiting."

"It's not that," Zoe said. She bent closer to the phone. "Can you hear me, Jill? Everyone?"

A chorus of yeses came from the phone.

"What is it?" Lesley asked.

Zoe looked at her. "It's your Stephen Carson. Your misper."

"Elsa thought he was more than a misper," Jill said.

Lesley frowned. "She did? I thought he was just her neighbour."

"She was. But she said something. It got me thinking."

Zoe was fidgeting in her seat, looking impatient. Frustrated, even.

"What is it, Zoe?" Lesley asked. "Is this relevant?"

"It is," Zoe replied. "It's highly relevant."

Lesley raised an eyebrow: *go on*.

"Stephen Carson," Zoe said. "I've come across his name in the files I've been going through. The Three Musketeers case. More specifically, Mark Ashforth."

"Are you sure?" Jill asked. "That's a completely different case."

"It looks like the Kelvin family might be involved in your case," Zoe said. "And they're definitely involved in mine... Ours..."

"What is it you found?" Katie asked. She cleared her throat. "Ma'am."

Lesley smiled, knowing how much Zoe hated that word.

"Stephen Carson is the holder of a bank account that was sending money to Mark Ashforth," Zoe said. "It was hidden behind two intermediary accounts, but his name's there alright."

"Stephen Carson?" Jill said. "You're sure it's the same one?"

Zoe's shoulders slumped. "Well, no. All I have right now is a name. But it's a hell of a coincidence. I'm hoping to access funding to bring in a forensic accountant I've worked with before. If anyone can find out for sure, it's him."

"There'll be digital records involved," Katie said. "Sunil's your guy."

"Katie," Jill said, her tone low.

"Sorry, guv," Katie muttered.

"I agree with Katie," Lesley said. "We need to use our own resources first" – she registered Zoe's disappointment – "but if that doesn't bear fruit, we cast a wider net. The important thing is getting the information, not who gets it."

"Of course," Zoe said.

"I'm sorry, boss," Katie said. "I didn't mean to..."

Lesley smiled. "Katie, it's fine. I ask for ideas and input, and I can always rely on you to provide them."

She placed her hands on the desk, thinking over what they'd discussed. Stephen Carson sending Mark Ashforth money... Did that mean he was working for the Kelvins, or the Musketeers' gang, in London?

She remembered something.

"Jill," she said. "You mentioned there was something Elsa said when you were interviewing her. Something that stuck with you."

"There was, boss," Jill replied. "She said that if Stephen Carson isn't our victim, then it's likely that he's our suspect."

"His prints are on that necklace," Stanley said. "And maybe he fled afterwards. Not just because of the petrol station robbery, but because he'd committed murder."

"And if he's tied up with the MCIT case..." Zoe added.

"It doesn't add up, though," said Mike. "What would his motive have been? And what's his connection with a five-year-old? Something close enough for Kyle to be there when he killed someone?"

"He didn't have to be there," Lesley said. "He just had to touch that pendant." She wasn't about to start speculating on that.

"What do you want us to do next?" Jill asked.

"The ID is crucial," Lesley said. "Mike, report back from the PM as soon as it's done. I want to know the cause of death, and I want to know if there's anything to help us identify the poor bastard. And Jill, your team needs to go back to missing persons reports from 1994. Every one of them needs to be checked out."

"No problem," Jill replied.

"And another thing, Jill," Lesley added.

"Boss?"

"I think you're right. I think everything we have so far points to Stephen Carson as the suspect."

CHAPTER THIRTY-FIVE

"Everything OK?" Sunil asked as Katie disconnected from the conference call. They were in his office at the forensics lab in Dorchester, a desk space lined with computer screens.

She shrugged. "Yes and no."

"It can't be both." He tapped on one of the bank of keyboards on a desk that ran along the longest wall.

"Can't it?" she replied. "It seems to be."

He sniffed. "Explain." He turned to look up at her with a smile. "Please. If you don't mind."

She laughed. "Very good social skills."

"Mine aren't the best. I am trying, though. I find it easier with you."

"Do you?" Katie felt her heart rate pick up. Sunil's reputation went ahead of him; he was a tech genius. She was slightly in awe of him.

Maybe more than slightly.

He gave her a long stare, longer than she was sure she felt comfortable with. Finally, the smile returned.

"Yes," he said. "You seem to... get me."

"I do?"

"Maybe you don't. But talking to you is definitely easier than talking to that lot out there." He gestured towards the wall separating his space from the main office.

Katie didn't like speaking ill of anyone. "They seem OK," she said. Gail was brusque, yes. But she was a busy woman. And Gavin and Brett seemed friendly enough.

Sunil stood up. "Good and bad, you said. Explain."

She shook her head. "Don't worry about that. Tell me about the trace you're running."

"That? It's just a trace. Glorified Google search. Not much point in telling you about it unless it works. But I'd like to know about your good and bad." He licked his lips. "If you don't mind."

"No. Of course I don't. Although if your trace gets results..."

"Don't worry." He smiled, his eyes joining in this time. "If one of these laptops pings, I'll be all over it like a rash."

Katie nodded. "OK. Well, Stephen Carson. I was just in a conference call with the rest of the team. He went missing at the same time those toilets were built. But he's definitely not our body."

"He is not," Sunil said. "Or I wouldn't have a dozen computers working together to track him down."

"No," Katie said. "But there's that necklace I found, with his prints on. It puts him at the scene."

"You reckon?"

She frowned. "You don't?"

"It puts his necklace at the scene. What if someone nicked it, or he gave it to someone? In that case, it would put them at the scene. Not him."

"There's only one other print on it," Katie said, "and that belongs to someone who was five years old at the time."

Sunil's eyebrows rose. "Carson had a kid?"

Katie stifled a laugh. "No. It's not Stephen Carson's kid. It's Frank Kelvin's kid. Kyle."

"What?"

She nodded. "I know. The more I think about it, the more ridiculous it seems."

"But Kyle Kelvin's... What happened to him?"

"He's in prison," Katie replied. "But that's irrelevant, when you're talking about a crime that took place over thirty years ago."

"Thirty-two years ago, to be precise."

Katie nodded. "So you see what I mean, by yes and no? The guv – that's DI Scott – thinks we should be treating Stephen Carson as a suspect. But the fact that Kyle Kelvin also handled that necklace... it complicates things."

Sunil sniffed. "Well, prints don't change. They're formed in the womb, so his prints when he was five would be the same as when they were taken on arrest."

"I know that. But how could Kyle Kelvin have handled a necklace that found its way to the crime scene, when he was five?"

Sunil looked at her, his gaze intent. She felt her stomach tighten.

"You don't need to worry about it," he said.

"No?"

"No. He was five. He's not the killer, is he? And he certainly won't talk to you about something that happened when he was that young."

"No." But Katie wasn't so sure. It created a link between the body at Mudeford Spit and the Kelvins. Between Stephen Carson and the Kelvins.

Sunil turned to face away from her. He raised a finger in the air. "Stop. Sorry."

"Have you got something?" She edged closer to him. He was wearing... What was his aftershave? She liked it, anyway.

Stop it. Be professional.

"Have you got something?" Katie repeated.

Sunil nodded. He zoomed in on images on one of the screens, flicking between them at speed.

"Wow," he said. "Hiding in plain sight. No wonder it was so quick."

"Who? Carson?"

"The very same. I've been trawling social media, news reports, police records. Finding photographs, where I can."

"But you've been talking to me."

He turned to her, his eyes bright. "When I say I, I mean the bot I created."

"Oh." Katie considered herself relatively knowledgeable about IT. She knew Sunil had automated the search process, and that throwing multiple computers at it would speed things up exponentially. "And you've found him?"

His eyes flashed. "He's not on social media, which means he's not completely stupid. And there are no police records after the missing persons report."

"So he's kept out of trouble," Katie said.

Sunil nodded. He was giving her that intense stare again. She decided to return it.

"So... What?" she asked.

"He bought a house. Used his passport to prove his identity."

"The one he got in 2006."

"Uh-huh. That'll have long since run out. A new one. But with the same photo."

Katie felt a grin spread across her face. "We've tracked him down."

"We have."

"Where?"

"Not local. Spain. Málaga, to be precise."

She snorted. "Who does he think he is, a train robber?"

"It is a cliché, yes."

"When?" she asked. "When did he buy the house?"

Sunil beckoned her closer. He zoomed in on a document, a title deed.

"Last year," he said.

"And it's a residential property?"

"Looks like it."

Katie rose from her seat. "Shit. Sorry. Sunil, you're a bloody genius. We can visit him. We can question him." She felt her smile drop. Had he been mentioned in news reports? Would he have been alerted?

Sunil leaned back in his chair, smiling up at her.

"Better get a move on, Katie. You've got a suspect to question."

CHAPTER THIRTY-SIX

"The pathologist is sure about that?" Jill glanced at her phone, sitting in its cradle on her car's dashboard.

"It's Dr Bamford," Mike replied. "I've worked with him before. He'll never give a cause of death if it's just a hunch."

"Still. It can't be easy, with a body that's been buried for so long."

"And it's not a cause we come across often," Mike added. "Not unless we find them in water."

Jill placed her hand over her mouth to cover a yawn. "Sorry. Sleep deprivation."

"Oh, I know the feeling."

"You finding it a challenge, being back at work?" she asked.

"Absolutely not. It's a juggling act, but Tina and I are managing it."

"Good for you." Jill felt like she and Meera were on the verge of dropping the balls every day. She knew she should stop feeling so guilty about it; Meera was the one taking most of the slack now.

"OK," she said. "So, suffocation. I'm assuming there's evidence of strangulation."

"There's nothing on the—" Mike replied.

Jill cursed beneath her breath. The signal was cutting out. "Say that again?"

"Sorry?"

"You said there was nothing on the... and then you cut out."

"Sorry, guv. I can hardly hear you."

She gritted her teeth. Living in the countryside was what she'd dreamed of all her life. But it came with its downsides.

"Mike, I'm going to call you back when I get home. Send me the pathologist's report, if you have it."

She realised he wouldn't have heard her. She raised her voice, enunciating clearly.

"I'll call you back on my home Wi-Fi."

"Got it. Speak soon." The line went dead.

She hoped Meera wouldn't be too disappointed at her jumping onto a work call the moment she got home. But it wasn't the first time.

There was always that field ten minutes away from the house, the one spot in their village where she could get a signal. The spot where she'd spoken to Eric Chiles for the first time.

And now Eric was in hospital. At least that explained the no-show. Should she visit him, show her respect?

No. Stupid idea.

She was in their village now. She felt her muscles relax as she turned into their road. There was a parking space right outside the house. The spot that Meera, who got home before most of their neighbours, usually used.

Jill frowned. Maybe someone had been in that space when Meera arrived home. A delivery driver, or a health visitor. Meera wouldn't have been happy, with Suzi in tow.

Jill parked in the tight space; she was an expert at parallel parking these days. She turned the car off and got out. The house was dark.

She frowned, then shook her head. They'd be in the kitchen, at the back. She placed her palm on the roof of the car and paused to breathe in. She could smell Mrs Aster's snowdrops from next door.

The only sound was a wood pigeon, from the trees beyond their row of houses.

No. She could hear something else. A nightingale?

Jill smiled. She closed her eyes and listened. God, she loved it here. Maybe she could persuade Meera to stay here, if they sorted out the damp and the plumbing... and added a modern extension at the back, like the one on Elsa Short's office. It had taken her breath away.

Stop dreaming and get inside. It was too cold to stand out here.

Jill grabbed her work bag from the back seat, locked the car, and walked to the house. She opened the gate and clipped up the path, her footsteps echoing in the quiet. She savoured every bit of it.

She unlocked the front door and went inside, quietly in case Suzi was already on her bedtime routine.

What time was it? Should Jill call Mike back before greeting her wife and daughter?

No. She'd message him, ask him to email her. Save the conversation for tomorrow. It wasn't like a few hours would make much difference.

The hallway was dark. Jill flicked a table light on, dropped her bag, and made for the kitchen.

The kitchen, too, was dark. It was silent.

Jill frowned. She turned the light on.

The table was empty. Nothing on its surface, no one sitting at it. On the draining board was the mug she'd washed that morning before leaving.

By now, Meera would have cooked. There would be a plate with a bowl over it, waiting for Jill.

No plate. No bowl. No cooking smell.

She pulled back and ran up the stairs, almost tripping on the squeaky step. Maybe they were in the bathroom, Suzi having her evening bath. She loved baths.

Jill flung the bathroom door open. "Why's the—"

The bathroom was dark. She flicked on the light, barely breathing. No Suzi. No Meera.

She turned towards the door. "Meera! Suzi! Where are you? If you're playing a game, please stop."

You're scaring me.

She ran into Suzi's bedroom, then hers and Meera's. Both empty.

Back at the top of the stairs, she called out again. "Please. This isn't funny."

No answer.

Jill clattered down the stairs. She stumbled into the living room, then the kitchen. She ran out into the garden, calling their names.

Where are you?

Back in the kitchen, she all but fell into a chair. Her breathing was shallow and her heart racing.

Where are you?

Clumsily, she pulled her phone from her jacket pocket. She dialled Meera's number.

It rang out, then went to voicemail.

She jabbed at the end call button, then tried again.

Where are you?

This time it went to voicemail without ringing.

"Meera, where are you?" she stuttered. "There's no one at home. I'm worried. Call me. Please."

She had a sudden, gut-wrenching thought. She ran upstairs and flung open the wardrobe doors, then Meera's bedside drawers.

All full. So at least her wife hadn't left her. Not that Jill had any reason to think she would.

But...

Where are you?

She sank to the bed, her mind numb. Nothing came to her. Maybe Meera had told her she and Suzi would be out, maybe Jill had forgotten.

She hadn't forgotten. She'd spoken to Meera at lunchtime. Meera had said she'd be making cottage pie tonight.

Jill fell back. She lay on the bed, blinking.

Meera, where the hell are you?

CHAPTER THIRTY-SEVEN

Lesley was greeted at the front door by Zoe's cat.

She crouched to give it a rub behind the ears. "Hello, puss. What's your name again?" She found the tag on its collar and smiled. "Yoda. You do have very big ears, it has to be said."

"Don't fuss over it, you'll only encourage it."

Lesley looked up to see Elsa standing in the kitchen doorway. She felt her body slump.

"What now?" she asked.

Elsa shook her head. "Nothing. Not really. I'm just... I'm in a funny mood."

Lesley followed her wife through to the kitchen, where she could smell something sweet and garlicky. "You cooked. Thank you."

Elsa sat at the island, shaking her head. "Not me. Zoe."

Lesley sniffed the air. "Really? Zoe hates cooking."

Elsa gestured towards a laptop, open on the counter. "She had help."

Lesley heard footsteps behind her and turned. Zoe stood in the doorway, Yoda purring in her arms.

"Nicholas has been walking me through his garlic chicken recipe," she said. "I hope you both like chicken?"

"Hello!" came a thin voice from the laptop. "Mum, you need to check on it. And it's time to boil the rice."

Zoe pulled a face and approached the laptop. A young man had appeared on screen, slim with wavy brown hair.

Goodness, he's grown up.

"Can't I use packet rice?" Zoe said to her son. "I only have to microwave it for two minutes."

Nicholas wagged his finger. Lesley looked at Elsa, who was smirking.

"Packet rice is a rip-off, Mum," he said. "Use the proper stuff."

Zoe rolled her eyes. "Alright, if you insist." She went to the island and rummaged through a Co-op bag.

"You went shopping," Lesley said.

Zoe looked at her. "There's a Co-op up by the bus stop, on the way here. I hope that's OK."

Lesley took a step towards Zoe. She put a hand on the younger woman's arm. "You don't need my permission to go shopping. But you've already given us money towards groceries. We should—"

"It's the least I can do," Zoe said. "I want to show you how grateful I am for your hospitality." Her gaze lowered. "How sorry I am for the damage Yoda did to your sofa this morning." She looked at Elsa. "I will pay for repairs."

Elsa shrugged. "It's fine. I overreacted."

Zoe gave her a long look. "Sorry."

"Like I said, it's fine." Elsa brushed Lesley's arm with her fingertips. "Can we talk?" She jerked her head towards the door.

"This rice'll take fifteen minutes at least," Zoe said. "If I don't burn it."

"You won't burn it, Mum," came Nicholas's voice from the laptop. "You've got me to make sure of that."

Lesley smiled. She couldn't imagine Sharon ever giving her cooking lessons. Elsa giving Sharon cooking lessons, yes, but...

"Sweetie?" Elsa was looking at her with a pointed expression.

"Sorry. We'll leave you to your cooking, Zoe."

Lesley followed Elsa out of the kitchen and into the living room. Elsa's laptop and files were on the coffee table; she'd brought work home again.

"What's up?" She approached her wife and put her hands on her waist. "Has something happened with Zoe?"

"No. Zoe's fine. It's your other DI."

Lesley frowned. "Don't tell me Jill needs a place to stay, too."

Elsa gave her a look. "That's not what I'm talking about, and I imagine you know it. She would have spoken to you before she and her colleague came knocking on my door."

"Go on?"

"Lanky, bum fluff where he should have a beard."

"That's Stanley. He's a better detective than people give him credit for."

Elsa pushed out a breath. "I don't care about that. I care about them turning up out of the blue and insinuating that I was an associate of their current suspect."

Lesley frowned. "Hang on. You expected me to warn you?"

Elsa craned her neck to look up at the ceiling. Finally, she looked down, her gaze level on Lesley's face.

"No," she said.

"No," Lesley repeated, her voice low. "I can't treat you differently from any other witness." She raked her fingers through her hair. "Christ, Elsa, you know that better than anyone."

Elsa sighed. "I know. I do. It's just... it all brought up memories of before. Harry's death. Ameena, before him. And all the crap with Arthur Kelvin." She glanced at the door, her voice low.

Lesley stepped forward. She placed her hands on her wife's shoulders. "I'm sorry, love. But this is a completely separate case."

Elsa nodded. "I barely even knew him. He was a neighbour. Not even that. He was going out with a neighbour. Before..." Her expression darkened.

Lesley chewed on her bottom lip. She desperately wanted to ask where that sentence had been heading. But that would undermine everything she'd just said.

Fuck, it was hard sometimes. Being married to someone with a habit of tangling herself up in cases.

She's a criminal lawyer, Lesley reminded herself. None of this was Elsa's fault.

"So you're not going to ask me how I ended up countersigning a passport application for your suspect?" Elsa asked.

Lesley shrugged. "No. Jill already asked you. That's her job, not mine."

Elsa stroked Lesley's face. "You're being very calm. Very professional."

Lesley snorted. "It's a struggle, believe me."

Elsa smiled. She wrapped her arms around Lesley and kissed her. "I love you."

Thank God, Lesley thought. She'd worried that this could escalate. She muttered into Elsa's hair, "I love you, too."

"Sorry."

Lesley looked up to see Zoe standing in the doorway. She looked agitated.

What's the cat done now?

"What's up?" Lesley asked.

"I'm really sorry to interrupt," Zoe said. "I know you're having a private conversation. But I think this is important."

Lesley pulled out of the embrace with Elsa. "What is?" she asked.

"Jill called me. She's been trying to get hold of you."

Lesley frowned. She patted her pockets. "My phone's in the kitchen." *Damn.* If she'd called Zoe, it was important.

She stepped towards Zoe, keeping hold of Elsa's hand. "What is it, Zoe? What's happened?"

"It's Meera," Zoe replied. "Meera and Suzi, their daughter. Jill thinks they've been taken."

CHAPTER THIRTY-EIGHT

TINA YAWNED as she entered the bedroom. Mike was lying on the bed, propped up against the pillows.

She smiled and plunked down next to him. "It's a bit early to be coming to bed."

He gave her a sidelong look. "You're made of tougher stuff than me if you're not longing for bed already."

She checked her watch and stifled another yawn. "At five past seven in the evening."

"Sounds like the perfect bedtime to me."

"The perfect bedtime for a nine-month-old. She's finally starting to go down at bedtime, thank God. Was Louis okay?"

"A little bit of grizzling over which story I read him, but he was fine." Mike scooted across to lean his head on her shoulder. "Let's not talk about the kids. How was your day?"

She laughed. "Talking about work instead of kids? We do know how to live." She stroked the increasingly curly hair on the top of his head. He'd snuggled up to her, arms wrapped around her waist.

"My brain doesn't have space for anything else right now," he said. "D'you think it ever will again?"

"Oh, it will. Look at my mum. She had two of us and her brain's full of all sorts of stuff now."

"Mainly trying to do our jobs for us."

"There is that." Tina's mum Annie had wormed her way into a series of investigations in Lyme Regis. The most recent had been only a couple of months earlier at Christmas.

"And she's retired," Mike pointed out. "I don't want to have to wait that long."

A sound came from the next room: Daisy? Both Tina and Mike stopped. The noise stopped.

"Should I go and check on her?" Tina whispered.

"You'll only disturb her. You know what she's like. If she needs us, she'll make it known."

Tina grunted. "So tell me about your day."

Mike rolled over onto his back, his head resting on Tina's thigh. He looked up at her.

"I'm on office duty on the Mudeford case," he said. "We still don't have an ID, but we now reckon the guy we'd thought was the victim could be our suspect."

"Really? Have you found him?"

"Not yet. But he applied for a passport in 2006, and he turned out to be a neighbour of the boss's wife." He shook his head. "I shouldn't be telling you this."

Tina mimed zipping her mouth. "It's not like I'm going to tell anyone. And the DIs confer, I've seen them."

"The guv gets on with your new DI?" he asked. "That's an improvement."

"DI Finch seems good," Tina said. "She gave me a bit of a pep talk, and she's dynamite with financial forensics."

"A pep talk? You're not in trouble, are you?"

Tina looked down at him. Mike had been in CID for years before she'd joined. She felt awkward about this.

"The opposite," she said. "She was pushing me to apply for the sergeant's exam."

Mike sat up. "Good. You should."

"You're sure? It doesn't bother you that I've—"

He grabbed her hand. "For God's sake, it doesn't work like that. You'd be a fantastic sergeant."

"It would be one hell of a juggling act," she said, "with the kids so little."

He shrugged. "We'd cope. You're not the first police officer to have kids, you know. Your new DI was a single parent. Still is."

Tina looked at him. "How do you know that?"

Another shrug. "Stan told me. He must have got to know her that time he went up to Birmingham with the boss."

Tina doubted that. But if the DI could do it...

"OK," she said. "I'll ask the DS what the process is." She swallowed, her stomach suddenly full of butterflies.

DS Tina Abbott. Was that a possibility? Did she even want it?

"Good." Mike kissed her cheek. "How did Johnny get on today, with his evidence? I heard he had to leave his dad's sickbed to go to court."

Tina brought a hand up to her face. "Oh, hell. I never checked up on him." She shook her head. "What kind of friend am I?"

"The kind who's busy."

She pursed her lips. "He hasn't been in touch with you?"

Mike shook his head. "I've been meaning to ask you about Johnny's dad."

"Me? You'd be more likely to know about the state of his health than I would."

Mike pulled himself up so their faces were level. "Not that. I've heard his name around the office. A couple of times. And the guv was asking me about him being in hospital, wondering how long he'd be in."

"DI Scott? Why?"

He shrugged. "No idea. Johnny's not in her team."

Tina frowned. "I haven't heard anything unusual, sorry. And Johnny... well, Johnny doesn't talk about his dad all that much."

"He was a desk officer," Mike said. "In Poole. Worked with the super."

"Have you been snooping around? Was he involved in your cold case?"

"The super was. But Eric... no." Mike wrinkled his nose. "Ignore me. I'm just making something out of nothing."

"OK." Tina was sure Johnny's dad didn't need them prying into his career. "I hope he gets better soon. It'd be a shame, what with Johnny moving here..."

"The man's not dead yet," Mike said.

"No. Let's hope not." Tina pushed herself off the bed. "Anyway, it is too early for bed. I'm getting a cuppa. I'll make you one, and we can have some quiet time."

CHAPTER THIRTY-NINE

Lesley reached out for Zoe's phone.

"Jill," she said. "Are you there?"

"Boss. Thank God. Has Zoe told you?"

"She's told me you think Meera's been taken. Tell me what's happened. Do you need a response team?"

"No. Yes. Maybe. I don't know. I don't know where she is. Both of them. But I got a text."

"From Meera?"

"I don't know who from. It just says: 'This is what happens.'"

Lesley frowned. She was standing in the middle of her living room, Elsa and Zoe hovering either side of her. The bloody cat had even come in, like it knew there was something going on. It stood on the arm of the sofa, staring at her, arranging itself neatly like it was some kind of Egyptian god.

"This is what happens?" Lesley repeated.

"Yes." Jill's voice was tight.

Lesley lowered herself to the sofa. The cat meowed and jumped down to the floor. Elsa grimaced at it.

"Jill," she said. "Zoe's going to arrange for a response team to be dispatched to your house." She looked up at Zoe, who nodded. "That's where you are, I assume?"

"Yes."

Lesley nodded at Zoe, who left the room. The cat trailed behind her. Lesley realised she had Zoe's phone.

Zoe'll find a way around that. She wouldn't have talked the woman into coming to Dorset if she couldn't manage that.

"OK, Jill," she said, keeping her voice steady. "Start at the beginning and tell me what happened."

"I got home at six thirty," Jill told her. "Six thirty-five, according to our doorbell. I was expecting Meera and Suzi to be here. Meera had told me she'd be cooking. But her car isn't outside, and there's no sign of them having been here at all. I've called her a dozen times. I've used the app we've got to track each other's phones. Hers is switched off."

"And you're sure she hasn't just gone somewhere and not told you?"

"Meera wouldn't do that. And there's this text."

Zoe reappeared, holding out Lesley's phone. She must have left it on the kitchen table. Zoe handed it to her, and Lesley jabbed in the passcode.

"Thanks," Zoe muttered. She started typing in a number as she walked back towards the kitchen.

"Tell me about the text," Lesley told Jill.

"It's from a number I've not seen before, and which doesn't respond when I call it. It says: 'This is what happens.' That's all."

"There's just one text?"

"Just one."

"OK. It could be a mistake. Do you have any specific reason to think this is related to Meera not being at home?"

"Boss, I—"

"I'm sorry," Lesley said. "I'm not trying to undermine you, Jill. I'm just being cautious."

Zoe appeared in the doorway. Elsa was on the sofa next to Lesley, a hand on her back.

"A team's on its way," Zoe said. "Twelve minutes away."

"A team will be with you in twelve minutes," Lesley told Jill.

"I'm not making this up, boss. Meera and I... we make sure our phones are charged up. We do a lot of juggling, what with Suzi and the job. We're in regular contact. And when you've got a little one, you never want to be unreachable."

"I know," Lesley said. She'd had a police-issue Blackberry when Sharon was young. And a pager. She'd made sure that the nursery, and then the school, had the numbers. And Terry, her ex, for what that was worth.

"Listen, Jill," she said. "If I didn't believe you, there wouldn't be a response team on its way. Do you want me to come over?"

"No," Jill replied, "I don't want to ruin your evening."

Lesley smiled, despite herself. "I'm a copper, Jill. You think I haven't had plenty of evenings ruined?"

There was silence, and then a sob.

"Sorry," Jill said. "It's just... I'm scared. What if it's the Kelvins?"

"What makes you think it's them?" Lesley asked.

"My meetings. With... you know who with. We've been careful, but... what if this is a threat?"

Lesley scratched her cheek. "You need to let forensics have your phone," she said. "Their digital guy."

"Sunil," Jill muttered.

"Yes," Lesley replied. "He'll take a look at the text, find out if it can be traced."

"OK."

"But our priority is to find Meera. Is there any CCTV near your house?"

Jill spluttered out a grim laugh. "No chance." A pause. "Hang on. The pub might have something. And there's our doorbell. Although I don't think she came home."

"She might have," Lesley said. "Can you check it?"

"It's got an app. Give me a minute."

Lesley sighed. If Meera was really missing, then she needed to go over to Jill's. Open an investigation, and the sooner the better.

Zoe was in the hallway, muttering into her phone. Talking to the response team, maybe.

Zoe headed up the MCIT now. It should be her that Lesley sent over. But Lesley was Jill's boss. And Meera's, indirectly. This wasn't a normal situation.

Elsa leaned in. "Is there anything I can do?"

Lesley put a hand on her wife's knee. "Make me a coffee?" she muttered.

Elsa nodded and stood up. "Caffeinated?"

"Yeah." It looked like it was going to be a long night.

"Boss." Jill was back on the line. "I've checked the doorbell, and there's nothing except for an Amazon delivery since I left for work this morning."

Damn. "OK. That doesn't mean she wasn't in your village. When the team arrive, tell them to send someone to the pub. And your neighbours, just in case."

"Will do," Jill replied. Her voice was steadier now. "Oh, that's the door."

"It'll be them," Lesley said. "Answer it. Zoe and I are going to come over."

"You don't need to—"

"We do. Now go and answer the door."

"Of course. Thanks, boss." Jill sniffed.

Lesley heard rustling sounds as Jill walked to the door. Elsa came in with a mug of coffee, and Zoe reappeared wearing her coat. It was a blue duffel, not the maroon leather one Lesley remembered from Birmingham.

"I can drive," Zoe said. "While you talk to her."

Lesley looked at Elsa. "Sorry, love, but could you put that in my travel mug? We need to get over there."

"Of course." Elsa picked up the mug.

"Boss." Jill was back.

"Jill." Lesley pressed her phone to her ear as she strode out of the room. "Are the response team there?"

"No. Well, yes, they are. But not just them."

Lesley stopped walking. "I don't get you. Is everything OK?"

"Yes. I mean, I think so."

Lesley was by the front door, reaching for her coat. Zoe was already outside, getting into her Mini.

"I don't understand," Lesley said to Jill. "Who's there? What's happened?"

"Sorry, boss. It's Meera."

"Meera?"

"Meera and Suzi. They're here."

CHAPTER FORTY

"I'm sorry, boss," Jill said. "I hope I didn't disrupt your evening too much."

"It's fine, Jill. I'm glad they're safe."

Jill put her phone down on the kitchen table. She could feel the sinews in her neck, taut and stiff. Meera was pulling off Suzi's gloves, making a game of it.

"Where were you?" Jill asked. She knew her voice was as taut as those sinews.

Meera, still trying to prise off the second glove, looked up. "I'm really sorry, love. Suzi had a play date with a new kid at the school. The mum didn't want us to leave."

"I thought you were cooking."

Meera stood up, her eyes dark. "Is that what this is about? You were expecting dinner on the table like a 1950s husband?"

Jill took a step towards her wife. She grabbed her hand. "I was worried. I called you. I..."

She thought of that text she'd received. Just a wrong number, probably.

"I was worried," she repeated.

Meera sagged. "I'm sorry. Suzi was getting on really well with the kid. And the mum was nice, kept making me cups of tea. Well, not the mum, but the aunt. But she's his guardian. In fact, all that tea... Give me a minute."

Jill watched as Meera patted Suzi, who'd climbed onto a kitchen chair, on the head, and hurried towards the stairs. She flexed her fingers, trying to ease the tension, and sat down opposite her daughter.

"Hey, Su-su," she said, trying to keep her tone light. "You have a good play date?"

Suzi gave her a definitive nod, one movement of the head up and down.

"Have you had something to eat?"

Suzi grinned. "Pizza."

Jill raised an eyebrow. Above their heads, the toilet flushed.

"Pizza, eh? Lucky you."

"Going back next week."

"Well," Jill said. "As long as I know next time." She stood up and leaned across the table to stroke Suzi's cheek.

The girl giggled. "Tickles."

Jill laughed with her and went to the sink. Meera reappeared as she was filling the kettle.

"Sorry about that. Too much tea."

Jill nodded. "I hear you're going back next week. You must have had a nice time."

"They've invited us, anyway." Meera put a hand on Jill's back, fingers splayed. "I'll put Suzi to bed then I can tell you all about it, if you'd like."

"It's OK." Jill wasn't sure she wanted to know the minutiae of a play date. "A boy and his aunt, you said?"

"Yup. Boy's name is Mason. The aunt is Brianna. Brianna Frobisher. She was really friendly. It was odd, though."

Jill turned towards her. She still hadn't shaken off the tension from earlier. "What was?"

Meera pursed her lips. "The reason I didn't call you was because I couldn't find my phone. When we were leaving, Brianna found it in her bag."

"Her bag?"

A nod. "She said her nephew does that. He's a bit of a magpie, apparently. She goes easy on him though, what with him..." she glanced at Suzi "...what with him being an orphan."

"Poor kid," Jill said.

"What's orphan?" Suzi asked.

Jill shook her head; *nothing gets past this girl*. "It's somebody who hasn't got a mummy or a daddy, Su-su."

Suzi frowned. "Am I an orphan? I don't have a daddy."

Jill felt a knot rise in her stomach. If she had a pound for every time she'd been asked about this...

"No, sweetie," Meera said. She scooped Suzi up from the chair and hoisted her up to her hip. "You have two mummies."

"Mason has his aunty."

"He does," Meera replied. "Brianna."

"Is aunty like second mummy?"

Jill exchanged a look with Meera. "No, Su-su," she said. "Aunty is your mummy's sister."

"Like Aunty Gee."

"Exactly," said Meera. "My annoying little sister."

"I like Aunty Gee," Suzi said.

Meera laughed. "So do I, lovey. It's just how people talk about their families sometimes."

"Like Mason talks about his aunty."

Meera raised an eyebrow. "I hope not. Come on you, bedtime."

Jill wrapped her arms around Meera and Suzi and kissed Suzi's forehead. "Night, Su-su. Sleep well."

"Night, Mama."

Meera and Suzi headed upstairs. Jill could still feel tension rippling through her, although a little more faintly now. She poured two cups of tea and took them into the living room.

She was hungry, she realised. No pizza for her. She was about to get up and head to the fridge for a rummage when she remembered something Meera had said.

Frobisher. That was the name of the aunt, the woman at the play date, wasn't it?

Brianna Frobisher.

Her phone buzzed. *Ignore it*. She closed her eyes.

Frobisher. Brianna Frobisher. Where had she heard that name before?

Think.

It wasn't Brianna. It was Amanda. Amanda Frobisher. Arthur Kelvin's wife, or she had been, before she'd died in her own Sandbanks bath. Suicide, supposedly. Not that anyone believed that, given that Amanda had been having an affair with Arthur's nephew.

Arthur's nephew Kyle. The man whose prints had been on that necklace Katie had found at the beach huts.

Another coincidence? Surely not.

Jill picked up her phone. She could be wrong. She needed to check Brianna's name. Was she Amanda's sister? The boy, the orphan... was he Arthur Kelvin's son?

"That was easy." Meera entered the room and dropped onto the sofa next to Jill. "She was exhausted."

"Mm-hmm." Jill was looking at her phone screen. The notification she'd ignored was another text.

She swallowed.

"You OK?" Meera put a hand on her knee. "You're breathing heavily."

Jill panted out a breath. She opened the text.

Meera turned towards her, sitting up straighter. "Jill. Everything OK?"

Jill stared at the text.

Next time, maybe they won't come home.

She squeezed her eyes shut. Meera grabbed her hand.

"Jill, what is it? You're scaring me."

Jill opened her eyes. She looked at Meera.

"I need to ask you some questions," she said. "About Suzi's play date."

CHAPTER FORTY-ONE

LESLEY SLUMPED down in her chair and plonked her bag on her desk. She'd overslept this morning, struggling to sleep after the conversation with Elsa last night.

Elsa had still been in a weird mood. After the panic with Jill had died down, Zoe had immediately retreated to bed, taking her cat with her, and Lesley and Elsa had sat staring at the TV for an hour, barely talking to each other. Things would be easier when Zoe moved out at the weekend.

Lesley knew her relationship with Elsa had these tensions. It was inevitable when a DCI and a criminal lawyer were married, but with Elsa having set up her own practice and taken on clients, mainly in Hampshire, she had been hoping the tensions would ease.

Perhaps that had been wishful thinking.

She reached for her bag and dipped her hand inside. She needed chocolate. She was just about to pull out a bar of Dairy Milk when there was a knock on her door.

She threw the Dairy Milk guiltily back into the bag and straightened up. "Come in."

The door opened and Jill appeared. She gave Lesley a tight smile, but her face looked drawn.

"Morning, Jill," Lesley said. "Are you OK? You don't look great."

Jill shook her head.

Lesley gestured towards the chair opposite her. "Sit down." She pulled the chocolate out of her bag. "Here, why don't you share this with me?"

Jill's eyes widened. "Don't tell Meera."

Lesley laughed. "As long as you don't tell Elsa."

Jill's face froze. "Is everything OK there?" she said. "I'm sorry. I had to go and speak to your wife."

Lesley waved her hand in dismissal. "My wife's name came up in a case, so you had to go and see her. It was right that you did it and not me. And as to any tensions it might have created at home, well, that's my concern, not yours. How are things with you? Was Meera OK after she got home?"

Jill shook her head. She unwrapped the Dairy Milk, looking down at it intently.

Lesley frowned. "Jill, is there something you're not telling me?"

Jill broke off a slab of the chocolate and put it in her mouth. She closed her eyes, not moving her jaw. Lesley knew that feeling, allowing a slab of milk chocolate to melt on your tongue, particularly when you'd been trying to wean yourself off the stuff.

"OK," Lesley said, "so your Mudeford Spit case, are you any closer to identifying the body?"

Jill shook her head. She pointed at her mouth. "Sorry, boss," she mumbled through the chocolate.

Lesley smiled. At last, Jill swallowed. She shook her shoulders out and cleared her throat. "Sorry, boss."

"No need to apologise," Lesley said. "It was me who gave you the chocolate."

"True. It's not the case I've come to talk to you about. Well, at least not this case."

"Ah," said Lesley, "our friend?"

Jill nodded.

"I know he didn't arrive for your meeting yesterday," Lesley continued, "and I'm assuming you know the reason for that."

She glanced at the door. She didn't want to mention that Eric was in hospital, in case anyone happened to be passing.

Jill nodded. "It's not about that. It's about Meera."

"I thought she came back."

"She did," Jill replied. "But—"

Lesley leaned forward, placing her elbows on the desk. "But what, Jill? You're starting to worry me."

"Sorry, boss."

"Stop apologising and tell me." Lesley realised her voice was sharp. "Please," she said, softening her voice.

"After the response team left," Jill told her, "Meera told me where she'd been. A play date with Suzi and a new friend from school."

"That sounds normal enough," Lesley said.

Jill nodded. "It does until you know who the play date was with."

Lesley frowned. "Who?"

Jill met her gaze. "The woman's name is Brianna Frobisher. The child is her nephew, Mason."

Lesley shook her head. "Never heard of her."

Jill raised an eyebrow. "Amanda Frobisher's sister."

"Amanda Frobisher being Arthur Kelvin's widow," Lesley said.

Jill nodded. "The nephew is Mason Kelvin, Amanda Frobisher's son. He was orphaned when his parents died, and it seems that Brianna, his aunt, is taking care of him."

Lesley leaned back. "Not the Kelvins? I thought they'd want to keep control of one of their own."

Jill shrugged. "Maybe they have joint custody, I don't know, but either way, Brianna invited Meera and Suzi round for tea, and it sounds like they did it at very short notice."

"Maybe it's a coincidence," Lesley said. "I mean, kids have got to go to school."

Jill put her hand on the desk. "Meera's phone," she said. "She lost it while she was there, and then Brianna found it in her bag."

"In Meera's bag?"

"No, Brianna found it in her own bag."

"Brianna's bag? How did it get there?"

Jill grimaced. "She claimed that her nephew put it there. Apparently, he's a bit of a magpie. But I think she did it deliberately. I think she didn't want Meera to get any calls from me. I think she was trying to scare me."

"Really?" Lesley said. "You're sure she just wasn't just a woman inviting a friend around for a play date? After all, Amanda Frobisher was a victim of the Kelvins. I don't imagine she'd be—"

"There's more," Jill said. "The text I got, remember?"

"Ah," Lesley replied, "have you sent that off to forensics?"

"Not yet," Jill told her. "That'll be my next move. But it wasn't the only text. There was another one later, from the same number."

"Which said what?"

"It said, *Next time, maybe they won't come home.*"

Lesley felt her jaw clench.

"Oh, Jill," she said, "why didn't you tell me that to begin with?"

Jill looked down at the desk. "Sorry, boss, I didn't mean to..."

"It's OK," Lesley said. "You're worried. You're scared."

Jill looked up. "Yes, I'm bloody worried. They know – the Kelvins know I've been seeing Eric Chiles."

"You don't know that," Lesley told her. "They could just be trying to scare you off the Stephen Carson case."

"Why would they do that?" Jill asked.

"There's the financial link," Lesley said. "Stephen Carson's name was used on some of the finances linking Mark Ashford and the Kelvins."

Jill frowned. "Have we got any more on that?"

"Zoe's been working on it overnight," Lesley said. "I—"

"She has? I haven't seen her yet."

"She's staying at my house right now." Lesley leaned forward.

"Let's get that text checked out. See who it's from. We can also do a background check on this Brianna Frobisher."

Jill nodded. "I think that would be a good idea."

"Are you going to tell Meera?" Lesley asked.

Another nod. "We've already talked about it."

"Good. I don't want Meera having any more contact with this woman without understanding what risks she might be getting herself in for."

Jill met Lesley's gaze. "Meera won't be going to that house again, not unless it proves to be—"

"Innocent," Lesley said.

Jill grunted.

"OK," said Lesley. She stood up. She needed a coffee. "So you get that phone off to forensics, one of your team can take it."

"Katie's already going over there," Jill said.

"Good. Get yourself another phone in the meantime and carry on with the Carson case."

"That's fine," Jill said. "That's my job. But Eric Chiles..."

"He's in hospital right now," Lesley said, her voice low. "You won't be able to meet him for a little while."

"It's not that," Jill said, "I can't put my family at risk."

Lesley sighed. She couldn't expect Jill to continue if there was a chance that the people she loved might become victims of the Kelvins. But she knew how important it was to find out what Eric Chiles knew, particularly about the disappearance of Frank Kelvin.

But Jill wasn't the only person who could handle that.

"OK," she said, "from this point on, there is to be no more contact between you and our friend."

Jill's shoulders slumped. "Thanks," she said, "I was really hoping you'd say that. I hope you don't think me unprofessional."

"I don't," Lesley said. "I think if there's a chance that they know what you've been doing, it's wisest to take you off that side of things, at least for now."

Jill smiled. "Thanks. I really appreciate it."

Lesley gave her a nod. She gestured towards the phone.

"Yeah," Jill said, "I'll get it straight over to forensics. Don't want to miss Katie leaving."

Jill left the room and closed the door behind her.

Lesley stared at the door.

Was this a blessing in disguise?

She'd felt uneasy about Jill conducting the meetings with Eric Chiles right from the start. It involved a level of risk that somebody more experienced should be taking. Somebody like herself.

And there was information reaching back into cases that Lesley had managed since she'd started here in Dorset. Information that might help put her mind at rest.

Information that might, finally, get rid of Vera Kelvin once and for all.

CHAPTER FORTY-TWO

Zoe turned to smile at Meera as they walked out of the office and along the corridor. Her own office was at the far end of the four doors on this corridor.

"Do you want a coffee?" Zoe said. "I know I could do with one."

Meera shrugged. "If you want one? Yes."

Zoe stopped walking. She turned to look at Meera. "You don't have to do that, you know," she said.

"Do what?" Meera asked.

"You don't have to go along with whatever I want. If you don't want a coffee, say you don't want one."

Meera smiled. "OK, Ma'am, I don't want a coffee."

"Fair enough," Zoe said. "I might think you're mad, but I respect you for telling me."

Meera's smile broadened.

"Come on," Zoe said. "Let's go into my office. I don't want to keep you any longer than is necessary."

"Thanks," Meera said. "I know there's work, on the Jackie Kendall case."

"That really affected you, that case, didn't it?" Zoe had noticed it, from the other woman's body language in the briefing.

Meera cast her gaze downwards. The two of them were standing by the door, neither of them having sat down yet.

"It was awful," Meera said. "Poor Jackie. She went to such lengths to keep herself safe, and Yiannis, too."

"Yiannis was her partner, right?" Zoe said.

Meera nodded. "Yiannis Kallias. At first, she went on the run without him. He launched a campaign to find her, a search. He gave up his job. It became his whole world."

"And then," Zoe said, "and then, she met me."

Meera looked up. "Oh, I'd forgotten about that."

Zoe gestured towards the desk. "Why don't we sit down?" She took one of the two chairs on the side of her desk nearest the door and gestured for Meera to take the other. This felt less confrontational than Zoe sitting on the other side of the desk in her larger office chair.

Meera sat down, her gaze on Zoe. "What was she like when you met her in Cumbria? She came into a police station, is that right?"

Zoe nodded. "Workington Police Station. She was up there for a while working in a hairdresser's, if I remember right, keeping her nose clean, keeping her profile low. She must have got scared."

Meera nodded. "She must have been terrified, and she was right to be."

Zoe gave Meera a sad smile. "It's not your fault, Meera," she said. "There was nothing you could have done."

"I don't think it was my fault," Meera said, "but Yiannis, I felt for him. He was devastated, turning up back at that hotel and finding his partner dead after everything they'd been through."

"I know," Zoe told her. "It's hard when you have to support people through the death of a loved one. But we're doing our best by Jackie. The Three Musketeers will be in prison very soon, and they won't be able to do that to anyone else."

Meera rubbed an eye. "Yeah, I suppose so."

"Is that what you wanted to talk to me about?" Zoe asked. She was wondering if this might have something to do with the call she'd received from Jill the previous evening.

Meera shook her head. "Something happened," she said.

Zoe nodded. "Go on."

Meera drew in a thin breath. "My daughter, Suzi, mine and Jill's. She's at school in Blandford. There was a new boy. He started last week. She's made friends with him and his mum, his aunt. She is his guardian now. She got friendly. She invited us over for a play date."

"OK," Zoe said. "That was where you were yesterday evening when Jill called the boss, right? Jill was really scared, you know."

"I know," Meera told her. "I would have called her, but, well, I lost my phone."

"You lost it?" Zoe said.

"Well, I found it again. Or rather, Brianna did. In her bag. Her nephew's a bit of a magpie, she told me."

"Brianna's the woman you went on the play date with?"

Meera nodded. "We went to her house, just a small house in Poundbury, but nice. She and her nephew have been living there for the last six months."

"OK," Zoe said. "So did something happen? Something that's worrying you?"

Meera swallowed. "It's not so much that something happened. It's what Jill was like when I got home."

"She thought you'd gone missing," Zoe said. "There was something about a text."

"Yeah," Meera replied. "That was probably just a wrong number or something."

"OK," Zoe said. "So, what is it that's worrying you? Is it connected to the Musketeers?"

She bit her lip. That had been harsh.

"Sorry, Ma'am," Meera said. "I probably shouldn't have—" She began to rise from her chair.

Zoe gestured for her to sit. "I didn't mean that to come out that way, Meera. If there's something worrying you about this situation, I want you to tell me about it, particularly if it's related to your work."

"It might be," Meera said. "Jill said that Brianna, that's the woman whose house I went to, is the sister of Amanda Frobisher."

"Who's Amanda Frobisher?" Zoe asked.

"Arthur Kelvin's widow," Meera replied.

"Arthur Kelvin was Vera Kelvin's son," Zoe said. "Ran the family business before he was murdered by his nephew."

Meera nodded. "And the nephew murdered him because of the affair that he was having with Arthur's wife."

Zoe let out a whistle. "Bloody hell. This is complicated. So do you think this Brianna, inviting you round to her house, has got something to do with the fact that we've been investigating the Kelvins?"

"Were we investigating them?" Meera asked. "I thought it was only last night that you discovered a link between Mark Ashforth and the Kelvins."

Zoe smiled. "You don't miss a trick, do you? Strictly speaking, we haven't been investigating them, not recently, but based on what the DCI has told me about them, I'm not surprised that their names have come up now."

"Nor me," Meera said, "but Jill was so jumpy when I got home."

"Did she tell you why she was jumpy?" Zoe asked.

Meera shook her head. Zoe leaned back in her chair and gave the DC a long look. "I can't spy on your wife for you, you know," she said. "There will be operational matters that Jill's involved in that I know more about than you do, because we're both DIs. I can't share those with you, and nor can Jill."

"I know." Meera's hands were in her lap, her fingers curling around each other. "I do know that. I just – well, you asked me if I was OK, and I'm not, and I just wanted to let you know why."

"I appreciate that," Zoe said, "but my advice to you would be to avoid this Brianna Frobisher woman until we know more about what her motives might be."

Meera's eyes widened. "You're going to investigate her?"

Zoe resisted a laugh. "What, for hiding your phone in her bag? No, Meera, we're not going to investigate her, but if her name comes up in the course of any investigations into Vera Kelvin and her wider family, then that might turn out to be relevant. But don't worry, I'm not going to ask you to spy on her at the school."

"I wouldn't mind," Meera said. "That seems like a good opportunity."

"No," Zoe told her. "It doesn't work like that. If we need to investigate Brianna, we do it properly. But for now, maybe it was just a genuine mistake that your phone ended up in her bag. Maybe her nephew is a magpie."

Meera laughed. "Yeah, four-year-olds are a nightmare, after all."

Zoe gave her a smile. "Yep, and they don't get much easier. Is that everything?"

"Yeah, thanks, boss." Meera stood up. "I appreciate this."

"That's OK," Zoe said. "Now why don't we get on with focusing on the Mark Ashforth case, and forget all about this Brianna, yeah?"

Meera said, "Sounds like a plan."

CHAPTER FORTY-THREE

Jill took a deep breath as she entered the Cold Cases Team room. All three members of her team turned as one to face her.

Katie looked expectant and eager, her back straight and her eyes wide.

Mike was hiding a yawn behind his hand.

Stanley had his phone in his hand and was glancing between that and her as she entered.

"Morning, all," she said. "Sorry I didn't come in first thing. I needed to speak to the boss."

"Have there been any developments?" Katie asked.

Jill sat down at the empty desk. She gave Katie a smile. "Nothing new, Katie," she said. "I'm expecting the three of you to brief me on where your parts of the investigation are."

Katie nodded. "Sunil and I have been doing more work on tracing Stephen Carson's movements since 2006. I'm heading back over there in a bit."

Jill nodded. "You sent me a message saying he'd bought a house in Spain last year. Is that right?"

"In Málaga," Katie replied.

"Have you followed it up?"

"I've got all the documents," Katie said. "He used a lawyer based in London."

"What about with somebody in Málaga?" Jill asked. "Have you contacted the local police?"

Katie looked at her. "You want me to do that, guv?"

"I wouldn't be asking you if I didn't."

"So you want me to call Málaga police and ask what?"

"I want you to ask if they can go to the address and see if Stephen Carson is at home. There's every chance he's our suspect."

"Shall I ask them to knock on his door?"

"No," Jill replied. "All I want now is to know whether he's there. Once we have that, we can decide how to proceed. We need more before we can bring him in for questioning."

"OK." Katie was writing in a notepad. She finished with a flourish and looked up with a smile.

"OK," said Jill. "Let's see what everybody else has got to share. Mike, any more from pathology?"

He nodded. "Toxicology report came back. There was heroin in the victim's system. Not enough of it to kill him, but it was there."

"So was he a drug addict?" she asked.

"There's no evidence of him having injected heroin on a regular basis," Mike replied. "No tracks or bruising according to pathology, but then, he is in a pretty bad way."

Jill nodded. "It would be difficult to tell after so many years. So, do you think someone gave him heroin in order to make him unconscious, and then took him to the beach huts?"

Mike nodded. "Given that he died of suffocation from being immersed in sand, I think that's probably likely."

Stanley winced. "Poor bastard."

"You're not wrong there," Jill said. "OK, Mike, I want you to go to the beach huts. See if there's anybody who had a beach hut there in 1994."

"It's a long shot," said Stanley.

Jill gave him a look. "It's not impossible."

"There's a warden," Katie said. "We met her when we went to the crime scene. Remember?"

Jill nodded. Panjit, the woman who'd directed them to the toilet block. "You're right," she replied. "Mike, get the details of the warden from Katie and track her down first. She'll know if there's anybody who's had one of those beach huts since 1994."

"She might not," Katie said. "They are privately owned. I'm not sure if the council keeps a log."

"Either way," Jill said, "there's going to be a record somewhere of who owns those properties. Surely they pay council tax or something. Mike, can I leave that with you? Find out if there's anybody who's been there since 1994 and if so, interview them. Find out if there was any habitual drug taking around there. Was there a group of people our guy might have been part of? Or if we're really lucky, can we find somebody who witnessed something?"

She drummed her fist on the desk. "I should have thought of this earlier."

"Sorry, guv," said Katie. "We should all have thought of it."

Jill looked up at her. "It's fine, Katie. You carry on working on Stephen Carson's whereabouts. Stanley, what have you got?"

"I've been looking at the robbery," he said, "the one that Stephen Carson was suspected of being involved in."

Jill felt her muscles clench. She hadn't told the team about the files she'd found, the redacted name, or the fact that Eric Chiles had written on it. She wasn't ready to share yet.

"OK," she said, keeping her voice level, "what have you managed to find out?"

"So there was a guy that was assaulted during the course of the robbery," Stanley said. "Joseph Tizzard. Only nineteen years old at the time, it was his evening job while he was studying. I was hoping to be able to speak to him, get a bit more information about Stephen Carson and what happened. But I can't find a record of him anywhere. It's like he never existed."

"Nothing?" Jill asked.

"Sorry, guv. Nothing. Only the robbery."

She pursed her lips. "OK. Keep digging. Maybe... maybe that's related somehow. Maybe he was using a false name."

"How old would he be now?" Katie asked.

Stanley shrugged, he screwed up his face. "Fifty-two."

"Old," Katie said.

Mike winced. "God, that's the same age as..." He frowned.

Jill smiled. "Don't go there," she said. "That's younger than the DCI. Only... well not all *that* many years older than me."

Mike grimaced. "Sorry, guv."

Stanley and Katie were chuckling.

"All right, all right," Jill said. "That doesn't make me old, just older than some of you."

The three DCs exchanged looks.

"Yes," Jill said, "older than *all* of you."

"Sorry, boss," Katie said.

"That's OK, Katie." Jill laughed. They needed some levity to break the frustration of not even knowing who their body was yet. "So we've got Katie speaking to Málaga, Mike working on the beach hut community, and Stanley, is there anybody else you can follow up from the robbery?"

"There weren't any witnesses," Stanley said. "It was a late-night thing, but the report said that there was more than one robber."

Jill swallowed. "I've seen that, too," she said. The question was, was the second robber the unnamed police detective whose name had been removed from the file? "Leave that with me," she said. "You help Mike with finding out what you can about potential drug taking around the beach huts at that time."

"OK, boss," Stanley replied.

Katie had her hands up. Jill gave her a *don't do that* look, and Katie plunged it back down into her lap.

"Sorry, guv," she said. "Just one more thing."

"Uh huh."

"Ursula Rowland," Katie said, "the woman claiming to be a forensic archaeologist who we met at the site. You remember her?"

"I do," Jill said. "She was keen, wasn't she? Has she found anything?"

Katie shook her head. "Quite the opposite. I was wondering why Gail hadn't heard anything from her, so I called the uni, and they said they'd never heard of her."

Jill thought back. "But she told us she was a PhD student, didn't she? Not an academic, so maybe they just haven't got her on their list of employees."

"I thought of that," Katie replied, "so I asked them to check their record of PhD students. There is no Ursula Rowland at Bournemouth University."

"Why would she lie?" asked Stanley.

"Very good question," Jill said. "Katie, did she give you any contact details?"

"No, guv," Katie replied. "I gave her my card, but she left before I got anything more from her than Bournemouth University."

Jill clenched her teeth. "Damn. So if she isn't a student or an academic at Bournemouth University, who the hell is she? And is she a forensic archaeologist at all?"

"Good question," said Katie.

"OK," Jill said. "Stanley, instead of helping Mike with the beach hut community, I want you to see if you can track Ursula down. Don't spend too long on it. Just do a quick search. See if you can get some contact details for me, yeah?"

"Sure, boss," Stanley replied.

CHAPTER FORTY-FOUR

Lesley had gone to great pains to avoid being followed to Dorchester Hospital.

She'd driven to Bournemouth Station and waited in her car until one minute before a Dorchester train was due. She'd boarded it at the last moment and paid the fare when the train manager had done her rounds, relieved not to be fined. Then she'd walked to the taxi rank at Dorchester Station and taken a cab to the hospital. She'd done all this whilst wearing her most anonymous raincoat and a grey woolly hat, at times even going so far as to hide under an umbrella. Thank goodness it was raining.

Lesley had never done undercover work. But she'd known officers who had, and she'd read a few Le Carré novels. She hoped all this, along with her copper's instincts, made her competent at going undetected, instead of making her look like Dorset's most conspicuous idiot.

Getting the ward details had been easy; Tina had them, of course, and had been happy to furnish them when Lesley had suggested she was sending flowers, in support of Johnny. What would be more challenging was ensuring she didn't bump into Johnny himself.

She found her way to the Robert White Building, where the oncology ward was, alert for signs of Johnny. She passed no one on the way there.

Once she'd found the correct corridor, she tucked herself in beside the double doors, right by the wall, and waited. Five minutes later, the only people to have come through those doors had been two nurses moaning about one of the consultants. She smiled at them as they registered her and walked in the opposite direction.

At the end of the corridor, she realised she'd gone the wrong way. She turned on her heel, alert for those nurses, and made her way to Eric's ward.

The woman at the nursing station looked up as she passed but didn't question her. Lesley slowed, listening for Johnny's voice.

Nothing. The ward was quiet: eight beds and just one visitor, a woman quietly knitting beside a sleeping patient. She gave Lesley a nod, which she returned.

Eric was in the last bed on the right. He looked like he was attempting to read a book and failing, eyes not moving from side to side. Instead, his gaze was vacant, boring right through the book.

Lesley cleared her throat. He looked up, momentary joy replaced by confusion.

"What have you come for? Where am I being taken this time?"

Lesley approached the bed.

"My name's Lesley Clarke," she said in a low voice. "I'm a colleague, of sorts."

She held up her ID so it was hidden from the ward's other occupants by her coat.

The confusion was replaced by recognition. He looked up at her.

"Johnny's guv'nor," he said. His face sagged. "And Jill's. I do hope she didn't wait long for me yesterday."

Lesley smiled. "Not too long. She sends best wishes."

"That's kind."

"I won't stay long," she said.

"That's wise." His gaze flicked to the nurses' station. Lesley resisted the urge to turn and look.

"I just want you to know," she said, "that you'll be dealing with me from now on."

His eyebrows rose. "I am honoured."

"Oh, I wouldn't be so sure about that. But I'll make contact. That is, if you're well enough?"

He nodded. "I am. Well, I'm probably not. But what's the point of not helping, eh? I'm dying. They don't scare me anymore."

Lesley didn't need to ask who *they* were. "I'm so sorry to hear that," she said.

He pursed his lips ruefully. "So am I. So am I. But it's Johnny I worry about. Him and the two little 'uns." He cocked his head. "But that's not what you came here for. What can I do for you?"

Lesley smiled. Eric Chiles might be sitting in a hospital bed. He might be dying. But he was still a copper, and a good one at that.

"Jill won't have had a chance to tell you about our case at Mudeford Spit," she said.

"I read about that in the local paper. Ain't got much else to do here. Fella dumped under the toilet block in 1994, right?"

"Exactly right. Do you remember the name Stephen Carson?"

Eric narrowed his eyes. "Career criminal. Robbed a petrol station in Pokesdown, roughed up the poor lad behind the till, then disappeared into thin air. Is he the fella you've dug up?"

Lesley shook her head. "We still don't have an ID. But we think Carson might be responsible."

"Wouldn't put it past him." Eric blinked at her. "But you're here about the robbery. The investigation I took over."

Eric Chiles, it seemed, had a bloody good memory.

"I am," Lesley said. "I'm after—"

"The name of the bent copper whose prints were found at the scene," Eric said.

"I'm impressed," Lesley told him.

"Oh, I don't remember everything. But that case... it was early in my career. Left an impression. His name was Ted Burns. Bent as a nine-bob bit. Hanged himself before I could prove it, though."

Lesley wasn't sure which was the most surprising: the revelation, or the casual manner in which Eric delivered it.

"He hanged himself? When?"

"Summer of 2001. I'm surprised no one's told you, it was all anyone talked about for months."

"Was it known that he was corrupt?"

"Only by me and a colleague, whose name I'm not ready to give you," Eric said.

Fair enough. "And was he involved in the robbery?"

"He bloody was. Used his position as a DS to get into places, conduct what he called community security checks. Then used what he'd learned to rob places, or to give information to others who did the robbing for him."

"And that was all? He wasn't involved in anything more serious?"

"It seemed pretty serious to me. A woman died in a Christchurch hotel. Gunshot wound, poor soul." He crossed himself. "But it's too late to bring him to justice, I'm afraid."

Lesley nodded. She'd stayed long enough. She'd made contact, and she'd learned more about the robbery.

"Thanks," she said. "I won't keep you any longer."

"I appreciate that," Eric replied. "And I'll reward you for it."

Lesley turned back to him. A nurse was at the next bed, talking to the patient in a loud voice.

"You will?" she asked Eric.

He nodded, then beckoned for her to come closer. She took a step towards him.

"The name," he said. "My colleague. Worked for me, unofficially, then... Well, he rose up the ranks like a rocket. Never betrayed me, though."

"Let me guess," Lesley muttered. "He was a PC in 1994, at the time of the robbery."

"He was. Made sergeant three years later. Then kept on going. And now," his gaze flicked past her, towards the ward, "he's a—"

"Superintendent," she whispered.

Eric looked into her eyes. "You know who I'm talking about."

"I do. Thanks, Eric. You look after yourself." She straightened up.

Eric shifted in the bed, then grimaced. He looked up at her.

"Don't mind me," he said. "And don't be a stranger."

Lesley smiled. "I won't."

CHAPTER FORTY-FIVE

THE COUNCIL, of course, had no idea who'd been in the beach huts as long ago as 1994. Nor were they able to give him a list of owners. The woman Mike had spoken to had all but laughed when he'd asked.

"You're probably better off going down there and doing a roll call," she said. "You don't need everyone to be there, they all know each other's business in those huts."

"It's February," he replied. "No one's allowed to stay there overnight."

She snorted. "Day use is permitted, though. And plenty of them have solar panels and chemical loos. I bet they're camping out, ignoring the restrictions."

Mike sighed. She was obstructive and rude, but she was probably right.

"Thanks for your help," he said.

"I haven't really helped you very much," came the reply.

Mike took his phone away from his ear and held it out in front of him. He stuck his tongue out at it.

At the next desk, Stanley laughed. "That bad, eh?"

Mike grunted. He put the phone back to his ear, but the woman from the council had hung up.

Mike sighed. He got up from his chair and stretched, then went to the coat pegs by the door and grabbed his fleece.

"I'm going to head over there," he told Stanley, who gave him a thumbs-up. Katie, who was deep in a call, gave him a grin.

An hour later, he was past the grind of Bournemouth town centre and heading for Southbourne, beyond which lay Hengistbury Head and Mudeford Spit. He wondered why they called it that, when Mudeford was on the other side of Christchurch Harbour.

His phone rang as he took the turn-off towards the coast, and he answered on hands-free.

"DC Mike Legg." He slowed down for a speed hump. This wasn't the quickest way, but he fancied a fix of sea view.

"Mike, it's Brett from Forensics."

Mike glanced at the phone. "Hi, Brett. What's happened?"

"You get a call from me, and you automatically assume something's happened? I might be calling to ask you a question, or a favour."

"Sorry." Mike slowed for another speed hump, wishing he'd taken the more direct route. "What can I do for you?"

"Nah, you were right the first time. Something *has* happened, or rather we've discovered something."

"OK." Mike slowed at a roundabout, where he kept right. The Isle of Wight appeared in the distance.

"I'm sorry, Brett, but I'm just about to arrive at the crime scene. Can you tell me what it is you've discovered?" Mike slowed again for a sharp left-hand bend signposted Hengistbury Head.

He'd driven these roads with his mum, as a kid. Hengistbury Head was one of her favourite places. He smiled. *I should bring her here, with the kids.*

"Of course," said Brett. "So the teeth you gave us, with your guy Carson's DNA."

"Which wasn't a match for the body," Mike said as he turned right again, Hengistbury Head itself finally visible.

"Which wasn't," Brett confirmed. "But as I'm sure you know, you can leave DNA on someone just by touching them. Especially if you touch them with enough force."

"Skin cells, sweat," Mike replied. "I know. It's why we all have to wear those horrible paper suits."

"Indeed. And what with Gail's team finding your Mr Carson's DNA on the victim..."

Mike's foot jerked onto the brake. The car stuttered and he quickly brought it under control, narrowly avoiding an elderly man and his dog, both of whom gave him a hard stare.

"Sorry," Mike mouthed. The man frowned, the dog barked, and they both walked away towards the golf course.

"Sorry, Brett," he said. "Can you say that again?"

"Sure. It took a while to extract, given the state of the body. But we sent swabs from his hands and ankles to Dorchester and Gail says there are traces of Stephen Carson's DNA."

Mike put a hand on his chest. "The body parts he'd touch if he was dragging the victim somewhere."

"Not for me to say," Brett replied. "But yes, it looks very likely that your Stephen Carson dragged the body somewhere."

CHAPTER FORTY-SIX

The man in the dock at Bournemouth Crown Court was elderly, his back stooped. But there was fire in his eyes and his jaw was set.

The CPS barrister, Zachary Hayes, was questioning him. Zoe watched intently; Hayes was someone she imagined she'd need to work with frequently in the future. She wanted to get a feel for his style.

His style was slow, but in a way that seemed calculated and considered. Each time Thomas Wolf finished a sentence, Hayes would wait a moment before jumping in with the next one, not wanting to fluster the witness. Mr Wolf, for his part, was calm, only betraying nerves by occasionally licking his lips. He allowed the silence to sit during the barrister's pauses, instead of indulging an urge to fill it with more words.

"Describe the level of visibility on the morning of the twenty-first of September last year," Hayes said. "From your vantage point near St Catherine's Chapel, what could you see?"

Thomas Wolf was a local photographer, a man Johnny Chiles had interviewed. Zoe listened as he described the conditions on Chapel Hill on the morning Mark Ashforth's body had been taken there. Light in the east, dark in the west, enough for him to make out people moving around but not enough for them to see him in his position huddled against the castle.

After Hayes had extracted as full an eyewitness account as he was going to get from the witness, he waved an arm to indicate the courtroom.

"Can you see the men you saw at Chapel Hill on that morning in this courtroom?"

Wolf screwed up his face. "I can't, sorry. Because I didn't really see them. Not clearly, mind."

"Did you have video recording equipment with you?"

Thomas's shoulders went back. "I did, Sir. I had my new Canon EOS 7D with me. Beautiful piece of kit, it is."

"And with the camera, you recorded footage of the men you saw, is that correct?"

"It is. Much clearer than anything I could see with the naked eye. Like I say, it's a marvel."

Hayes smiled. "Thank you." He faced the judge. "I would like to admit into evidence the prosecution's second video recording."

"Very well. Play it, please," the judge replied.

Hayes gestured towards a man in a tight-fitting suit standing by a table at the front of the courtroom. The table held a laptop.

The man pressed the trackpad and an image of the Dorset coast appeared on a projector screen to one side of the judge's desk. Zoe leaned back in her chair. She'd watched this footage before. What would be more interesting was the reaction of the Musketeers. Not to mention the jurors.

The video appeared to do its job. One of the Musketeers, the youngest, twitched when he and his co-conspirators appeared onscreen. The jury members watched intently, repeatedly looking from the screen to the accused in the dock and back again.

The video was high quality and made the scene appear lighter than the witness had described. The men were undoubtedly the same three men who stood in the dock.

Zoe punched her knee in celebration. Sure, they didn't know yet who the Musketeers were working for. And she hadn't been directly involved in their arrest. But this was a win.

"Can you confirm that this is the video footage you recorded on the morning of the twenty-first of September last year?" the barrister asked.

"I can," the witness replied. "It is." He glanced towards the dock, his face giving nothing away.

"Thank you. That will be all."

The volume increased in the courtroom; spectators muttering to each other, the Musketeers' three barristers approaching their clients for a quiet conflab. The jury sat in silence. Three of them stared at the Musketeers with undisguised contempt.

The judge cleared her throat. "Break for lunch. Reconvene at two pm."

Zoe sat in her chair for a moment. When the three men arrested in the Canary case had been in court, she hadn't been there; that had been Lesley's job, along with David Randle. And only one of them had been convicted. Today, in a different courtroom over a hundred miles away, reminded her of that.

Hopefully this time, they would get a better result.

She joined the crowd heading out of the courtroom and walked out onto the street. Coming here had done what she'd hoped it would. She felt energised and optimistic. There were bigger fish to be fried, and the MCIT would get them.

Her Mini was a ten-minute walk away, in the only car park she'd been able to find. She would get to know Bournemouth better, but it would take time.

As she crossed the road outside the court building, a maroon Bentley pulled up opposite. Zoe stepped back onto the pavement and watched, intrigued. The car was grander than anything she'd seen since arriving here, even if its grandeur was a little faded.

A man in a grey suit emerged from the driver's door and opened the door behind it. Zoe could make out the shape of a short woman with red hair, largely obscured by the car.

The driver escorted the woman around the back of the car and the two of them crossed the road, heading straight for Zoe. Zoe took a few steps backwards.

The woman was old, probably in her eighties, the faintest of grey roots showing on her hairline. When she looked up and down the road there was a cold intensity to her gaze. She wore a reddish-brown fur coat over a fitted blue dress.

Zoe knew this woman. She'd read her file, learned all about her family.

Vera Kelvin.

Wasn't she supposed to be giving evidence tomorrow?

Zoe watched as the woman and her escort passed, approaching the doors to the court. As they reached them, the woman turned to look at Zoe.

"Getting an eyeful, DI Finch?"

Zoe felt her breath catch. So she wasn't the only one who'd done her homework.

"Don't look so surprised, girl," Vera continued. "Your reputation precedes you."

Zoe allowed herself a smile. She could only hope her reputation – all those evil men she'd taken down – gave Vera Kelvin pause for thought.

Vera spat onto the pavement. She wrinkled her nose, still eyeing Zoe.

"What are you waiting for, girl? Come on inside, get a look at the spectacle of me in the witness box."

So Vera Kelvin was scheduled to give evidence today, after all.

Zoe clenched a fist and nodded. *This should be interesting*. She followed the older woman inside.

CHAPTER FORTY-SEVEN

"I AM SORRY, but we visited two times. Nobody there."

Katie grimaced. This was the third call she'd had with Málaga police. It seemed that having Stephen Carson's Spanish address hadn't brought them any closer to finding the man himself.

"*Gracias*," she said, trying to remember her GCSE Spanish. "Thank you for trying."

She was about to hang up when the officer, Gabriella Lora, spoke, causing her to bring the phone back to her ear.

"It is not finished," Gabriella said. "We ask questions. Speak to... people in near houses?"

"Neighbours?" Katie asked.

"*Las vecinas*. Neighbours. *Si*. They see your Señor Carson. Saw."

"The neighbours have seen him?"

"*Si*. Him, and his wife. Friend. I don't know."

Katie felt her jaw fall open.

"Wife?" she said. Since when was Stephen Carson married?

"*Si*. *La mujer*. Woman. I have photo. From neighbours, your people are in... what is the word? Background."

Katie bit down on her bottom lip and winced. She grinned, ignoring the metallic taste of blood.

"Please," she said. "Can you send me the photo?"

"Yes. I can. Give me email and I will send."

Katie gave the woman her email address. A moment later, a new message appeared in her inbox.

"Got it," she said. "Give me a minute."

She clicked on the email and then the attachment, cursing the time it took to run it past security filters.

At last, the photo was open in front of her. A man, looking like a significantly older version of the man in Harold Carson's photos. Standing against a scuffed white building, smiling. He had his arm draped ostentatiously over the shoulders of a woman with blonde-brown hair, also smiling. The woman had her face turned away from the camera and was looking up at Stephen. Smiling into his face.

Katie slumped back in her chair, staring at the photo.

"Bloody hell," she breathed.

"Katie? Are you there?" Gabriella's voice was tinny; Katie had dropped her phone on the floor.

She bent down and fumbled for it.

"Gabriella," she said. "Sorry. I have it. The photo. Thank you."

"You need us to go visit again?" Gabriella asked. "Only I am not certain my boss, he will..."

"It's OK. You don't need to go back. Thank you."

The odds were slim that Stephen Carson would be returning to that house. To anywhere the police could find him.

And his companion. The wife, or friend... She was already in the UK.

Damn. She hadn't asked when the photo was taken.

No matter. Sunil would be able to extract that from the metadata.

Katie continued staring. At Carson, but mostly at the woman smiling up at him.

"Bloody hell," she repeated.

Stanley was at his desk. He looked over. "You OK, mate?" he asked.

She nodded. "Yeah. Yeah."

He pushed his chair over so it was next to hers.

"Is that Carson?" he asked.

"Yup. Outside his house in Spain."

"You tracked him down." He gave her a slap on the shoulder.

Katie winced. "He's not there anymore."

"Ah. Bugger. You're sure?"

Katie nodded. She pointed at the photo, her jaw set. "But I know where she is."

"The woman? She his girlfriend, or something?"

Katie turned to Stanley. "Maybe. Probably. But I know her name. At least, the name she gave us."

Stanley's eyes widened. "Go on then."

Katie looked back at the screen. Last time she'd seen that woman, she'd been dressed in more layers, her hair pulled back. But it was definitely her.

"Ursula Rowland," she said. "She told me and the boss that her name was Ursula Rowland, and she was a forensic archaeologist ."

CHAPTER FORTY-EIGHT

Vera Kelvin's gaze on the CPS barrister was sharp and steady. Zoe didn't know whether to smile at the fact that the woman was everything she'd expected and more, or to run ten miles in the opposite direction.

But Zoe had met people like Vera Kelvin before. Men, admittedly.

But Zoe had taken all those men down. She wasn't going to let Vera Kelvin scare her.

"Can you tell us what you were doing on the night of the twenty-fourth of September?" Zachary Hayes asked, his hands shoved lightly in his pockets.

Vera Kelvin shrugged. "I'm afraid that's months ago, young man. How can you possibly expect me to remember what I was doing on a random evening?"

He cocked his head. "That was the evening on which Jackie Kendall died. The evening on which your vehicle was stolen and used in the murder of Jackie Kendall."

Vera grunted out a laugh. "Were you telling me it was used to run her over?"

Hayes's expression darkened. There was a ripple among the jury.

"No, Mrs Kelvin," he said. "The three men on trial here," he pointed to the Musketeers, "used your vehicle to travel to the hotel where Jackie Kendall died, and then to leave it. It seems that they then dumped the vehicle on a road between the hotel and your property in Lulworth."

Another shrug from Vera. "That was what they were doing. I still can't tell you what I was doing. What day of the week was it?"

Hayes looked at his notes. "It was a Tuesday, Mrs Kelvin."

She screwed up her face. "Tuesday, I like to have a bath. On a Tuesday, I was probably having a bath."

"Very well," he said. "So you had no knowledge of your vehicle being used in this crime?"

She shook her head. "No knowledge whatsoever."

He glanced over at the jury, and then at the Musketeers, and then back at Vera. "And are you aware that your name and credit card were used to book a room at the Premier Inn, which was where the crime was committed?"

Again, Vera shrugged.

"Well, I can tell you one thing for sure," she said, "I wouldn't be taking my bath at a Premier Inn."

A titter ran through the courtroom. Zoe felt her jaw clench. *Bloody hell. She's getting them on her side.* Even the Musketeers were smiling.

"Regardless of where you prefer to take your baths, Mrs Kelvin," the barrister said, "can you tell me if it was you who made that booking?"

Vera leaned forward, elbows on the dock in front of her. "Definitely not."

"You sound very certain."

"I am. Do you think I make my own hotel bookings? I've got a hundred people working for me. Probably more, I lose track, but I'm sure one of them makes hotel bookings for me. And if they decided to book me a Premier Inn that night, I'm sure they had their reasons."

She frowned. "They were probably using the room to shag somebody else from the staff." More laughter.

The judge turned to Vera. "Mrs Kelvin, this is a court of law and a very serious matter we're dealing with. I'll ask you to take it seriously and not use this as an opportunity to make jokes at your employees' expense."

She looked up at her. "Very sorry. Won't do it again."

Zoe bit her lip. If they ever got Vera Kelvin into court on charges of her own, was this how she would behave, and would it work? In fact, was Vera only doing this to show Zoe that arresting her would be a complete waste of time?

Zoe grunted. Making the jury think you were funny only got you so far, particularly when you were the kind of woman Vera Kelvin was and had overseen the kind of crimes she had.

"So you're telling the court that you have no idea who booked the hotel room, and that you have no knowledge of the fact that your vehicle was used by the three men in the dock when travelling to and from the Premier Inn where Jackie Kendall died?" the barrister said.

"That sounds about right," Vera responded.

He licked his lips and threw his head back for a moment, as if in thought. Zoe had seen enough barristers at work to know that this was entirely artificial.

"So tell me," he said, "do you have any theories as to why these men used your name, your credit card and your vehicle in the execution of their crime?"

Vera glanced at the Musketeers. She looked back at Hayes, and then sent her gaze over to the Musketeers again. She allowed it to rest on each one of them in turn.

Slowly, two of the men fidgeted, looking down to avoid her gaze. One of them, the oldest, stared straight back at her.

Had they met her before? Were they working for her? Zoe wasn't sure, but she was hoping the financial records would help her work it out.

"Theories," Vera said. "I was visited by a police officer who gave me some theories. She seemed to think that those three over there were fitting me up, or rather, the people that they work for were. I think that's a bit far-fetched. I just think it's coincidence."

"Coincidence?" Hayes said. "You think it's coincidence that they used your credit card, your name, and your vehicle when committing a murder?"

The judge cleared her throat. "Alleged murder, please, Mr Hayes."

"Sorry. When committing an alleged murder," he said to Vera Kelvin.

Vera shrugged. "Like I say, coincidence. They didn't want to use their own vehicle in case they were caught, so they used mine. And as for the hotel room, well, who's to say they made the booking? Maybe they spotted there was an empty room. Maybe whoever makes my bookings, boyfriend didn't turn up to shag her."

Three members of the jury suppressed smiles, one laughed. Four of them, all in the back row, looked stern. *Good,* Zoe thought. *She's not winning them all over, at least.*

"Do you have anything concrete to ask this witness?" the judge asked Hayes.

Hayes looked at the judge, then at Vera, and then back at the judge. He shook his head. "That's all I have."

"Good." The judge looked over towards the defence barristers, who all shook their heads. "Mrs Kelvin, you can leave."

Vera gave the judge a nod. "Thank you very much, and a pleasure it has been."

Zoe felt her skin tighten. She knew how nasty Vera Kelvin could be, but here she was acting like some monarch of the courtroom. It made her teeth stand on edge.

In the inevitable hubbub that accompanied the changing of one witness for another, she took the opportunity to leave the courtroom. As she reached the back door, she spotted Johnny shuffling along the back row.

"Johnny," she said, "I didn't know you were here."

He gave her a sheepish look. "Sorry, boss, I should have told you."

"That's all right," Zoe said. "You wanted to see Vera's evidence, given that it was you who arrested the Musketeers."

He nodded. "Not that she actually gave any evidence. Bloody hell, Ma'am, did you see the way she wound the jury up?"

Zoe sighed. "She's quite the performer, isn't she?"

"Yeah. God knows what it'll be like when we get her in the dock on her own charges." They were walking along a corridor towards the doors to the street.

Zoe glanced at Johnny. "I was thinking the exact same thing," she said. "But I'm surprised you're here. I thought you were with your dad."

Johnny shrugged. "He was getting sick of me, Ma'am. I figured it was best to leave him alone for a while, and he's having some tests. No point hanging around by his bedside while they wheel him off to various places."

Zoe put a hand on his shoulder. "If you need anything from me," she said, "just shout, yeah?"

He looked into her eyes. She could tell he was weighing her up, trying to work out if she was being sincere.

"I mean it," she said. "Having this happen to you is not fun. I've been through it myself. Trying to juggle it with a young family and the job makes it even harder."

They were at the doors now. Johnny looked down at the ground. "Yeah, Ma'am, you're right there."

Zoe gave him a sympathetic smile. "Don't forget, Johnny, keep talking to me. If you need time off, or you need to change your hours, or you need some support, just say. I don't want you suffering in silence, right?"

He shrugged. "Suppose so, Ma'am."

CHAPTER FORTY-NINE

IT WAS two hours since Lesley had left the office. Would her team miss her if she made one more stop en route?

Jill knew where she was, and Jill was busy herself, with the Mudeford case. And Zoe had sent her a message saying she was heading to court to observe the trial. None of their team members would come running to Lesley anytime soon.

And there was the fact that her office was on a separate floor from theirs, which might as well be a different time zone as far as she was concerned.

No one would miss her.

She pulled up outside the familiar 1930s semi. She hadn't phoned ahead – all this was far too sensitive – so she was relieved to see Dennis's car in the front drive. No sign of Pam's green Aygo.

Perfect.

Lesley looked up and down the street as she got out of her car, aware that she was being paranoid. Also aware that paranoia was justified, under the circumstances. She wondered if Jill had had those text messages checked out yet.

The door was open and her old DS was waiting for her as she strode up the path.

"It's two in the afternoon," he said. "What's the emergency?"

"No emergency." She frowned. "Just a change of personnel on a case you've been advising on."

"Oh. Well, in that case, you'd better come in. There's some lemon drizzle cake in a tin somewhere."

Lesley patted her stomach as Dennis closed the front door behind them. The house was quiet, not even the sound of a radio.

"Even I know that too much of your wife's delicious cake isn't good for me," she said. "Is Pam not in?"

He shook his head, leading her into the kitchen. "Meeting a friend for coffee in Wareham."

"Wareham? I didn't know Wareham had the kind of places you could meet someone for coffee."

"There's Nellie Crumb," Dennis said.

Lesley pictured Pam in her immaculately ironed, brightly coloured blouses and neat trousers. Those trousers she wore were in a flattering cut, not from the classic range.

"Pam's never the Nellie Crumb type," she said.

Dennis flicked on the kettle and laughed. "There's also the Salt Pig."

Lesley nodded. "Ah. That's a bit more Pam. I pictured her in Love Cake in Swanage." The café served the best cakes in Purbeck.

Dennis pointed out a pile of cake boxes on the counter. "She's started supplying them."

"No."

"Really. Only a few cakes a week so far, but she's hoping it'll grow."

"Surely your police pension is—"

"It's not about the pension, Lesley." He gave her a *work-it-out* look and then turned to the kettle, which had boiled.

"I'm sorry," Lesley said. "I thought you'd be one of those rare couples who enjoy spending more time together after retirement."

"Oh, we are. Don't worry about that. But you can have too much of a good thing, don't you agree?"

Lesley tried to imagine spending twenty-four hours a day with Elsa. She loved her wife, but...

She grimaced. "You're right. Well, I'm glad she's got a focus. And you? How are you occupying yourself, three years in?"

Dennis poured hot water into a teapot. "Don't remind me. You're making me feel old."

"You retired early." Lesley's gaze flicked down to Dennis's left leg. An injury had precipitated his retirement.

"Only a year early," he reminded her. "But it's doing a lot better, thank you for asking. I'm finally doing proper walks again. Which makes Pam very happy."

"That was always something you enjoyed doing together." Lesley took the tea Dennis offered her.

He smiled. "We might even register for the Jurassic Coast challenge next year."

Lesley almost spat out her tea. "What, all hundred miles of it?"

"Don't be daft. Just the first bit, it's twelve miles."

"That sounds more sensible." Lesley didn't want her old DS curtailing his retirement by killing himself on an endurance walk.

"It is." Dennis jerked his head towards the door. "Anyway, you didn't come here to talk about cakes and walking. Let's go into the conservatory and you can tell me about this change in personnel."

"The conservatory, in February?"

"I've got the heater on."

"It's your heating bill." Lesley followed him through and took her habitual seat. She couldn't quite believe how quiet this house was, without Pam. Almost eerie.

"So," Dennis said as he shuffled into his chair. "What's happened to bring you here at this time of day?"

"It's Jill."

He stopped, cup halfway to his lips. "Jill? Is she alright?"

"She's fine. Well, no. She's scared." Lesley took a breath. "The Kelvins have threatened her. Her family, specifically."

Dennis crossed himself. "Goodness me."

Lesley smiled. "*Goodness me.* Is that the best you've got, Dennis?"

"How?" he asked. "When?"

"Just last night. Meera – she's married to a DC in the MCIT – and their daughter Suzi were invited on a play date at very short notice."

"Sounds innocuous."

Lesley sipped her tea and shook her head. "By Amanda Frobisher's sister. Brianna. The other child at the play date was—"

"Don't tell me. Arthur Kelvin's orphaned son." Dennis's cup was on the table, he'd turned to face her.

"Yes."

"Could it be a coincidence?"

She shrugged. "It's not just the identity of the boy and the aunt," Lesley said. "Meera's phone went missing while she was there, it turned up in Brianna's bag."

Dennis frowned. "So she stole it."

She shrugged. "She claimed that her nephew's a bit of a magpie and that he must have put it there."

"Hmm, indeed."

"And it gets worse."

"Go on then."

"Jill got two texts, one while Meera was out, and one after she got home." Lesley opened up her phone and showed Dennis the screenshots of the texts that Jill had sent her.

Dennis let out a breath. "That's not good."

"Indeed, it isn't," Lesley replied, "which is why I'm here. Jill's spooked, and I don't blame her. She wants off the Frank Kelvin case for now at least," she gestured towards herself, "which means I'll be taking over."

Dennis gave a wry smile. "I have to admit, I did wonder how long it would be before you managed that."

"I didn't engineer this, you know."

"Oh, I'm not saying you engineered anything, but... Well, you do know how to take advantage of an opportunity."

"I hope you don't think that I consider Jill being threatened by the Kelvins an opportunity."

He shrugged. "Have you had those texts checked out?"

"Forensics are looking at them right now."

"Good."

Lesley's phone rang. If it hadn't been already in her hand, she would have ignored it, but she couldn't fail to notice that the caller was Gail.

She held it up and raised her eyebrows at Dennis in a question.

"Answer it," he said.

Lesley put the phone to her ear. "Gail," she said, "what can I do for you?"

"It's more what I can do for you," Gail replied. "I've got some new information about the DNA analysis we've been doing."

"I don't mean to be funny, Gail, but why are you calling me? Why don't you call Katie or Jill?"

Gail laughed. "I miss our chats. I thought I'd use this as an excuse to say hello."

Lesley looked at Dennis. Here she was sitting with one old colleague and chatting to a woman who'd been her friend since she'd moved to Dorset.

It felt good.

She smiled. "You're talking about Carson's DNA being on the victim's skin, right? It's been added to the case notes."

"Right, so Bamford has told you about that," Gail said. "Good. But it's not that I'm calling about."

Lesley frowned at Dennis, who gave her a shrug. "OK, then Gail," she said, "what have you found?"

"So," Gail said. "We still don't have a definite ID on the body, but we have extracted his DNA. I searched through the database and found the same DNA profile, on file from another crime."

Lesley sat up straighter in her chair. "What other crime?"

"One from not long before the body was left under that toilet block."

"The petrol station robbery," Lesley said. "One of the perpetrators?"

Dennis had sat up straighter in his chair.

"One of the victims," Gail said, "but—"

Lesley shook her head. "There weren't any victims. Were there?"

"Nobody was killed," Gail replied. "Not killed, but traumatised. The man who was serving in the petrol station... his DNA is a match."

"Shit," Lesley said. "So you're telling me that the body buried under the beach huts at Mudeford Spit is the same man who was the victim of the petrol station robbery in 1994?"

"It's not my job to tell you anything," Gail said, "but the evidence seems to point that way."

CHAPTER FIFTY

Katie picked up her phone and dialled a number that was becoming increasingly familiar.

"Hello," came the reply. "This is a nice surprise."

Katie smiled. She hadn't known Sunil was capable of flirting.

"I've got a photo," she said. "If I send it to you, can you check that it's legit and let me know when it was taken?"

"What format is it in?" Sunil asked. "Is it digital or physical?"

"Digital," she said, "although I'm not sure if it's a scan from a physical."

"Have you got it in front of you?"

"Yeah."

"OK, take a look at it. Zoom in. What happens when you get up close? Does it blur or become pixelated?"

"Pixelated," Katie said.

"Good," Sunil replied. "That means it's a digital image. There'll be metadata in there, which will tell me when it was taken. I'll also be able to check whether it's been doctored at all."

"Thanks," she said.

"Email it over now and I'll prioritise it."

"I thought you'd be busy," Katie replied as she was composing the email.

He laughed. "Your team certainly are keeping me busy. The cold cases, your governor sent me over some texts to analyse."

Katie frowned. She knew nothing about any texts.

"What texts?"

"Uh." Sunil sounded less confident now. "Nothing. I don't think it's related to your Mudeford case. Something else. Don't worry about it."

"OK."

It was the guv's business what she sent over to forensics, but it was weird if she was working on another case that they didn't know about.

"I've just sent the email," she told him. "You should have that photo in a couple of moments."

"Got it," he replied. "I'll take a look at it. Let you know if it's genuine."

"Thanks," Katie said. "I appreciate it." She could feel her cheeks flushing.

"Not a problem," he said. "In fact, I think I can get this done today and then bring the results to you later on."

"That would be a big help. You're heading over towards Winfrith?"

"I live in Poole, but I thought, I thought maybe we could meet for a drink and I can show you what I've found?"

Katie covered her mouth, allowing herself a chuckle. "That would be lovely," she said. "You show me the photo, and we can have a drink. Have you got somewhere specific in mind?"

"There's a place on the beach," he said, "in Bournemouth. I'll send you the details."

Katie could feel her breath hitching. Was this a date? She hadn't been on a date in years.

"Sounds good," she said, and hung up before asking him if he thought it was a date.

CHAPTER FIFTY-ONE

Jill was packing her bag when Lesley got back to the office.

She looked up, her eyes wide. "Boss," she said, "what can I do for you?"

Lesley smiled. "I think there's something I can do for you."

Jill straightened up and cocked her head. She looked flustered.

Lesley frowned. "Are you OK? Are you still bothered by those texts yesterday?"

Jill shook her head. "I'm trying not to be, but I'm waiting on the analysis from forensics."

"Have they given you any preliminary information?"

Jill shook her head. Her grip on the top of her bag tightened. "Not yet. I'm just... I'm not sure what to tell Meera." She gave Lesley a meaningful look. "She knows nothing about what I've been doing with Eric, but if she's in danger, she deserves to be told."

Lesley stepped towards the desk. "Let's cross that bridge when we come to it. Jill. Meanwhile, you focus on the Mudeford case and don't worry about Eric. I'll deal with all that."

Jill closed her eyes for a moment. "Thanks, boss. I hope you don't think I'm a wimp."

Lesley put a hand on Jill's shoulder. "You're not a wimp, Jill. You have legitimate cause to think that your family is at risk, and therefore you'd be foolish to continue working on this case."

"You really think so?"

"I know so," Lesley told her. "And besides, I've got something to tell you that I think you'll like."

"Oh, what?"

Jill looked expectant. Lesley smiled. "Gail's just given me an ID for your body at Mudeford Spit."

Jill's mouth fell open. "At last, who is it?"

"The victim in that robbery from 1994," Lesley said. "Joseph Tizzard."

Jill slumped down into her chair. "God, he was only nineteen. Poor man." She looked away, her gaze unfocused. "What do we tell his family?"

"I presume he either doesn't have a family, or they reported him missing in 1994," Lesley said.

Jill looked up. "He wasn't local. He was from... oh, I can't remember. Scotland, I think."

"I guess that's why there was no report of a missing person." Lesley nodded. That made sense. "Well, at least now you have your ID, and I think you've probably got a motive."

Jill's jaw was tight. "Stephen Carson killed him so that he wouldn't give evidence against him in that robbery case."

"Uh huh," Lesley replied. "Now all you have to do is find Stephen Carson."

Jill's face brightened. "We're getting further with that, boss. Katie spoke to police in Málaga. He bought a house there a year ago, and you'll never guess who he's been living there with."

"Tell me," Lesley said.

"Ursula Rowland, the woman who told us she was a forensic archaeologist and offered to help out at the crime scene."

"Seriously? But she was from Bournemouth University, wasn't she?"

Jill shrugged. "Turns out she was a student at Bournemouth University twenty years ago. She hasn't been near the place for decades."

Lesley whistled. "Wow. Well, I have to hand it to her. The woman's got some brass. Where is she?"

"That's the problem," Jill replied. "We're assuming she's still in the country and not gone back to Spain, but we don't know. We've got the registration number of the car she rented and there's an ANPR call out for it. That's all we can do right now."

"What about the father?" Lesley said. "Harold, wasn't it?"

Jill nodded. "I've sent Katie over there. He needs to know that his son's alive and living in Spain. He also needs to know that he's at risk." Another nod. "Don't worry, boss, Katie won't be going alone. We're going to post uniformed officers outside his house and hope that his son turns up."

Lesley grasped Jill's shoulder, more firmly this time. "Good work, Jill, you and your team. You're closing in on him."

"He's slippery," Jill replied.

"They're all slippery," Lesley told her, "but you'll get him. Don't worry."

CHAPTER FIFTY-TWO

"Huh? What was that?"

Harold Carson woke from his nap with a start. He blinked a few times, looking around himself. He was getting this more and more these days, that sense of not knowing where he was when he woke. Even lying in bed, he sometimes imagined his bedroom door was on the opposite side of the room to where it was. He'd slept in that bed for decades. Why was his mind playing tricks on him now?

At least this time, there was a reason for it. He'd nodded off in his chair again. *Countdown* had finished. Now it was... what was it?

He yawned and reached for the remote control on the side table beside his armchair. He turned the TV off and the house went quiet.

He didn't like it when the house was like this. He'd go into the kitchen and turn the radio on. There was something about silence that made him think of Betty.

He pushed himself up from the chair, groaning as his back complained at the movement. Falling asleep in his chair was bad for him. He should give in to the idea of the afternoon nap, take himself up to bed. No. Afternoon naps were for babies. He was a grown man, and he wasn't surrendering to old age yet, even in his nineties.

As he approached the door to the living room, he heard a sound from above. He stopped, looking upwards. A movement?

He waved a hand in dismissive annoyance at himself. "Don't be daft, you old bugger."

He was imagining things, his mind wearing out and playing tricks on him. *Bloody mind.* Why did it have to do this to him? Why was it betraying him just when he needed it most?

He shuffled towards the door and opened it. A cup of tea would sort him out. He shouldn't drink caffeine in the afternoon, but he needed perking up.

As he walked into the hallway, he stopped, his legs almost giving out from under him.

There was a man on the stairway. He'd had stopped halfway down, clearly in the middle of running down.

He looked at Harold, his eyes wide, his knuckles white where his hand had frozen on the banister.

Harold put a hand on his chest. He forced himself to breathe.

Then he said it.

"Stephen," he croaked.

Bloody mind, playing tricks on him again. Stephen had died thirty years ago, but this man, this man looked like Stephen, Stephen as he would look if he was thirty years older.

"Stephen," he repeated, his voice hoarse.

The man's eyes widened. He moved his jaw as if speaking, but no sound came out. Then he moved. He sped down the stairs, approached Harold, and hit out.

Harold flinched, throwing his hands up in front of him to protect himself. "Stephen," he cried. Why was his voice so weak?

"Stop it," the man barked.

"Stephen, is that you?"

The man looked around the hallway. There were ornaments on the table by the front door: a woman, a shepherdess and a child. Betty had bought them years ago. Harold liked to stroke them as he walked in through the door, reminding himself of the day she'd brought them home.

The man, Stephen, grabbed the shepherdess.

"No!" Harold shouted. "Don't, lad, you'll only—"

His words were cut off by a sharp pain in his head. Stephen had ignored him. He'd grabbed that ornament, and he'd flailed at Harold's face with it.

Harold felt his legs buckle. He dropped to the floor, throwing his arms up. He couldn't see. Was that blood in his eye?

"Stephen," he repeated, his voice wavering.

"Shut up," the man said. He turned and opened the front door, leaving it swinging on its hinges as he ran out into the cold air.

CHAPTER FIFTY-THREE

"I NEED to speak to my team," Jill said. "Do you mind?"

The boss nodded. "Go. Do you want my help?"

Jill shook her head. "I'll be fine."

Katie was already heading over to Harold Carson's house, but Mike and Stanley, if she was lucky, would still be in the office.

She ran out of her office and along the corridor, and into the room next door.

Mike and Stanley were both inside.

"Thank God, guys," she said. "We've had a development."

The two DCs looked up.

"Yeah?" said Stanley.

Jill nodded. She leaned against the closed door, suddenly aware that she was panting.

"You all right, guv?" Mike said.

"Fine," she gasped. "I'm fine. We've got an ID for the body."

Stanley straightened in his chair. "The body at Mudeford?"

Jill nodded. She felt a smile break out on her face.

"At bloody last," Mike said.

Jill looked at him. "It's the man who was the victim in the armed robbery at the petrol station," she told him. "Joseph Tizzard. Gail managed to extract the old files and match them up."

Stanley whistled. "Brilliant. Now we know who did it."

Jill looked at him. "We can't be a hundred per cent certain," she said.

"Yes, we can," said Mike. "We've got Stephen Carson's fingerprint on that necklace that was found there. And we've got the fact that he buggered off to Spain immediately afterwards."

"Not immediately afterwards," Jill corrected. "He went to London first."

"But we don't know whether he was in London in 1994," Mike said.

Jill shrugged. "It's not relevant."

"But then there's Ursula," said Stanley, "the forensic archaeologist ."

Jill took a deep breath. He was right. The fact that Ursula had attempted to inveigle her way into the investigation and was clearly a close associate of Carson's only made them both look more guilty.

"OK," she said. "Katie's already heading over to Harold Carson's house."

"But what if Carson's there?" said Mike. "Stephen Carson, I mean. What if Ursula is there? What if Katie's in danger?"

Jill looked at him. "What if Harold's in danger? He's an elderly man."

"Shit," said Stanley. He grabbed his phone. "Do you want me to call Katie?"

"Do it," Jill said. "Mike, I want you to keep digging on that armed robbery."

"And we need to find Joseph Tizzard's next of kin," Mike said. "Inform them."

Jill nodded. "They were in Scotland, I think."

"Leave it with me, boss," he said. "Do you want me to look into Ursula's background, too?"

"Yeah."

"Will do."

Jill looked at her watch. "It's half past five. Mike, you need to get home to your family."

"I'll speak to Tina," he said. "Her team haven't got a huge amount on at the moment, just the Musketeers trial. She can be on childcare duty tonight."

Jill smiled. She knew that feeling.

"OK," she said. "You speak to Tina, sort out your childcare. Let's make sure that our victim's family know what happened to him and then let's see what we can find out about Ursula."

CHAPTER FIFTY-FOUR

Katie arrived at Harold Carson's house to find the door swinging on its hinges in the wind. She swallowed, steeled herself and stepped inside.

Harold lay on the floor in the hallway, slumped around the bottom of the stairs.

She hurried towards him and bent to feel for a pulse.

Thank God. His heart was still beating, but he was unconscious. She grabbed her phone and made the emergency call. A marked car was already on its way, officers due to be stationed outside the house to protect Harold, but it was too late for that.

She knew better than to move him. She straightened up, not shifting her feet from their position, and looked around the space. It was dark, the only light coming from the TV in the living room. She crouched down again, not moving her feet an inch, and peered at the floor around Harold. There were fragments of china near his head, and...

There was a wound on the side of his head, the side facing away from the door. It looked bad, matted hair and blood seeping into the carpet.

Kate stood up again, turned, still not moving her feet, and looked towards the front door.

"Where are you?"

How long would an emergency call take, this far out of Bournemouth? Would they even come from Bournemouth, or from Christchurch? Maybe the car that had already been on its way here was nearby. She could only hope so.

She wanted to go outside and wait for it, to stand in the street and holler until the car arrived along with an ambulance. But she knew that what Harold needed was somebody with him if he came to.

"Harold," she said, keeping her voice low. "Can you hear me?" She held his hand.

It was cool, but not cold. God knows what the effect of that open door would be on a man of his age, lying here on the floor. How long had he been here?

"Come on," Katie muttered, "come on." At last, she saw blue lights, faint outside.

She gave Harold's hand a gentle squeeze. "I'm here, Harold. I'll be right back."

She strode towards the front door, careful not to disturb anything, and ran out into the street.

Lights had come on in the house opposite, and a man stood in a doorway wrapping a dressing gown around himself.

"Please go back indoors," she called. "Stay in your house. We may need to take a statement from you." He nodded, looking puzzled, and withdrew.

The police car stopped outside the house, followed right behind by an ambulance. Katie felt her shoulders drop in relief.

An officer got out of the car. "PS Dillick," he said. "Who are you?"

Katie held up her ID. "DC Young, Major Crime Investigations Team. The man inside this house is a witness, Harold Carson. Were you called here to protect him?"

The sergeant shook his head. "We're on a 999 call."

Katie nodded. "He's been attacked. He's got a head injury."

The paramedics were outside the ambulance, gathering their kit together. One of them, a woman in her late twenties, called over to Katie.

"He's in the hallway, you say, head injury?"

Katie nodded. Her mouth felt dry. "Be careful, please," she said. "He's very elderly."

The paramedic gave her a grim smile. "Don't worry, love, we know what we're doing." She ran towards the house with her colleague.

"Where are the access points?" the sergeant said.

Katie stared back at him. "I don't know." She swallowed. "We need officers stationed at the front and back of the house in case whoever attacked him comes back."

"Any idea who attacked him?"

"I've got a pretty good idea," she replied, "but I don't know for sure. I don't even know if he's in the country." She frowned. "I might need one of you to come with me up to the beach."

"The beach?" said the sergeant.

She nodded.

If Stephen Carson had been here, and fled the scene, he might have headed up to Mudeford Spit. If his girlfriend was sniffing around, then he might be, too.

How far was it from here? A mile, two miles. How long would it take to run?

"Yes, the beach," she said. "If you can take me in the car, I'd be grateful. Or one of your team. I need to go up to Mudeford Spit. There's emergency vehicle access."

Katie closed her eyes. She'd never done this before.

"How many of you are there?" she asked.

"Three," he said. "I'll take you and the others will stay here."

"Thank you," she replied. "Sarge."

He gave her a long look. "If you're sure."

Katie clenched her jaw. She began to walk around the car, heading for the passenger seat.

"Stephen!"

Katie turned at the sound of the voice. A woman stood on the pavement opposite the Carson house, the blackness of the sand dunes and the beach behind her.

Ursula.

"Ursula!" Katie called. "It's me. DC Young. We met at the—"

"Stephen!" the woman cried.

Katie turned briefly to the PS and gestured at him to stay where he was. She turned back towards Ursula and ran towards her.

"What's happened?" Ursula called. "What's going on? Have they arrested him?"

Katie stared at Ursula. Was there evidence this woman had committed a crime? Could she arrest her?

No, but she could certainly take her in for questioning.

"Ursula, I need you to come with me," she said.

Ursula looked at her, her eyes wild. "What are you talking about? What's going on?"

"Ursula," Katie said. "Please, I need you to get into the back of this police car. I've got some questions for you, but first—"

"Why should I get in the car with you?"

Katie licked her lips. "Ursula, did Stephen tell you that he'd killed a man in 1994? Did you know that the body we found underneath that toilet block was the man he killed?"

Ursula stared at her for a moment, then let out a high-pitched laugh. "Don't be ridiculous. That was Stephen's friend. He wanted me to find out who'd killed him so that he could grieve properly."

Katie shook her head. "He lied to you, Ursula. Stephen's a killer. You're in danger if you go back to him."

"Don't be ridiculous. Stephen's no killer. Somebody else killed that man, and you need to find out who."

"Ursula," Katie said, "please get in the police car with me, and then I can explain everything." She had a thought. "In fact, if you come with me, you can help me tell Stephen who killed his friend."

That wasn't a lie, was it? Telling Stephen who killed the man, when it was Stephen himself who killed the man.

Ursula stared back at her. "OK," she said, "But my Stephen's not a killer. I'll prove it to you."

"You do that," Katie said, giving her a smile that she hoped looked genuine.

She reached out, and Ursula allowed her to take her hand.

"This is Ursula Rowland," Katie told the PS. "She'll be riding in the back of the car with us. Don't let her out."

"I should think not." He said, "You stay there, madam."

Ursula shrugged and got into the car.

Katie breathed a sigh of relief. Harold was in good hands, and she'd found Ursula.

But would she find Stephen Carson at the beach huts?

CHAPTER FIFTY-FIVE

JILL WAS LEAVING the team room, heading back to her own office, when her phone rang.

It was Sunil, the digital forensics guy.

She answered it, feeling her heart rate pick up.

"Sunil," she said, "is this about those texts?"

"It is," he replied. "I'm assuming you're not the person I should be talking to about evidence in the Mudeford Spit case."

"Oh, no," she said. "Katie's your liaison there. Why, has something come to light?"

"No, no," he replied. "Nothing in particular. Sorry, this is about those texts."

"Right. Give me a moment," she said. She pushed open the door to her own office and closed it behind her. She needed to be sitting down for this. She rounded the desk and sat in her chair, taking a moment to shuffle into a comfortable position.

She was putting this off, she knew. At last, she took a deep breath and put the phone back to her ear.

"Sunil," she said, "sorry about that. I just needed to get somewhere private. What have you got?"

"Well," he replied, "first up, those texts are definitely from the same number."

"I knew that much," she told him. "That's what my phone told me."

"You'd be surprised," he said. "Sometimes people can disguise numbers, make texts from two different phones look like they came from the same place."

"OK," she said, "consider me educated, but I was already assuming they were from the same number. Is there anything else?"

"Yes," he replied. "The number in question is unregistered. It's a burner phone."

No surprise there, either, Jill thought. "OK," she said. "Were you able to find out anything more about it?"

"You're lucky," he told her. "I've got contacts."

Jill rolled her eyes. She'd heard about Sunil's reputation. He was a geek, someone with very few social skills. Katie seemed to like him, but then, Katie's social skills weren't something to shout about.

"So what have your contacts told you?" she asked him.

"I know it was bought in the Bournemouth area," he said.

Jill felt her chest hollow out. *OK. OK, don't panic*, she told herself. It could just be two messages sent in error, two messages from a phone that happened to be local. That wasn't that big a deal, was it?

"OK," she repeated.

"It was bought three days ago," Sunil said, "in a shop in Pokesdown."

"Pokesdown," she repeated. Pokesdown. That was where the armed robbery had taken place, the one that Stephen Carson had been involved in, not that that had anything to do with it.

"This shop," she said, "what kind of shop? Is it a legitimate phone shop, or something else?"

"Legitimate phone shop," he replied, "but one with a significant under-the-counter business."

She nodded. "Can you tell me the name of the phone shop, who it belongs to?"

"I can," he said. "In fact, you'll find I'm a step ahead of you there."

Jill gritted her teeth. "In what respect?"

"Brett found out the name of the shop. I've got its address. We've looked up the company that owns it, and I followed the Companies House trail to the company that owns that."

"OK," she said. "What company?"

"Well, the phone shop is owned by a company called FonesRU, that, in turn, is owned by another company called Dorset Communications, and that is owned by a larger company going by the name of Sunrise Holdings."

"I've heard of that," Jill said.

"I'm not surprised," Sunil told her. "Sunrise Holdings is owned by the Kelvins."

Jill sucked in a breath. So the phone that had been used to send her a message threatening her family had come from a shop owned by the Kelvins. Surely that wasn't a coincidence.

"Can you trace this phone?" she said. "The physical phone?"

"That's extremely unlikely," Sunil told her. "It'll have been destroyed by now."

"Right," she said. "So is there anything more you can tell me?"

"No, sorry."

Jill sighed. "OK, thanks, Sunil. Look, don't tell anybody about this, will you? It's not to do with the case. It's something else, something sensitive."

"Fair enough," he said. "Not sure who I'd tell anyway."

The line went dead.

Jill slumped back in her chair, staring at the door. What was she going to tell Meera? Did Meera need to know that she was at risk because of the work Jill had been doing, or had Jill done enough to keep her family safe, by passing the liaison with Eric Chiles up to the boss? Had she just put the boss's family at risk? Was she being selfish and irresponsible?

After all, Eric had information on a cold case – the disappearance of Frank Kelvin. It was part of her job to find out what had happened to Frank Kelvin, to know whether he was alive or dead. But she knew this was bigger than that. It was linked to multiple cases the MCIT had investigated, and DCI Clarke had oversight of all that.

"You're doing the right thing," she told herself. The boss had said so, after all.

She rose from her chair and walked slowly to the door. She needed to forget about this, for as long as it took to bring Stephen Carson in. She opened the door and dialled Katie's number. It rang out.

"Oh, hello."

Jill looked up halfway between her own room and the team room. Meera was standing in front of her, smiling.

Jill felt relief wash through her body. She and Meera tried to avoid each other at work, but right now, Meera's face was the one thing she wanted to see, even if she was putting her wife in danger.

"Meera," she said.

Meera frowned. "Are you OK? You look pale."

Jill closed her eyes. She felt Meera's hand on her arm, rubbing it. The warmth was soothing. She couldn't lie to her wife. She couldn't let her walk around as if she was invulnerable when the truth was that the Kelvins were watching her.

Jill opened her eyes. "Meera, love," she said, "I need to talk to you about something."

Meera stopped rubbing. "What's up? Is it Suzi? Have you had a call? Has something happened?"

Jill shook her head. "No, it's not Suzi. Don't worry. Suzi is fine."

"OK." Meera withdrew her hand. "So what is it?"

Jill looked her wife in the eye. "Come into my office a moment, and I'll tell you."

CHAPTER FIFTY-SIX

It took the response car ten minutes to get up to the beach. Most of that time was spent getting the code to unlock the gate leading up to the access road.

Katie drummed her thighs with her fingertips as she waited, aware that letting Dillick see how frustrated she was wouldn't get them there any faster. Ursula sat in the back of the car the whole time, silent.

As they arrived at the beach hut, Katie's phone vibrated. She looked down to see a text message from Sunil: *Hey, I'm at the bar. Let me know when you get here.*

Damn. She was, what, twenty minutes late now? It had taken her ages to get here. But in truth, she'd forgotten all about him.

She shoved her phone back in her pocket. She'd text him back in a moment, when she'd done an initial reconnaissance of the area.

She turned to Sergeant Dillick. "Let's get out. Ursula can stay in the car." Katie turned in her seat. "You don't go anywhere, alright?"

Ursula shrugged. "Not many places to go, are there? I'll see you back here. Don't worry."

Katie narrowed her eyes, unsure whether to trust the woman, but really, she had no choice. "Good," she said, and got out of the car. The sergeant was already waiting for her.

"What now?" he said. "There's only two of us, and there's a hell of a lot of beach huts."

"We're not looking in the beach huts," she said. "There's a toilet block along there. They're in the process of rebuilding it. If he's here, maybe that's where he's gone."

"If you're sure," Dillick replied. He gestured towards the path leading alongside the beach huts. "Lead on, you know the way?"

Katie looked at the sergeant. Was he mocking her?

Well, he was here. He was doing as she asked, and that was the important thing. She could only hope that they'd find Carson.

She hurried towards the toilet block, Dillick keeping up with her easily. Katie always wore sensible shoes, and since this investigation had begun, she'd taken to wearing her Doc Martens every day. She was glad of it now. Not only were they comfortable and sensible, they were warm. It was bloody freezing up here, at the very easternmost point of the county, with the wind ripping off Christchurch Harbour.

At last, they were in view of the toilet block. She put out a hand.

"Stop here please, Sarge," Katie whispered. She crouched down behind a rubbish bin and peered over the top towards the block.

The area had been levelled now, all signs of the old building gone. The council hadn't started building its replacement yet. Maybe they'd had to stop because of the body. Either that, or these things simply took time.

She scanned the area around the toilet block, wishing she had binoculars. She turned to Sergeant Dillick. "Have you got any binoculars or night vision goggles?" she asked.

He gave her an incredulous look. "Who do you think I am? Rambo?"

Katie pushed back a frown. "Doesn't do any harm to ask," she said.

"No, sorry," he replied. "I don't have anything like that. We'll just have to use our eyesight."

She shook her head. "I can do better than that."

She brought out her phone, suddenly remembering the text from Sunil, and held it up in front of her. She used her fingers to zoom in, hoping that would help her see better. But no, it was too dark up here, the only source of illumination a couple of dim security lights near the café further up. Nobody came up here on a February evening. Why would they?

She sighed. Maybe she was wrong. Maybe Carson hadn't come up here at all. Maybe it wasn't even him who'd attacked Harold.

A lump formed in her throat. Maybe it had been Ursula. Had she been duped by a woman feigning innocence?

"Christ, Katie, you're an idiot." She stood up.

"What are you doing?" asked Dillick.

"Going back to the car," she snapped. "I need to check if she's still there."

He raised an eyebrow. "I'll stay here."

"Thanks," she replied.

"Keep in touch, yes?" He waved his mobile phone at her.

Katie nodded and started running back towards the car. As soon as she rounded the last beach hut and it came into view, she could see the back door was open.

Damn. She stopped running.

"Ursula, what have you done?"

She scanned the area, trying to see the woman. They were over a mile away from the road. But this place was a labyrinth, beach huts scattered irregularly through the sand dunes. There was no way she'd find Ursula.

She pulled out her phone and dialled Dillick. "My witness," she said. "She's left the car. Do you have colleagues with a drone that we can use to find her among the beach huts?"

"So she's a suspect now?" he asked.

"Yes," Katie replied.

"Leave it with me." He ended the call, and she plunged her

phone back in her pocket. She took a few steps towards the car. Maybe Ursula was still in there. Maybe she'd seen Katie coming.

She caught movement beside one of the beach huts and turned towards it. Ursula was standing in its shadow. Katie felt her breath hitch in her throat.

"Ursula," she called. "I told you to stay in the car."

Ursula said nothing. Katie couldn't even see if she was looking at her. She was facing her, yes, but could she hear Katie calling her? The wind whistled around these beach huts, catching her voice and sending it off in unexpected directions. The sand was billowing around her feet, and she could hear the clanging of boat masts behind her. She shivered.

She took a few steps forward. "Ursula," she called again. Ursula moved, turning towards her.

"Yes, Ursula," Katie called. She advanced on the woman, picking up pace. "Ursula, stay there."

Ursula disappeared behind the beach hut.

"No." Katie started running.

She reached the beach hut she thought Ursula had been standing next to and rounded it. There was nobody there. She caught a flash of movement to one side and turned towards it. Was that Ursula, disappearing behind another hut?

This was a waste of time. She'd never find her amongst all these huts. She needed to stay where she was and wait for Uniform to bring a drone. But by the time that happened, Ursula could be back in Southbourne.

Katie stood, breathing heavily, thinking. She was in the middle of a group of beach huts, neither the sea to the east nor the harbour to the west visible. You could easily get lost here.

The harbour was behind her. She stumbled in that direction, heading back towards the car. That would be the best place to wait.

As she emerged from the beach huts, she spotted a figure running towards the car.

Ursula.

Katie knew better than to call out this time. She picked up pace, running as quietly as she could along the sand. Her heavy boots made it hard work.

Ursula rounded the car. Katie squinted to try to get a better look, but it was too dark. Had Ursula got in the car, or was she running away from it, back in the direction they'd come?

"Hey."

Katie turned at the sound of the voice. Was that the sergeant?

"Hey," came the voice again.

Katie planted her feet in the sand. She turned from side to side, confused.

"Sarge," she called, "where are you?"

"Hey," came the voice again.

Katie wanted to cry out. *Don't be scared*, she told herself, *you're a bloody police officer. Don't be such a wimp.*

She turned back towards the police car. She heard footsteps behind her. Felt movement.

She turned back again. There was a figure, Ursula, no, larger, running towards her. The sergeant – no. The figure wasn't in uniform.

It was a man wearing a hoodie, holding something, raising his arm. What did he have in his—

Katie turned and started running towards the car. She could hear the man behind her, his footsteps, now his breath.

Carson, she thought, *it's Carson.*

It has to be.

Katie focused on her feet, terrified of tripping. She just needed to get to the car. To get inside, lock the door and call for backup.

Why the hell had she come up here with just one sergeant?

The footsteps got closer. Katie picked up speed. She felt her toe hit something.

She looked down quickly, a rock, no, her ankle went sideways, no, her leg crumpled underneath her, no, her hip hit the ground.

She threw her hand up, not sure if it was for balance or to protect herself, but he was over her.

She felt two blows to the head. The first was the concrete beneath her, the path leading to the car, hitting the back of the head as she crashed to the ground.

She shrieked, and then she felt the second blow. Something sharper, smaller, hitting her temple.

Katie screamed as the world went black.

CHAPTER FIFTY-SEVEN

"GAIL, SLOW DOWN."

Lesley was talking into her phone as she navigated the wet roads past Bournemouth town centre.

It had started raining about ten minutes earlier, the downpour so intense that her windscreen wipers could barely cope with it.

"I had a call from Sunil," Gail said. "He was supposed to be meeting Katie."

"What, at your lab?" Lesley asked.

"No. I think Sunil and Katie might have been dating. He said he was in a bar waiting for her and she hadn't shown up."

"Which bar?" Lesley asked.

"One in Bournemouth," Gail replied. "Sorry, I don't know which. I'll get the details from him, but the important thing is, he can't reach Katie. He's been calling her for the last half an hour, and there's no reply."

"OK," Lesley said. "Well, it's half past six, and Katie's a grown woman. Do you think there's a reason I should be worried?"

"I've met Katie," Gail said. "She's keen. When she learned the identity of the victim, she'd have gone back to the crime scene."

"I think she was sent over to the family house," Lesley said. "I can check with Jill, though."

"Hang on."

The line went quiet. Lesley tapped her fingers on the steering wheel, idling at traffic lights. The red of the lights was a blur, occasionally smoothed out by her windscreen wipers.

"That was Sunil," Gail said. "I had to put you on hold. He's been talking to Uniform. A Sergeant Dillick."

Lesley frowned. "Who's he?"

"I don't know," Gail said, "but he's with Katie. They're at the beach huts."

"OK," Lesley said, "so what's the emergency?"

"He said she'd been attacked."

Lesley stopped tapping the steering wheel. "Who's been attacked?"

"Katie," Gail replied. "But they've got Stephen Carson, and a woman."

The lights turned green. Lesley didn't move. After a moment, a horn honked behind her.

"Oh, fuck off," she called in her rear-view mirror. "OK, Gail, I'm heading straight there. I'll speak to Katie, find out what happened."

"Are you nearby?" Gail asked. "I just thought, with you living not far from the beach huts..."

"You did the right thing," Lesley said.

Strictly speaking, Gail hadn't done the right thing. She should have called this in, had it dealt with officially. But thinking of Lesley made sense.

"I'm ten to fifteen minutes away now," she said. "I'll go straight there."

Twelve minutes later, she was at the barrier to the access road that led to the beach huts. She stopped her car, walked out and jiggled the access gate. It moved.

"For once, I'm grateful for idiots," she muttered to herself as she swung it out of the way.

She got back in her car, shaking off the rain as she did so, and crawled through. Quickly, she got out again, closed the gate and dived back into the car. She'd need to get her waterproof out of the boot if it didn't stop raining like this.

She drove along the access road as quickly as she dared, aware that there was a speed limit along here. She could see blue lights in the distance, glowing over the trees that separated the access road from the beach and, as she approached the beach huts, she realised that this was no ordinary scene.

Four police cars and an ambulance. The ambulance was at the back. Lesley pulled up behind it and got out of her car. She whipped the boot open to grab her waterproof and ran towards the beach huts, pulling on the coat as she went. She passed the emergency vehicles and saw a huddle of police and paramedics up ahead. She ran towards them.

"Who's in charge?" she barked.

Two paramedics and a police officer turned towards her. "Who are you?" one of the paramedics asked.

"DCI Lesley Clarke," she replied, "Dorset Police. My colleague, Katie Young, should be here."

The paramedic paled. Lesley frowned at her. "What? Where is she?"

The paramedic glanced at her colleague, then pulled to one side. Lesley stepped through the gap that had formed. Up ahead were five uniformed police officers. A sergeant was talking into his radio, facing away from her. He seemed to be the most senior officer on the scene.

"Sergeant," she called, "what's happened here?"

He turned towards her. His lips stopped moving, and he lowered the radio. "Are you DCI Clarke?" he asked.

She nodded. "Where's Katie? Where's my DC? She can give me a—"

The sergeant shook his head.

"I'm so sorry," he said.

Lesley felt heat rise to her chest. "What do you mean, you're sorry?"

He looked back at her. "I'm afraid DC Young was attacked. She received a blow to the head, and—"

"And what?" Lesley said.

The sergeant shook his head.

"She was dead before the paramedics arrived."

Lesley felt her legs weaken. "Say that again."

"I'm sorry, Ma'am," the sergeant said. "I'm afraid DC Young is dead."

CHAPTER FIFTY-EIGHT

Zoe was sitting in Lesley and Elsa's living room, her mind going over what she'd read in the files from Mark Ashforth's business and banking.

She was getting closer to understanding who the man had been working for. She was sure of it, but sometimes she felt like she was going round in circles, finding information that contradicted itself. There were documents that pointed towards the Kelvins, but there were also documents that pointed towards the London gang and the Musketeers.

None of it made sense. There were records of Ashford having received payments. Not only that, there were phone calls, messages and Post-it notes. He'd written names that he'd tried to disguise on those notes, but he hadn't made a very good job of it.

Mrs K, for example. It didn't take a genius to work out who that was.

Elsa appeared in the doorway. "Have you heard all the noise?" she asked.

Zoe looked up. "What noise?"

Elsa gestured towards the window. "Didn't you see the blue lights going past? There've been at least four police cars go past the end of our road. I looked out the front door, and I could see a glow on the horizon."

Zoe's brow furrowed. "A blue glow?"

Elsa replied, "The blue glow that you get from multiple emergency vehicles."

Zoe stood up. "Which direction?"

"Hengistbury Head," Elsa replied, "up towards the visitor centre and the beach huts."

"Show me," Zoe said.

Elsa led her out of the room and opened the front door. They both went out onto the driveway. Neighbours had gathered in their doorways, on driveways, and a couple were in the road. It seemed that rain didn't stop people who lived out here.

"Does anybody know what's going on?" Elsa asked.

A man looked at her. "I thought you'd know, what with your wife being a copper."

Elsa shrugged. "She's not home from work."

Zoe looked at her. "Do you think she's involved with that?"

"No," Elsa said. "Lesley spends most of her time behind a desk these days, managing people. That'll be uniform up there."

"Maybe I should go and look," Zoe said. "It might be connected to the Mudeford Spit case."

"OK," Elsa said. She looked Zoe up and down. "But you need to put something warmer on."

"You're right." Zoe hurried back into the house, where she grabbed her duffel coat.

"I'll drive you up," Elsa said.

"Are you sure?" Zoe asked her. "I mean, Lesley could be home any time now."

Elsa smiled. "Lesley has her own key. She's a big girl, you know, and I'd like to know if she's up there."

"OK," Zoe replied. She had no idea where Hengistbury Head or

Mudeford Spit were. She hadn't ventured further than this house, and she was grateful. "Thanks," she said. "I appreciate it."

"No trouble," Elsa said, as she grabbed her car keys. The two of them hurried out to the car.

Zoe got into the passenger seat, eyeing her Mini. Elsa's Cupra was significantly more modern and efficient, but Zoe loved that Mini. She knew it was getting closer and closer to the day when she would have to give it up, but every time she took it for an MOT, she would spend a fortune on getting it fixed, desperate not to lose that last link with her dad.

They drove towards the northern end of Lesley and Elsa's road and stopped for a police car passing from the east.

"That's coming from Hengistbury Head," Elsa said.

Zoe nodded. She'd seen a figure in the back. "Someone's been arrested," she told Elsa. "There was a man in the back of that car."

Elsa leaned forward, craning her head to get a good look at the receding lights of the police car. "I wonder who," she said. "Maybe they caught their suspect." She looked at Zoe. "Can you find out?"

Zoe looked back at Lesley's wife. Since when was it her business? She wasn't sure what was a healthy level of interest, when your other half was a criminal lawyer. She picked up her phone as Elsa turned right out of the road, heading towards the blue glow.

Lesley's number went straight to voicemail. She tried Nathan. He picked up on the second ring.

"Ma'am," he said, "everything OK?"

"Nathan," she replied, "I'm in Southbourne, and there seems to have been an incident near the scene where the body was found at Mudeford Spit. Do you know anything about it?"

"Sorry, Ma'am," he said, "nothing."

"OK," she replied. "See if you can find anything out."

"OK," he said. He hung up.

Zoe turned to Elsa. "I think the best way for us to find out is to head up there."

"OK," Elsa continued driving along a straight road heading

directly towards the blue lights, then took a right-hand bend, immediately followed by a left-hand turn that took her straight on. They passed a car park on the right, and then Elsa stopped at a barrier.

"I can't go any further than this," she said.

"That's fine," said Zoe. "You've brought me more than half the way by the looks of it."

"I did," Elsa told her. "Good luck."

"Thanks," Zoe said as she got out of the car. As Elsa drove off, she stood shivering, staring back at the receding car.

Was this a good idea? Was she simply interfering? Or could she be of help?

Only one way to find out. She pulled up the hood of her duffel and started running.

CHAPTER FIFTY-NINE

"WHERE IS SHE?" Lesley said. "Take me to her." The sergeant nodded and pushed through the crowd. Lesley followed him, her breathing shallow.

Katie dead.

He had the wrong person. Surely Katie was...

Katie was far too tough to be dead.

After a few moments, the sergeant stopped. He turned towards her, his face grim.

"Ma'am," he said, "I'll ask you not to go any closer."

Lesley glared at him, then softened.

He was right. *Don't contaminate the scene.* Even with Katie...

She stared past him towards the figure slumped on the ground. It was a young woman with dark hair, even darker in the dim bluish light.

"Get lights here now," she said. "We need to be able to see what we're doing. All I can see are those bloody blue lights."

"Ma'am," he said, looking sheepish, and walked away.

Lesley grunted. She needed to be alone, alone with whoever the woman on the ground was. She wouldn't accept it was Katie until she saw for herself.

Two uniformed officers stood on the other side of the body, gazing downwards. The rain was easing up, thank God.

"Have you identified her?" Lesley asked. "Are you sure?"

One of them looked up. "Excuse me, but who are you?"

"DCI Lesley Clarke," she said. "Her senior officer."

The constable nodded. "She identified herself to us when we arrived at the scene. Her ID badge, it's still around her neck."

Lesley took a step forward. The second constable, a young man who looked barely old enough to be out of school, cleared his throat.

"I'm sorry, Ma'am, we've been told to keep people away from her for now. There'll be forensics."

"I don't care," Lesley said. "I need to check."

"Ma'am," the male constable said.

The woman walked round him, taking a wide arc to pass around Katie and towards Lesley. "If you come to this side, Ma'am," she said, "you can get an angle that allows you to see her face."

Lesley blinked at her. "Thank you," she said. "What's your name?"

"Sue," the woman said. "PC Sue Jarrett."

"Thank you, Sue," Lesley said. She stood where the constable had indicated, then squatted down, careful to bring nothing but the soles of her feet into contact with the ground. The sand in front of her was disturbed, footsteps, sweeping marks, signs of a struggle. At the centre of it all, completely still, was the young woman.

"Have the paramedics looked at her?" Lesley asked. "Are they sure?"

"They've looked, Ma'am," PC Jarrett said. "They are sure. I'm sorry."

Lesley swallowed. It was too dark. Still too damn dark.

She got her phone out and switched on the torch.

"I'm sorry, Katie." This was such an undignified way to be identified.

She lifted her phone and shone the torch towards the woman. She let out a tight breath.

It was Katie.

Lesley plunged her phone back into her pocket, too clumsy to turn off the torch, and stood up straight.

"It's her," she said. "It's her."

She strode back towards the crowd of Uniforms and paramedics. "Why are you all standing here?" she asked. "Why aren't you doing something?"

"Ma'am," PS Dillick said, "there's nothing we can do. Not until the crime scene manager gets here."

Lesley swallowed. *Shit.* Gail. Gail and the rest of the MCIT would have to investigate Katie's death.

"Who did this?" she asked.

"We've already arrested him," Dillick said. "He's on his way to Poole in a police car right now."

Lesley's jaw tightened. "Who? Do you know who he was?"

The sergeant nodded. "His name's Stephen Carson. I visited his house, with your DC." His shoulders dropped. "I'm sending a team over there now."

Lesley shook her head. "He doesn't live in that house. He left that house thirty-two years ago, and tonight he came back and he killed one of my most promising officers."

The sergeant looked down at the ground and then back up at Lesley. "I'm so sorry, Ma'am."

Lesley turned at the sound of voices. Two police officers were approaching, a woman in handcuffs between them.

"Who's this?" she said.

"Ursula," one of the officers told her. "DC Young was chasing her."

"I've done nothing," Ursula cried out. "I don't know why you're arresting me. All I did was come and see what had happened to Stephen's friend."

Lesley stepped forward. "You're Ursula Rowland," she said. "You pretended to be a forensic archaeologist so you could gain access to a crime scene."

The woman squared her shoulders. "So what if I did? I just wanted to be able to tell Stephen what had happened to his friend."

Lesley raised herself up to her full height. Luckily, she was taller than Ursula. She glared down at the woman.

"That man was not Stephen Carson's friend. That man was a poor, unfortunate victim who happened to be in a petrol station on a night when your boyfriend decided to rob it. That man was going to identify your boyfriend to the police, so your boyfriend, Stephen Carson, killed him."

Ursula's face flickered. She struggled to regain composure.

"You're lying," she said.

Lesley shook her head. "I'm not lying about a word of it."

She turned to the constable. "Take her to Poole, put her in a cell until I'm ready to question her."

CHAPTER SIXTY

As Zoe approached the beach huts, she spotted Lesley's car in the middle of the emergency vehicles. She looked up and down the row of vehicles, wondering what could have happened to bring so many of them out here. There were voices beyond the beach huts up ahead.

Zoe continued running. She could feel wind whistling through the gaps between the beach huts, and she could hear the harbour lapping to her left.

Which harbour was this? It wasn't Poole Harbour, she knew that much, but she wasn't aware of another one. She needed to do more research on Dorset. Surely it couldn't be as hard as Cumbria to get to know.

There was a crowd up ahead, Uniforms huddled. Zoe stopped and scanned them, looking for Lesley.

"Zoe, is that you?"

Zoe turned to the sound of the voice. Behind her was a white CSI van with a woman sticking her head out of the window.

"You must be Gail," Zoe said.

"That's me. Can you get somebody to move so that I can get through?"

"Do you know what's happened here? Why have you been called out?"

"Oh, hell, Zoe. Don't you know?"

Zoe walked towards the van. She shook her head. "Know what?"

Gail leaned on the open window. "A woman's been attacked. Murdered."

"Another one?" Zoe said. "Is this related to—"

"Probably," Gail replied. "The woman's a police officer."

Zoe felt herself teeter. She put her hand on the bonnet of the van.

"Who?" she asked.

"DC Katie Young," Gail said. "Do you know her?"

Zoe shook her head. "She's... She's one of Jill's team. What happened?"

Gail shrugged. "I don't know. All I know is that I need to secure that scene as quickly as I can and get to work."

"OK," Zoe said. "I'll go and speak to the Uniforms."

"Thanks."

Zoe ran towards the group of uniformed officers and told them to let Gail through. As they began to move, Lesley emerged from the crowd, her face drawn.

"Lesley," Zoe called. "I'm so sorry."

Lesley looked up. "Zoe, what are you doing here?"

"I saw all the lights heading in this direction. Elsa and I were worried."

Lesley looked past Zoe. "Is Elsa here?"

"She gave me a lift and then went back home."

"Good," Lesley replied. "This isn't the place for..." She sighed. "Have you been told?"

Zoe nodded. "DC Young."

Lesley pulled in a faltering breath. "My God, Zoe, she'd only been in the Cold Cases Team for less than a year. I don't even know if she's got any family."

Zoe stepped forward. She put her hand on Lesley's arm. "Jill and I will help you with this, Lesley."

Lesley's eyes widened. "Jill, she doesn't even know. Oh, God, Zoe, you and me and Jill, we all need to talk, but not now."

"What about..." Zoe asked, "what happened here?"

Lesley screwed her eyes shut. "Stephen Carson was here. He's under arrest. It was him who—"

Zoe nodded. "He attacked her?"

"Yeah, fucking bastard. And Ursula."

"Ursula?"

Lesley opened her eyes. "Ursula Rowland, Carson's girlfriend, she tried to inveigle her way into the investigation to find out what we knew. And then she came here." Lesley gasped. "Oh, fuck, his father. Somebody needs to talk to his father. Uniform have gone to the house, but..."

"I can do it," Zoe said.

"Thank you." Lesley put a hand up to her face. "Somebody will give you the address."

"OK." Zoe squeezed Lesley's arm. "Do you want me out of your hair? I can move to a hotel tonight."

"God knows, Zoe, I need you in the house. In fact, I want you to stay until you've bought your house."

"I'm not doing that, Lesley," Zoe said. "I've signed a tenancy agreement starting from the weekend, and I'm going to be out of your way from next week."

"OK," Lesley replied. "I can't think straight."

"No," Zoe said. "I don't blame you. Look, I'll speak to Jill. I'll tell her what's happened, and then the three of us can talk in the morning."

Lesley pulled closer. "This case," she said, "Stephen Carson, there's a connection."

"I know," Zoe said. "That bank account."

Lesley shook her head. "It's more than the bank account. I can feel it in my blood. Stephen Carson was working for the Kelvins. I'm sure of it."

"You think he'll tell you when you get round to questioning him?"

"Of course he bloody won't," Lesley said. "Would you?"

Zoe gave her boss a grim smile. "Probably not. Why don't you get home, and I'll speak to Jill and to the Carson family."

"Thanks, Zoe. I know I should do this. I'm the senior officer."

"It's fine," Zoe said. "I didn't know her. I'm the best person to do it."

Lesley straightened up. "I appreciate this, Zoe, I really do."

CHAPTER SIXTY-ONE

"Are you sure you're going to be OK?" Meera asked, as she followed Jill to the door.

Jill turned to her, one hand on the door handle. "I'll be fine, sweetie," she said. "Please try not to worry."

Meera glanced back towards the kitchen, where Suzi was finishing her breakfast. "I'm sure they'd understand if you didn't go in today."

"Don't be ridiculous," Jill said. "My team need me today, of all days, and besides, there'll be official things to do, reports to make, evidence to give, HR stuff." She rubbed her forehead. "Oh, God, I don't even know where to start." Jill bashed her hand against the door. "She never talked about her family, Meera. I don't even know where her parents live."

Meera grabbed her wife's hand. "You'll find out, love, and it'll be fine. I know you, you'll be able to support them. We all will."

Jill sniffed. "I bloody hope so. Oh, God, why did I send her over to Harold Carson's house?"

"It's not your fault," Meera said. "You had information that

Harold Carson needed, and you sent a member of the team over to impart it. It's perfectly normal."

Jill shook her head. "It was dark. I should have sent two people."

"Katie knew what she was doing," Meera said. "And besides, it wasn't at the Carson house that she died."

Jill stared at her. "Died. Oh God, that word."

Meera swallowed. "Do you want to wait a bit and then we can drive in together? I'm worried about you driving."

Jill shook her head again. "I'm fine, Meera, I'm absolutely fine. I need my car in case I have to go anywhere today."

"OK," Meera said, "but call me when you get to the office."

"I will." Jill gave Meera a kiss and then left the house.

Meera turned back towards the kitchen. She spent a few moments gathering her composure, then pushed the brightness into her face. She walked through to the kitchen, trying not to drag her feet. "Come on then, lovely," she said. "Time to go to school."

"Not finished," Suzi replied.

Meera rolled her eyes. "You need to eat faster," she said. "Come on, or we'll be late, and you don't want to get a lateness point."

Suzi gasped. "No, Mummy, no lateness points."

Meera smiled. She wondered how long Suzi would be this keen to follow the school rules. Hopefully for a good many years yet.

At last, Suzi finished her cereal. "Come on then," Meera said. "Your coat's in the hall."

Suzi jumped down from her chair and ran through to the hall. Meera helped her on with her coat and grabbed her rucksack. Quarter to nine. They would only just make it.

Ten minutes later, they were outside the school. She bundled Suzi through to her classroom and waved her goodbye as the girl skipped inside. Once Suzi was out of sight, Meera slumped against a fence.

"Hey, Meera, you OK?"

Meera turned to see Brianna approaching her. She was a tall, solidly built woman with blonde hair and features that made her look posh, in a way that Meera struggled to define.

Meera pulled on a thin smile. She didn't want anybody here knowing about Katie, although they would find out soon enough. "I'm fine," she said. "Don't worry."

"You can always talk to me, you know," Brianna replied. "I know it's tough having a little one." She gazed towards the classroom their children had disappeared into, and Meera wondered what was going through her head. Missing her sister, no doubt.

"Thanks," Meera said. "I need to get to work."

"Of course," Brianna said. "I'm jealous. I wish I had a job to go to."

"You haven't got a job?" Meera asked, remembering Brianna's house. Maybe there'd been an insurance policy. Maybe she was being bankrolled by the Kelvins.

Brianna shrugged. "I have Mason on weekdays, his gran has him at the weekends."

"Does she?" Meera asked, then bit her lip. She didn't want Brianna knowing that she knew who Mason's gran was. "Sorry," she said. "None of my business."

Brianna smiled. "That's OK. I'm glad to have the help. To be honest, my mum's been amazing since Amanda died."

Meera felt relief wash through her. So Suzi's little friend wasn't spending half his time living at Vera Kelvin's house. She wondered if he ever saw that side of his family, and if so, how much he knew about them.

How much Brianna knew about them.

Brianna smiled. "Anyway, don't worry about me. I'll let you go off to work. We'll have to have another coffee sometime."

"Yeah, it was nice catching up the other night."

Meera hesitated. Jill had told her about the texts, about the danger that getting to know Brianna was putting her and Suzi in. But she also knew that the MCIT wanted to know more about the Kelvin family and their operations.

Maybe Meera had an in.

"OK," she said, "coffee would be nice. Maybe one day next week."

Brianna smiled, looking surprised. "Next week, that sounds perfect."

CHAPTER SIXTY-TWO

Lesley didn't want to use either of the team rooms. She didn't want them associated with this conversation. So she'd found a meeting room, a neutral space, somewhere that she hoped wouldn't lodge in anyone's mind.

Of course, everybody already knew what had happened. For starters, Katie hadn't come into work this morning. But Jill and Zoe both knew the details, and Gail and her team did, too.

Lesley had suggested that both Jill and Zoe quietly tell their teams before they all gathered in this room to discuss Katie's death. She knew that Carpenter thought what she was doing was pointless. Why rake over the coals when the team members had already been informed of their colleague's death?

But Lesley knew better.

She'd seen colleagues die in the past, and she knew that talking about it and asking questions helped people come to terms with it. Otherwise, it would hang over the entire team like a shadow for weeks, months, maybe even years. She couldn't change the fact that they would grieve, but the least she could do was help.

She sat at the front of the meeting room, her phone beside her on the table. For once, there was no laptop, no slides, no evidence photos, no briefing. The super had already identified a DI from another team, who was on his way to open the investigation.

Lesley leaned forward in her chair, her hands clasped in front of her. She'd thought the hardest part of being a DCI would be sitting behind a desk and having to manage people instead of getting out there, solving crimes and speaking to witnesses. But she'd been wrong. This was the hardest part.

Zoe's team arrived first, Zoe taking the lead, Nathan behind her, and Tina, Johnny and Meera filing in after them. All of them looked downwards, none of them speaking.

"Morning, folks," Lesley said.

Zoe gave her a grim smile. "Morning, boss." She glanced towards her team members. There were muttered "Good mornings."

Nathan pulled his shoulders back, trying to look authoritative, but failing. Lesley eyed him. She still didn't know what to make of Nathan.

Jill filed in, with her tiny two-person team. Lesley swallowed the lump in her throat.

Mike and Stanley both walked stiffly, their movements jerky, their heads down. Mike glanced over at Tina and blinked a few times. She threw him an encouraging smile, which he didn't return. Stanley threw himself into a chair and leaned over the desk in front of him, his face in his hands. Mike sat next to him, leaning back, eyes closed. Jill took the seat in front of them, staring forward, blinking and swallowing repeatedly.

Lesley stood and walked to the front. This room was too big for them. It would have been too big even when Katie was here. There were two rows of empty desks at the front. She leaned against one of them.

"You don't have to sit in your silos," she said. "If you need to sit with your friends or loved ones, please do."

Mike and Tina exchanged glances, and then Tina stood up and

walked over to stand behind Mike. She put her hands on his shoulders.

"Here," Jill said. She stood up, pushed her chair round to where Tina was, and offered it to the DC.

Tina muttered a *thank you* and sat down. She reached out and clutched Mike's hand. Jill hesitated for a moment and then walked across the room to sit in the empty chair beside Meera. Meera put a hand on her knee.

"You OK?" she muttered.

Jill nodded and sniffed. She glanced across at Stanley. "Stan, do you want to sit over here?"

Stanley shook his head. "I'm all right here, guv, don't worry about me."

Lesley took a deep breath. "Right, everyone," she said. "You've all heard the tragic news about Katie. Jill has already spoken to her parents on the phone, and they'll be coming down here from..." She looked at Jill.

"Leicester," Jill said.

"From Leicester later today," Lesley finished. "So," she continued, "here's the good news. Stephen Carson is in custody. There were witnesses to his attack on Katie. A uniformed sergeant saw him hit her over the head with an ornament that he'd taken from his father's house. He also attacked his father, Harold Carson."

Stanley looked up. "How is the old geezer?"

Lesley smiled. "He's in critical care right now, but he's hanging on. He's very elderly, so the doctors can't make any promises, but they're hoping he recovers."

"Poor bastard," Mike muttered. "If he does recover, the shock of finding out his son was a bloody murderer'll probably finish him off anyway."

Lesley nodded. "His daughter's with him. He's got all the support that can be on offer. Don't worry about Harold, worry about yourselves. Losing a colleague like this can be traumatic. It'll make you angry. It'll make you wish you could have done things differently."

She glanced at Jill. "But the truth is, none of you could have done anything differently. Katie was doing her job. She was a damn good detective, and she was trying to catch a killer."

"The killer got to her first," said Stanley.

"He did," said Lesley, "and we have to find a way of living with that. So I've made the calls, and counsellors are available to all of you. I expect every member of Jill's team to undertake at least one counselling session and consider more. Anything you say in there will be confidential, and it's designed to help you, rather than judge you or impact on your work. This is the twenty-first century, folks. If you're struggling mentally, we will help you. We won't condemn you."

Meera sniffed. She tightened her grip on Jill's knee.

Jill looked up. She turned her chair, the noise incongruous in the quiet room. "Mike, Stanley," she said. "We'll have a job to do, pulling together the evidence so that Stephen Carson goes down for a bloody long time."

"I hope," said Mike.

Jill looked at him. "We need to be professional," she said. "We need to be considered and objective. Carson killed Tizzard, thirty-two years ago. He then killed Katie last night."

"Surely another team will take on the investigation for Katie?" Stanley asked. "Why do we have to get involved?"

Jill stood up. She glanced at Meera and then walked over to her team on the opposite side of the room. "They will," she said. "It won't be us. But I'd like to assist them, where we can. Anyone who can't face that is not obligated to do more than simply answer questions about Katie's movements yesterday and what we knew about Carson. Most of which will be on file. And you can be transferred to the MCIT for a while if that's what you need."

Stanley looked up at her. "I don't want any transfer," he said. "I want to stay right where I am."

"Good," Jill replied. "There will be evidence to process relating to the original case, but that's all."

"Do we think he'll be convicted?" Johnny asked.

Jill's head snapped round to look at him. "Why do you think he wouldn't?" she said.

He shrugged. "I don't know. I..."

Zoe and Jill exchanged glances. Lesley knew that they were thinking about the Kelvins, about the fact that Carson was somehow associated with them. That necklace, and the bank transactions...

But even Vera Kelvin couldn't keep Stephen Carson out of prison now.

Lesley pushed herself upright. "Stephen Carson will go down for a very long time. The evidence against him is incontrovertible. He killed a copper, for God's sake."

"Juries hate coppers," Stanley said.

"What makes you think that?" Lesley asked, and he shrugged.

"Everybody hates coppers," Johnny added.

"Not in Dorset, they don't," said Lesley. "This isn't the Met."

Johnny grunted. "Yeah, suppose so."

This hadn't been what Lesley was expecting. She'd been expecting anger. She'd been expecting energy, a desire to take charge of the situation and make sure that Stephen Carson saw justice, but it was like they'd just given up.

"We've all still got jobs to do," she said. "I know it's going to be hard, but Jill, Zoe and I are here to support you, and there's counselling available. If you need to take some time off over the next few days, please do, but if you feel the need to take more than that, speak to me first, and make sure you get counselling."

There were grunts around the room. Lesley could see that if she kept them here any longer, it would just make things worse.

"I..." she tried to smile, "I appreciate your hard work, all of you," she said, "on the Musketeers case and the Mudeford Spit case, you've all done sterling work. And there will be arrests and convictions."

"Let's hope so," Mike muttered.

"There will," said Tina. "We'll make sure of it."

Mike looked across at her. He smiled. "You're right, T," he said. "You're right."

CHAPTER SIXTY-THREE

Jill leaned back in her chair and stretched her arms above her head. She'd had one-to-ones with both Mike and Stanley, spoken at length with the DCI, and talked to Katie's mum on the phone. Her parents were on a train from Leicester and would be in Bournemouth this afternoon. Jill was intending to pick them up. They didn't want a marked car coming for them.

The post-mortem on Katie's body hadn't been carried out yet, but the cause of death was obvious. Either way, Katie's poor parents would have to go to the mortuary and identify her. Jill was planning to escort them.

She sighed, pumping her fists open and closed. *What a mess.* Katie had shown such potential; she'd been keen. Yes, they'd been annoyed by her at times, but she was clearly someone who would progress. And so young.

Jill grabbed a tissue from the box on her desk and wiped under her eyes. She needed to be strong. There were other people around her, people she needed to support, people who were worse affected by this.

There was a knock on her door. Jill sighed. "Come in," she called.

The door opened and Meera appeared. Jill closed her eyes. It was good to see a friendly face, someone she didn't need to handhold.

Meera closed the door behind her and walked around the desk. She crouched down beside Jill and grabbed her hand on the arm of the chair.

"How are you?" she asked. "I've been thinking about you all morning."

Jill rubbed her forehead. "The honest answer? I have no idea how I am. I feel like I don't have time to be upset by it myself, because there are so many other people I've got to help." She looked at her watch. "I've got to leave in half an hour, to pick Katie's parents up from the station."

Meera grimaced. "Do you want me to come with you? I know DI Finch won't mind."

Jill shook her head. "That's kind of you, sweetheart, but I'll be OK. Doing the job is what keeps me going."

Meera nodded. She stood up and bent over to give Jill a hug. "I'm here if you need me."

"I know," Jill gave her wife a smile. "How was Suzi this morning?"

Meera, who was heading towards the door, turned back towards her. "Fine. She doesn't know anything about this, does she?"

"Of course not." Jill shuddered. "No, I was just wondering how things were at school with that new friend of hers and his aunt."

Meera stiffened. "Oh, fine. I didn't see them."

"Hopefully they won't bother you again," Jill said.

Meera nodded. "Let's hope so." She blew Jill a kiss and left the room.

CHAPTER SIXTY-FOUR

"You're right, Lesley," the super said. "You and I do need to have a chat about that robbery and my involvement in the investigation, but I can tell you now, I was just a lowly PC at the time. I had no idea what was going on with Cotton."

Lesley eyed him across the desk. They'd been talking for over half an hour, making plans for what would happen following Katie's death. There was a vacancy to be filled. But there had to be a respectful period before that process started, and besides, the Cold Cases Team had just wrapped up their latest investigation. Hopefully, there wouldn't be another one for a little while.

"I understand that, Sir," she said, "and I understand that this is sensitive. But you know that Jill was seeing our friend."

He smiled. "Our friend. The first friend, I assume?"

"Yes," she said, with the first glimpse of levity she'd felt since last night. "We still don't know what's happened to our second friend."

Our first friend was Eric Chiles; *our second friend* was Frank Kelvin.

Lesley still had her work cut out getting to the bottom of what had happened to him, or even if he was still alive.

"We'll talk, Lesley," the super said. "Jill can be involved, too."

Lesley shook her head. "I had to take her off that case."

He frowned. "You did?"

She nodded. "Her family are at risk. It's a long story, but it looks like the Kelvins got to her wife."

"Hang on," Carpenter said. "Isn't her wife one of your DCs?"

"She is," Lesley replied, "but they've got a young daughter as well. I couldn't authorise one of my team getting involved in an operation that would put her family at that kind of risk."

He pursed his lips, eyeing her. "But you've got a family, too, Lesley. I'm assuming that what you're telling me here is that you're taking over and conducting the meetings with our mutual friend yourself."

"I've already spoken to him."

He sucked through his teeth. "Be careful, Lesley. These are dangerous people you're getting involved with, and they've shown that they won't baulk at killing people they see as a threat."

"We've investigated the Kelvins before," Lesley said. "I've squared off against Vera Kelvin plenty of times. I can handle myself."

He snorted. "Well, let's hope you can."

"I can, Sir, and if I think there's going to be a problem, I'll let you know."

He leaned forward. "But you don't want to tell me all of the detail of what you're doing."

She shook her head.

"Not until you have more answers."

She nodded. He sighed. "Do you trust me, Lesley?"

Lesley stiffened. There had been plenty of times in the past when she hadn't trusted Carpenter. When she'd started in this job, she'd suspected he might be behind the death of her predecessor, DCI Tim Mackie.

Lesley licked her lips. "I do, Sir. I'll be honest with you. I haven't always. I've had my doubts. But I trust you absolutely, and that's the truth."

"I believe you," he replied, "and I trust you, Lesley, so be careful."

She nodded. "I—"

"That's all for now," he said. "I've got to attend another planning meeting. Who'd have thought that these things could continue, given what's happened, eh?"

Lesley nodded. She stood up.

"You take care of yourself, Lesley," he said. "I know you'll have been offering your team counselling if they need it, but it's available to you, too."

"I know, Sir," she said. "I'll be OK."

Lesley's mental health hadn't always been great. She'd moved down to Dorset following an attack in Birmingham that had left her with PTSD. In theory, she'd come here for a quiet life, but somehow it hadn't turned out like that. Regardless, the fresh air and change of scene, and possibly the slower pace of policing here, even in the face of murders, had led to her recovery. And she had to credit Elsa, too.

"Thank you, Sir." She left the room, realising her phone was ringing.

She picked up. "Dennis," she said, "you don't normally call at this time of day."

"I hope I'm not interrupting," he replied, "but I heard about Katie Young."

Lesley was standing opposite Carla's desk, Carpenter's PA. She turned her back to the woman and clenched the fist of her free hand at her side. "I'm more worried about my team, Dennis," she said. "It's a hell of a blow."

"They'll be OK," he told her. "They've got you and they've got each other. I may not have worked with all of them, but I know they're good people. They'll rally round."

"I hope so," she said.

"Don't forget, Lesley, they've got a damn good boss in you."

Lesley resisted a laugh. There had been times when Dennis would have described her as anything but a damn good boss.

"Dennis," she said, "did you just swear?"

He laughed. "I wondered if you'd notice. Desperate times call for desperate measures, eh?"

Lesley snorted. "I might just get the swear box out."

Dennis chuckled. "You do that, Lesley, and come and visit me soon. We need to chat."

CHAPTER SIXTY-FIVE

"THE CAR's just over there, Dad," Johnny said, pointing towards Alice's Polo. She was in the driving seat, flashing the lights to get their attention, parked on double yellow lines. Everything was double yellow lines around the hospital.

He'd been on the verge of telling his dad they had to hurry in case she got a parking ticket before he realised that would be cruel. "OK, Dad," he said, "take your time. I'll carry your bags."

"I should think so, too, son," said Eric. "Why else do you have kids, other than to have somebody to carry your bags for you when you're old and sick?"

Johnny grimaced. Eric seemed quite comfortable talking about his illness and his prognosis. It was almost as if he found it entertaining, something to chat about, something that made him interesting.

But to Johnny, this was his dad, and he was going to lose him.

"Here we are, Dad," he said, stopping at the car. He opened the passenger door and guided his dad inside.

"Hang on, son," Eric said. "Since when do I sit in the front?"

"The front is more comfortable," Alice said. "You sit here with me, Eric, we'll be fine."

He grunted but didn't move out of the front seat. Johnny hurried round to the boot, placed his dad's bags inside, and then got into the back seat.

"Let's go home," he said to Alice. Eric turned his head to look at his son, then winced and turned back to face the front.

"That's not right," he said.

Johnny frowned. "What do you mean?"

"What do you mean by home?" said Eric. "Your home or my home, our home."

Alice said, "We've made up the spare room for you. You've even got your own bathroom."

Eric wagged his finger at her. "I'm not having any of that."

Alice looked at him, puzzled. "You're not well enough."

"I don't care if I'm well enough," Eric said. "If I need caring for, I want professionals doing it. I'm not going to be a burden on you two."

"You're not a burden, Dad," Johnny said. "You looked after me when I was a kid."

"That's different, son. Like I say, I'm not going to be a burden. If I need to go into a home or a hospice or anything like that, I will." He chuckled. "Even if you have to pay for it."

Johnny looked out of the side window of the car. They were leaving the hospital now, heading onto the A35. Did his dad really not want his help? Did he really not want him to care for him?

"I don't get it, Dad," he said. "Why won't you let us?"

Eric raised a hand to stop him. "I'm not having this conversation again, son. Now Alice, why don't you put the radio on, give us something to distract us? Radio Two, none of that news nonsense. I don't want to know the bad things that are happening in the world. There's nothing I can do about them, so I might as well forget about them in the time I've got left."

CHAPTER SIXTY-SIX

Lesley arrived home to find the hallway full of boxes. She stared at them, perplexed.

Since when did Zoe have this much stuff?

Elsa appeared in the kitchen doorway. "Hi, sweetie. You're early."

Lesley looked at her watch. "Six pm. I'm not early. I just left on time."

"I made everybody else leave on time, too, including me," said Zoe, coming down the stairs with another box in her arms.

Lesley looked up at her. "How come you've got so much stuff? You didn't have this much when you moved in."

Zoe exchanged a conspiratorial look with Elsa.

"I've been having a clear out," Elsa said.

Lesley rolled her eyes. "Another one. We'll be calling you Marie Kondo next."

"Hope you don't mind," Elsa said. "It's just, with us having pooled our stuff, we have way too much kitchen equipment, crockery and cutlery, that kind of thing. Saucepans. We've even got two microwaves. I thought Zoe might like some of it."

Lesley looked at Zoe. "Didn't you bring stuff down from Cumbria?"

Zoe shook her head. "I felt bad leaving Carl up there on his own, so I let him keep everything. All I took was my clothes."

"And the cat," Lesley said.

Zoe smiled. "And the cat."

Elsa came out of the kitchen. She approached Lesley and wrapped her in a hug. "How was it?"

Lesley leaned on her wife, glad to let somebody take her weight. "Awful," she muttered. "Truly, truly awful."

Zoe came down the stairs and put a hand on Lesley's back. "I'm so sorry about Katie," she said. "I feel bad not feeling everybody's grief, but—"

Lesley turned to her. "Don't fake it, Zoe. You don't feel grief for Katie because you didn't know her, and that's fine, but if you try and pretend you did, people will see through it."

"I know that," Zoe said, "and that's why I'm not pretending to be as upset as my team." She ran her hand through her hair. "They're in a right state, especially Tina."

"Tina?" Lesley raised an eyebrow. "She's the strongest of the lot of them."

"She's also the most caring," Zoe replied. "That's part of what makes her such a good copper. I told her she should go for sergeant."

"Good move," Lesley said. "I've been trying to encourage her for a while. Did she listen?"

"I think so," Zoe replied. "Let's see. I'll keep encouraging her."

"Good," Lesley said, "and thanks for supporting them. The next few weeks won't be easy."

"I know," Zoe told her, "and in a way, having me there should help – somebody who can just look after the rest and take up the slack."

"It should."

Zoe looked at her for a moment. "Would it be inappropriate to share some good news?"

Lesley looked between Zoe and Elsa. "Is this something to do with your house move?" she asked. "Or the cat? Where is the cat, anyway?"

"Oh, she's upstairs sleeping on my bed," Zoe said. "No, this is nothing to do with my house move. It's about the Musketeers case."

Lesley felt her chest rise. "Good news?" she asked.

Zoe nodded. "It seems the evidence against them was so damning, they've decided to change their plea."

Lesley's mouth fell open. "No."

"Yep," Zoe said. "They've pled guilty."

Lesley clasped both of Zoe's shoulders. "Really?"

Zoe nodded.

"That's fantastic news," Lesley said.

"I know it comes at a bad time," Zoe told her, "but, well, it's something."

"Yeah, it certainly is," Lesley replied.

Elsa put an arm around Lesley's shoulders. "I've made beef stroganoff," she said, "your favourite, and I've bought a bottle of really good wine. I thought you deserved it."

"I don't deserve it," Lesley said. "I feel responsible for what happened to Katie."

"So does Jill," Zoe said, as she followed them into the kitchen. "She feels terrible for telling Katie to go to the Carson house."

Lesley sat down at the island. "She really needs to stop thinking like that," she said. "Katie was just doing her job."

Zoe shrugged. "That's what I told her. But it's Jill."

Lesley nodded. "I'll have a chat with her in the morning, make sure she understands that nobody blames her."

"Good," Zoe said.

Elsa placed a glass of wine in front of Lesley and another in front of Zoe. "Let's drink to the memory of DC Katie Young," she said.

Lesley felt a tear come to her eye. "That sounds like a good idea."

She closed her eyes and lifted her glass, waiting for the other two to hold theirs against hers.

"To Katie Young," said Zoe and Elsa in unison.

"To Katie Young," added Lesley.

Thank you for reading *The Beach Hut Murders*. If you'd like to read more about Lesley and the team you could download a free ebook or audiobook called *The Lyme Regis Murder* from my website at www.rachelmclean.com/lymemurder

And keep reading for a Q&A with me about *The Beach Hut Murders* and a few hints of what's to come next.

Happy reading! Rachel.

AUTHOR Q&A WITH RACHEL MCLEAN

Q: Where did the idea for *The Beach Hut Murders* come from?

A: I've always been fascinated by those quirky, expensive beach huts at Mudeford Spit – what a location. What would it be like to be part of such a secluded community? The idea of a body buried under a toilet block just popped into my head one day and I couldn't let it go. I loved the contrast between the idyllic setting of Mudeford Spit and the dark secrets hidden beneath it.

Q: Did you always plan to kill off one of the team?

A: Honestly? No. That decision came quite late in the writing process, and it wasn't easy. The person in question (I'm not going to name her in case anyone reads this before reading the book) had grown on me – they were bright, ambitious and full of heart. But I felt the story needed a real emotional punch, and the death becomes a turning point for the whole team. It raises the stakes and brings out so much in the other characters. And it will have ramifications in the next book.

Q: Why bring Zoe Finch to Dorset now?

A: Zoe's been a fan favourite since her first appearance, and I loved writing her dynamic with Lesley in the 'Deadly' books. The Cumbria Crime series had come to an end so Zoe's story there had been told, so I needed to decide whether to rest her as a character or move her to another series. Bringing her down to Dorset gave me a chance to explore how she's changed – and how she fits into the Dorset team. Plus, she's brilliant at seeing the big picture, which is exactly what the MCIT needs with the fallout from the Three Musketeers.

Q: Is Stephen Carsons based on anyone real?

A: Not at all, no! But I'm intrigued by people who fall off the grid – people who just vanish and reemerge years later. Stephen's character came from the question: "What if someone disappeared for decades and then turned up with murder in their past *and* present?"

Q: What's going on with the Kelvin family? Are we going to see more of them?

A: Oh yes. The Kelvins are like a rot that runs deep through Dorset's underworld – and the police force, historically. Vera's role is going to grow, as I love writing her. If you think Lesley takes no prisoners, she's got nothing on Vera. We're only just scratching the surface. Eric Chiles has more stories to tell, and Lesley's starting to dig into some very dangerous ground.

Q: Will Jill and Meera be OK?

A: Good question! They're going through a rough patch, for sure, and the pressure of the job doesn't help. But they're strong, and they care about each other deeply. I'm not done exploring their relationship, and I think readers will see growth there in future books. Some hard times will bring them closer together... eventually.

Q: What's next in the Dorset Crime series?

A: Without giving too much away, the next book picks up some threads from *The Beach Hut Murders*, especially around the Kelvins and the fallout from the death of a member of a team. There's also the risk of things becoming personal for someone else on the team. Expect tension, secrets and a few surprises.

Q: How do you keep track of all the characters and storylines?

A: With a LOT of notes, a story bible and a huge amount of help from Joel, my editor. I get things wrong sometimes... remind me again, what car does Dennis drive?

READ A FREE NOVELLA, THE LYME REGIS MURDER

DCI Lesley Clarke is back, and she's got not one, but two teams to head up.

When the body of a prominent local business owner washes up in Lyme Regis Harbour, Lesley must lead her new team through a murky investigation revealing the darker side of the picturesque town.

As she navigates betrayal, secrets, and the challenges of managing two teams without her old sidekick, Lesley grapples with her own past while racing against time to uncover the truth. Can she filter through the evidence to sort fact from fiction and find the real killer?

Read *The Lyme Regis Murder* in ebook or listen to the audiobook for free by downloading from rachelmclean.com/lymemurder or buy the paperback from book retailers.

READ THE DORSET CRIME SERIES

The Corfe Castle Murders

The Clifftop Murders

The Island Murders

The Monument Murders

The Millionaire Murders

The Fossil Beach Murders

The Blue Pool Murders

The Lighthouse Murders

The Ghost Village Murders

The Poole Harbour Murders

The Chesil Beach Murders

The Beach Hut Murders

The Gold Hill Murders

...and more to come

Buy from book retailers.

ALSO BY RACHEL MCLEAN

The DI Zoe Finch Series – buy from book retailers.

Deadly Wishes

Deadly Choices

Deadly Desires

Deadly Terror

Deadly Reprisal

Deadly Fallout

Deadly Christmas

The McBride & Tanner Series – buy from book retailers.

Blood and Money

Death and Poetry

Power and Treachery

Secrets and History

The Cumbria Crime Series by Rachel McLean and Joel Hames – buy from book retailers.

The Harbour

The Mine

The Cairn

The Barn

The Lake

The Wood

The Port

The Marsh

Read the London Cosy Mystery Series by Rachel McLean and Millie Ravensworth – buy from book retailers.

Death at Westminster

Death in the West End

Death at Tower Bridge

Death on the Thames

Death at St Paul's Cathedral

Death at Abbey Road

The Jurassic Coast Mystery Series by Rachel McLean and Millie Ravensworth – buy from book retailers.

The Swimming Club

The Empty Easel

The Shattered Bauble

The Frozen Carriage

The Roscoe & McBride Series – buy from book retailers.

Veil of Secrets

...and more to come